I0658040

A SOUND OF FREEDOM

WALTER GRANT

PO Box 221974 Anchorage, Alaska 99522-1974
books@publicationconsultants.com
www.publicationconsultants.com

ISBN 978-1-59433-038-4
eBook ISBN 978-1-59433-228-9

Library of Congress Catalog Card Number: 2005909307

Manufactured in the United States of America.

Dedicated to Charlene

Thanks to Tom and David.

TABLE OF CONTENTS

BACKGROUND

Walter's flight crew shown in front of their P5M seaplane, LM9.

Walter joined the navy in 1956 and was schooled by the navy for almost two years before he was assigned to VP-44 at Breezy Point and became the junior crew member on a P5M seaplane, LM-9—his job code required a secret clearance. Back then aircrews were families; each crew maintained, flew, and operated the mission equipment on their own aircraft.

Walter's career in avionics took him from vacuum tubes to microchips, from subsonic propeller driven aircraft to supersonic jets, from a sleepy farming town to real-life scenes straight out of *National Geographic*.

He entered the navy unaware of the free world's dependency on America's prestige and military might; the term cold war had little meaning—his fall from innocence was at hand.

Soviet threats were reshaping world opinion, fear of nuclear attack was affecting the daily routine of many Americans, DOD was pushing for newer and more sophisticated weaponry, and the military was redefining the rules of engagement—this was the real-life world Walter was thrust into when he entered the navy.

After the soviet's moved nuclear missiles into Cuba, a mere ninety miles from America's shores, Walter realized the communist threat was real. It was then he began collecting and reading books on the cold war, which introduced him to the shadowy world of espionage.

NO TURNING BACK

The solarium on the big Alaska state ferry, open to the rear with glass overhead and on both sides, offered an unobstructed view. Whereas a person traveling the Inside Passage for the first time might stand in awe, Maxwell Kayne, settling into his lounge chair, was aware of the majesty surrounding him, for a moment only, as he reminded himself he was not here to enjoy the beauty of this vast land—he was here to kill.

The *Matanuska* slipped her mooring, eased out into Gastineau Channel and slowly moved off into the semidarkness. Alpenglow, playing along 6,000-foot peaks above Juneau, signaled an end to this late October day. In the Lower Forty-eight the sun was still high in the western sky, but Alaska's Panhandle days were growing shorter; winter was fast approaching. Already nights were below freezing along Lynn Canal and snow, now down to 1,000 feet, gave off an eerie glow as evening faded, giving way to the night.

Radiant heaters overhead, glowing red, kept the chill out of the solarium and with a stretch of the imagination one might even consider it warm, except when the wind, carrying an icy hint of the impending winter, whipped in across the stern. Passengers here, however, preferred fresh air to the smoke-filled observation deck or sleeping lounge, and dressed accordingly. Max Kayne was not unprepared.

He pulled the drawstring on his mummy-style sleeping bag until only his face was left uncovered, and closed his eyes. In the fleeting seconds before sleep came, he thought about the past, about the events that had brought him to this space and time.

As sleep took control of his body, subconsciousness took control of his thoughts, and he drifted back into the past, back to an early June dawn.

A yellow school bus sat on the parking lot in front of a large white stone building. In two-foot-high letters above the archway leading to heavy double doors was the name, Shelby County High School. On the school bus a banner read, "Senior Class Trip, Washington, D.C. or Bust."

A half dozen kids were outside near the bus; twenty-five or so were already inside. "Hey J.J., hurry up, we're gonna leave without you," someone yelled.

A tall, skinny kid carrying a cardboard suitcase in one hand and a Brownie Hawkeye camera in the other walked slowly toward the bus. The suggestion of being left behind did nothing to increase his stride. He was always late, and everyone always waited. As he approached, the kids hanging around outside hurried onto the bus. He followed them inside, tossed his suitcase in back with the rest of the luggage, and looked around for a place to sit. Peggy Jean watched him, the seat beside her vacant, as he knew it would be. But today he did not want to talk about James Dean, or Elvis, or what everyone had done on Saturday night. He saw an empty seat and quickly sat down. Several minutes passed before he glanced in the direction of Peggy Jean. She had been joined by her best friend and they were both glaring at him.

As the bus rolled along the empty main street of the small farming town, Jack Johnson had no way of knowing he was seeing it for the last time. By the time they made the turn onto the state highway the strains of "Hail, Hail, The Gang's All Here" were dying away and most of the kids, tired from the previous night's graduation party and last-minute preparations, were trying to sleep. But not Jack. Only twice had he been further than fifty miles from home and never out of the state. This wasn't just a trip; this was a milestone.

Their visit to the nation's capital had been well planned and in just three short days Jack learned more about his country's history than in all the time he'd spent in school. As he began to understand the true cost of freedom and what America was all about, the unfamiliar emotions of pride and patriotism crept, slowly at first, then flooded through every fiber of his being. As he visited museums and monuments and listened to the words of tour guides, his thinking seemed to merge with that of the men who had framed his country's constitution and he began to share their hopes and dreams. Through dedication and sacrifice they had forged a nation out of wilderness and shaped those dreams into reality. Jack wondered if the leaders of tomorrow would have the wisdom and dedication of those past. Not only would America's future be determined in this very city but the fate of the world as well. Jack Johnson, for a brief moment, glimpsed the future and although he did not know what role he would play, he knew he would be part of that determining force.

———

An hour before they were to board the bus and begin their long trip home, Jack confided his plans to his best friend and gave him three letters he had written the night before, one for Peggy Jean, one for his parents, and one for the class chaperone.

Anxious to get going, the bus driver had been counting heads and complained, "Everybody's here except J.J.; you might know he'd be late."

At that moment a kid with sandy-colored hair and a sunburned face stepped forward, handed a letter to the chaperone, and with a flippant smile announced, "J.J. ain't late, he ain't comin."

———

Three months ago, as J.J. watched the school bus carrying his friends and classmates merge into traffic and disappear, two hundred eighty dollars had seemed like a lot of money, everything he'd earned working weekends and the two previous summers. He didn't know why he had brought his savings with him in the first place, and hadn't thought about what he would do when the money ran out or even that it would. It didn't matter now, his plan had been to see and learn as much about the nation's capital as he possibly could while his money lasted, and he had done just that.

Concerning him now was an empty stomach and the prospect of another night with no place to sleep. There was nothing left to do but follow through on his decision, a decision he had made after spending a day in the National Cemetery at Arlington. He sat on a bench savoring his last moments of freedom, the carefree type of freedom only a youth can experience, but fun and games were all behind him now. There was no turning back. His next act would be that of an adult.

After considerable time Jack Johnson stood up, walked across the street, up the steps and through the door, never looking back. As he approached a desk a few feet inside the office, a Marine captain, looking all spit and polish in his dress uniform with rows of medals on his chest, looked up from paperwork on his desk and asked, "Well?"

"I guess we've got a deal, sir." Jack Johnson replied. The officer pushed back his chair and stood up and said, 'Raise your right hand and repeat after me."

Jack raised his right hand as instructed and the officer continued, "I, Jackson Jefferson Johnson, do solemnly swear that I will support and defend the Constitution of the United States against all enemies, foreign and domestic; that I will bear true faith and allegiance to the same; and that I will obey the orders of the President of the United States and the orders of the officers appointed over me, according to regulations and the Uniform Code of Military Justice. So help me God." After Jack had repeated the oath the officer extended his hand and said,

"Welcome to the Corps, Private Johnson."

NO RIBBONS

The six-foot, 185-pound, rock-hard Marine sprawled on the couch wearing nothing but gym shorts bore little resemblance to the skinny kid of four years before who'd stood in the recruiter's office with his right hand held high, proudly taking an oath to give his life if necessary in the defense of his country. Jack lay with his head propped up on pillows watching a man at the bar scrutinizing photocopies of a classified military document.

Behind the bar a tall, slender brunette wearing a tank top stretched tightly across her ample breasts, leaving little to the imagination, was mixing martinis. Aware that Jack had shifted his attention to her, she continued shaking the martinis a full twenty seconds longer than necessary, her breasts straining at the confines of the tank top with her every movement. She filled two glasses, dropped an olive in each drink, picked them up and moved slowly away from the bar. Carrying both drinks in one hand she picked up a pillow and tossed it on the floor in front of the couch, placed one of the drinks in Jack's hand, took a sip from the other, and sat down on the pillow.

Satisfied, the man at the bar stood up, placed the photocopies inside a magazine, removed an envelope from his pocket and held it up for Jack to see. "I believe you will find this satisfactory."

He dropped the envelope on the bar as he spoke. "I look forward to our next meeting."

Aware of the implications, Jack did not respond. Without further hesitation the man said, "I can show myself out."

The man walked quickly across the room. A few seconds later they heard the door open and close.

"Do you want to count it?"

Again, Jack did not reply.

"Oh, come on, it can't be all that bad."

"It's bad enough." Jack's words were barely audible.

"Next time will be easier, you'll see."

Shifting to a kneeling position she took another sip of her martini and then set it aside. "Just think of all the fun we can have spending that money."

Her lips, warm and moist, were slowly tracing circular patterns across his bare torso while her hands gently tugged at the waist band of his gym shorts.

"So this is how you recruit a traitor," he hypothesized. "Seven thousand dollars and the favors of a beautiful woman." He wondered how many others had sold out their country for the same price. It was an age-old game and it worked very well. How could anyone say no to Jeanne?

———

In a small but plush room hidden away inside the Russian embassy in Brussels, three men were congratulating themselves and toasting each other with vodka. They now had eyes and ears deep within NATO headquarters. The Marine sergeant had not been bought easily and might be difficult to control, but like any fish, once bait is taken and the hook is set, you can reel it in any time you please. They were confident he would serve them well and long.

Meanwhile, not far across town in the office of NATO commander Brigadier General Thomas P. Boaden, three men were toasting with brandy. "Son, you have placed yourself in a very dangerous position. A position, you understand, where one mistake could cost you your life?"

"Yes, sir," came the quick reply.

"The information you passed on to the Communists today was outdated, and we have reason to believe was already compromised. However, it was correct in every detail. It is important to continue giving them authentic material until we feel they are convinced you are, indeed, a traitor, at which time we can begin to alter, omit, and add false information. In this way we not only confuse and disorient their intelligence-gathering systems, we also cause them to put money, time, and energy into areas we already know are counterproductive. Mr. Tosi," the general nodded toward a man wearing gray slacks and a blue pullover, "is with the Central Intelligence Agency. Mr. Tosi will work out whatever is necessary to keep you in the good graces of the KGB. Mr. Tosi will be your only contact. You and I are not likely to meet again. Any questions, Sergeant Johnson?"

"No sir."

General Boaden stood and extended his hand. "I wish there was a medal for this occasion. Unfortunately, Sergeant Johnson, there will be no ribbons for your uniform. Like Cyrano de Bergerac, you must wear your adornments on your soul."

The door had barely closed behind the general when Henri Tosi set his brandy snifter down, picked up a heavy briefcase and said, "Shall we get started?"

GOING HOME

In Moscow spring is a time that lifts the spirits. Ice has broken up on the Moskva, trees are budding in Sokiniki Park, crocus and freesias are starting to bloom in Ostankino Gardens and it feels good just to be alive, to have survived another winter without freezing or starving to death.

For Jack Johnson it might just as well have been the dead of winter. In his eight years behind the Iron Curtain since his defection to the Soviet Union—orchestrated by the CIA—he had acquired the same fear shared by all Russian citizens, the fear that today was the day the cheka would call.

Everyone had a file and a number. Jack suspected his file was quite thick and monitored very carefully, with new entries daily and close attention given to every detail. As a captain—a rank of privilege, rather than authority, a reward for spying against his country—in the Foreign Intelligence Directorate, he was aware of the Counter Intelligence Directorate that focused its energies cn citizens inside the Soviet Union. No one was exempt.

Foremost on Jack's mind, however, was the life he had left behind. Starting slowly and building until it was his first thought upon awakening in the morning and the last thing on his mind when he closed his eyes at night.

He wanted to go home. Twice within the last six months he had sent the coded request with no response. Each day he felt the bone-chilling cold of communism intensify and he wanted desperately to return to the warmth of America.

He lived well in Russia. As a junior officer in the KGB he was paid four times more than a college professor, with services and privileges not only nonexistent for the average Soviet citizen, but unheard of and unsuspected as well. These perks ranged from chauffeurs to vacations, from laundry service to call girls, all freely provided by the State.

Had Jack been born and raised in Russia, he might have felt fortunate for his position. But he remembered the luxury of having a friend he could trust, the warmth of smiles and laughter, and of not being concerned with whom he talked, where he walked, what magazine or newspaper he read, and he had reached the point where he was willing to make a deal with the devil himself for just one hour of freedom.

His thoughts were interrupted by a knock at the door of his small, austere apartment in the KGB living quarters overlooking Mozhayskoye Chaussee. Startled, he sprang to his feet, his mind racing. He had become more paranoid with each passing day and every event, and now with a knock at the door a dozen questions raced through his mind. Who was calling? Why at this hour? Did they know? Did he talk in his sleep? Was his room bugged? Could they read his very thoughts? He was already moving across the floor when the knock came again. Before he could reach the door the knock came a third time with a sound of urgency. Jack grabbed the knob, snatched open the door and found himself looking at a young lieutenant he recognized as an aide to Colonel Vladimir Chevshenko, section chief of illegal operations. The KGB operated a spy network using ambassadors, trade representatives, and other diplomats who entered and exited countries with legal passports; however, members of the illegal section worked strictly undercover and involved foreign nationals, citizens working against their own countries, double agents, and agents from their own section.

"Comrade Captain," the lieutenant saluted smartly, a courtesy Jack's rank demanded of the young officer. "I am here to escort you to the hospital at Dzerzhinsky square."

Jack knew his years of training would never allow the sudden rush of adrenalin to reflect in his face. The most feared of institutions in all of the Soviet Union stood at number 2 Dzerzhinsky Square—the infamous Lubianka prison. What the lieutenant referred to as a hospital was nothing more than an infirmary where, through the use of drugs and torture, men were known to confess to crimes they never committed and implicate others who had no previous knowledge of the crime or even knew that a crime had been committed. People interrogated at Lubianka always confessed in the end, so said the KGB.

With calm and a show of indifference Jack demanded, "What requires my personal and immediate attention at this late hour, Comrade Lieutenant?"

"I have no information, Comrade Captain. My instructions are to personally escort you to the hospital without delay. I have a car and driver downstairs. Shall we go?" It was not a request.

The lieutenant opened the door of the sedan for Jack, and then closed it again after he settled into the back seat. The lieutenant climbed into the front with the driver. Jack sat quietly wrestling with his emotions during the short trip to Dzerzhinsky Square. When they arrived at Lubianka the lieutenant opened the door and waited for Jack to exit the sedan, then escorted him past the guards and through several doors with more guards and down several passageways before opening a door and stepping aside so Jack could enter. He then closed the door and remained outside. As Jack stepped into the room his years of training and experience automatically took control of his emotions and actions. In the time required to take three steps toward four men sitting at a table about twelve feet long, he had surveyed and mentally recorded the entire scene.

Besides the chief of Illegal Operations, Colonel Chevshenko, he immediately recognized his own boss, Colonel Viktor Galuzin, chief of the Western Hemisphere Intelligence Section, along with the chief of Special Operations, Colonel Vasily Ivanovich. The fourth man, wearing a white hospital coat, he surmised was a doctor. Behind the table a nurse stood beside a gurney. There was little doubt that underneath the sheet draping the gurney was a body. Jack was in what appeared to be an operating room with an overhead gallery. Behind the glass, although no lights were on in the gallery, he could see half a dozen shadowy figures. At least one wore a general's uniform.

Colonel Chevshenko motioned for Jack to step closer and said, "Ah! Come in, Comrade Captain. I regret calling you out at this late hour but a matter of urgency has come to our attention and it must be resolved without delay."

Knowing microphones would carry his every word to a recorder as well as to the audience above, Jack replied nonchalantly, but with the sincerity of a dedicated Communist, "There is no need for an apology. I have not been inconvenienced. How can I be of service, Comrade Colonel?" He was feeling more at ease now—he was not here as a suspect. You did not assemble an audience of colonels and generals at his time of night to bring a mere captain up on charges. Something major was going down and he was becoming curious as to how he was to be involved.

"Are you loyal to the Party?" inquired Colonel Chevshenko.

There had been a time when the question would have chilled his blood, but not now. The CIA and KGB had trained him well. He was in his element and whatever his fears might be, his emotions would not betray him. He played this sort of game very well and was in complete control of his emotions.

When your life depended upon how well you played the game, you played very well, indeed. His fourteen years as a player and the fact that he was still alive were a testament to his ability to play the game. He felt the familiar rush and, like the dope addict sticking a needle into his arm, felt the high coming on—center stage was his and the curtain was going up. His answer weighed and reweighed in the space of a nanosecond came across composed with the conviction of a patriot of communism. "I am dedicated to the Party, I desire only to serve."

Numerous questions raced through his mind, but he knew he had been summoned here to answer questions, not to ask them. It didn't matter, all his questions would be answered in due time. All he had to do was be patient and wait for the scenario to unfold.

"Do you have any desire to return to America?" Chevshenko asked.

Could they possibly know that he was a double agent and that he had a burning desire to go home? If so, how? Perhaps he was wrong—this was beginning to take on the appearance of a full-blown investigation. Every agent in the field always worried that he would be exposed by a mole. It had long been rumored a mole was deep within the CIA. Maybe it was true. Maybe the interrogation was about to begin in earnest. But he didn't think so. The setting just wasn't right. He made a show of resenting the implications, but not enough to be disrespectful of the colonel. "I chose the Soviet Union over America eight years ago. I am proud to be a Communist. I have no desire to return to a capitalist world."

He wondered if he was laying it on a little too thick as he made sure the word capitalist was accented with disgust.

"Would you be willing to return in the interest of the State?"

"I'm happy here. However, if the party so desires, I will make the sacrifice," Jack replied, his voice melancholy for the benefit of the gallery. He had a feeling they were about to expose their hand and the time had come to express some anxiety. He didn't want to appear too much in control. "If I am required to leave my beloved homeland, will I be able to return soon?"

The question was for effect. The colonel continued, as Jack knew he would, as if the question had not been asked. "We find ourselves with a problem. This problem, however, provides us with a unique opportunity, an opportunity to embarrass the United States and bring worldwide attention to the glory of communism."

Without taking his eyes off Jack the colonel commanded, "Remove the sheet."

It took all his concentration to maintain control of his emotions. His spirits were flying higher than he could have ever imagined. He could only guess at their plan. No doubt it was insane—an insane plan formulated by insane men—he didn't care. They would lay it all out for him and he would make sure it succeeded. Well, part of it anyway; the part that served him, and serve him it surely would, of this he had no doubt whatsoever. One glimpse was all it took and he knew he was looking at his ticket to the West.

All the years as a double agent and the torturous training preceding those years had not prepared him for this moment. He was afraid to move or speak. What if his voice broke, or showed even the slightest tremor? He felt flushed, then chilled, his skin suddenly clammy. Beads of perspiration were dangerously close to forming on his brow and worst of all, his eyes were becoming moist. Would a tear, of all things, betray his emotions? He was on his way home if only he could survive the next few seconds.

The naked corpse on the gurney could have been his twin brother. Five years older, maybe, slightly heavier, and possibly an inch or two shorter, yet except for hairstyle and a mustache the dead man was his double. His fear that emotion might somehow give him away was unfounded. Years of training provided his subconscious the ability to react as would be expected of a true patriot of communism.

As quickly as panic had raced through his being he regained control of his emotions as well as his confidence. There was nothing to fear. His dedication to the State had never been in question—after all, none of the other officers summoned here tonight wore the Order of the Red Banner or the coveted title "Hero of the Soviet Union" on their uniforms. His only concern now was to convince them he could successfully carry out their foolhardy plan, and this he most certainly would do.

Chevshenko softened his tone as though sympathetic to Jack's reluctance to return to America and said, "There are some minor details to be worked out. Doctor Chekhov will simulate superficial wounds to your head and face. This will warrant shaving your head and mustache, and some attention must be given to the throat as well. This will excuse any difference in speech. We have some audio-and videotapes of Mr. Harte taken during his visit to Moscow. You will study them while Doctor Chekhov is preparing his staff."

The colonel spoke directly to Jack as though he had been asked and had agreed to cooperate. Jack had no say in this whatsoever and he knew it. The decision was made long before the lieutenant was sent to his apartment, and to refuse or even question the wisdom of his superiors was unthinkable. There was no reason to ask. It was understood, everyone always agreed.

No one in the Soviet Union had ever been more in agreement with any decision by the KGB than Jack at this moment and he didn't even know the details.

The colonel concluded, saying, "We are gathering as much information as we can about Mr. Harte. It will be passed on to you as quickly as possible. We have very little time to prepare. You must be ready tomorrow."

The media had the story correct in every detail, with one exception. The United Nations delegation, after a six-day tour in the Soviet Union, was en route to Sheremetyevo International Airport in Moscow when a pedestrian suddenly stepped into the path of one of the cars in the motorcade. The driver, a member of the security police, was killed as he swerved into an oncoming truck. The passengers had been seriously injured, but all would survive without long-term disabilities.

Doctor Chekhov, the hospital chief of staff, allowed the reporters to visit and question the U.N. delegates, restricting them to just five minutes with the most prominent of the delegation, David Harte.

And that one incorrect detail? David Aaron Harte had not survived. Unknown, except to a select few within the hierarchy of the KGB, Captain Jack Johnson was now masquerading as United States ambassador to the United Nations.

The KGB had an ingenious plan: David Harte would return to America glowing with admiration for the Soviet Union and spend several months expounding the virtues of communism and the great socialist successes—which, of course, did not exist since there had been few successes in the Soviet Union—at the same time condemning capitalism and criticizing the democratic system at every opportunity to anyone of the media willing to listen. The media, having socialist leanings themselves, were always willing to listen to left-wing fanatics.

The Kremlin considered the American media among their best propaganda tools, if not allies. Via the media, Communist fronts spread disinformation and were able to influence the thinking of many Americans, who, in turn, pressured their legislators—some of whom were already sympathetic to socialism and communism—to vote for or against certain bills pending in Congress.

Ambassador Harte's lectures and news conferences, however, would only set the stage for the big event. When the KGB bosses decided the time was right Ambassador David Harte would, in front of prearranged television coverage from around the world, address the United Nations General Assembly, denounce the United States as an imperialistic aggressor and ask the Soviet delegation for political asylum. This would embarrass and humiliate the conservative administration that had appointed Harte to the U.N. and would most certainly be the headline of the decade.

In this election year, the impact would be doubly devastating to the United States, and the advantage for the Soviet Union would be immense. The Democrats were running an ultraliberal candidate and this would almost certainly assure his election to the Oval Office. During the four years to follow, the Kremlin would be able to further undermine the economies of the free world, expand its boundaries, advance its military position, and usurp American prestige throughout the world. Under the guise of détente, the Soviets would be able to win favorable arms limitation treaties, purchase high-tech equipment, install puppet governments in many third-world nations, and step up infiltration of sensitive positions in our own government. It was indeed an admirable plan. No doubt, congratulations were being passed around as everyone involved was vying for credit.

The new David Harte had gone without sleep for the better part of three days. Briefings had continued around the clock, interrupted only by the media and U.S. officials. Benzedrine had kept him awake and alert for those three days, but now he was coming down fast. Even so, he would force himself to stay awake until his "Freedom Bird" was airborne. He surmised men would always lie on stretchers wherever the struggle for freedom existed. He remembered lying on a stretcher some fifteen years ago at Tan Son Nhut waiting for another Freedom Bird. It wasn't his doing and he had no say in it, but he felt he was deserting the people in Southeast Asia and vowed to continue the fight against oppression. That vow had deprived him of his own freedom for the last eight years. During those eight years he had sent thousands of coded messages and documents to the Central Intelligence Agency, risking his life every day of those eight years. Now he felt no remorse or guilt in his desire to go home.

The scream of jet engines interrupted his thoughts. Turning his head he could see a big C141 without identification markings and painted in standard air force camouflage, taxi to a stop just fifty feet away. In an unprecedented decision the Kremlin had granted the president's request and allowed the air force to medivac Ambassador Harte directly from Moscow. The pilot did not cut power and the big engines continued to whine. The rear cargo ramp was lowered and had barely touched the pavement before an air force doctor followed by a nurse and two medics hurried down and walked directly to where the ambassador lay. Talking briefly with his Russian counterpart as he examined his new VIP patient, the air force doctor appeared relieved to find no major injuries. A few parting comments, a handshake, and they were on their way up the cargo ramp.

The litter smelled clean and fresh as did the nurse, her perfume reminding him of many things past and of dreams yet to be fulfilled. The nurse noticed Jack watching her as she leaned across to tighten the safety harness. "I just want to make sure you don't fall out of bed.

We've come a long way to get you and we want to make sure nothing happens to you on the way home."

Fighting now to stay awake, he was determined not to give in to the much-needed sleep until they were airborne. He heard the ramp come up, the hatch close, the whine of the jets increase, and felt the plane begin to move. They taxied for only a couple of minutes before stopping momentarily at the end of the runway. To Jack it seemed an eternity, but now, at last, the engines went to full power and with afterburners thundering the big aircraft gathered speed quickly and sprang into the air. As the Starlifter turned its nose skyward he heard the gear retract, the wheel well doors slam shut, and felt the acceleration as the safety harness strained to hold him in position on the litter; his Freedom Bird was on the wing.

"Welcome aboard, Mr. Ambassador, I'm Doctor William Edwards. We'll try to make your flight as comfortable as possible. Our orders are to proceed to Andrews, where you will be transferred to the Naval Hospital at Bethesda. We'll touch down briefly at either Keflavik or Goose Bay for refueling; otherwise you have an express all the way to Washington." Jack had heard only two words before falling asleep, "Welcome aboard."

"Any personal requests, sir?" There was no reply as Jack was already dreaming. Dr. Edwards wondered why the ambassador was smiling. Nurse Brooks thought he was smiling at her.

More than five thousand miles and seven time zones had slipped beneath their wings in the last twelve and a half hours. Flying east to west they would gain eight hours. Takeoff from Moscow was at ten thirty and even though flight time would be approximately fourteen hours, they would land at Andrews Air Force Base at about four thirty the same afternoon.

Intending to awaken the ambassador with a gentle nudge, Dr. Edwards had barely touched the sleeping man's arm when his eyes popped open, and his attempt to bolt upright was stopped short by the safety harness. Giving the startled man a few seconds to collect himself, the doctor asked, "How do you feel, Mr. Ambassador?"

"Hungry," came the quick and pleasant reply.

"I'm not surprised, you've been sleeping for over twelve hours." The doctor continued speaking as Nurse Brooks leaned over and loosened the restraining strap across Jack's chest. "Well, I think we shall be able to ease your hunger pangs. We're preparing a nice lunch for you. In the meantime would you like something to drink?"

"Please!"

Handing the ambassador a large paper cup filled with a slightly yellowish liquid the doctor explained, "This little concoction is full of minerals, proteins, electrolytes, and lots of other goodies. The stuff may not look very appetizing but it doesn't taste too bad and your body will thank you for drinking it. It's kind of like Gatorade."

"Like what?"

"Gatorade, you know, the stuff all the athletes drink."

"Oh yeah, sure." He raised the drink to his lips and took a sip, then without stopping, drank until the cup was empty.

"Where are we?"

"Somewhere off the New England coast. We passed over Cape Sable, Nova Scotia, about an hour ago; we should be touching down in another hour and a half." The nurse had placed a couple of pillows behind the ambassador's back, making it comfortable for him to sit upright. Another pillow on his lap made it easy to balance the lunch tray. Doctor Edwards was entering David's vital signs in his chart as he spoke. "I've recommended a few days' bed rest and observation along with various blood tests. I'm sure the navy will have their own ideas about your care; however, I see no reason for concern. I'll leave you to enjoy your lunch and to collect your thoughts. I'm sure you want some time to prepare for the press. No doubt you'll be the lead story on national television tonight. If you need anything, just let Nurse Brooks know."

"Thanks."

Prepare! Hell, he didn't need to prepare. He knew exactly what he was going to say. "Surprise, surprise! I'm not David Harte. The ambassador is back in Moscow, dead as a mackerel. I'm Sergeant Jack Johnson, United States Marine Corps. If you don't believe me, check my fingerprints." Oh yeah, it would be the headline of the decade all right, but not the one the KGB had in mind. He just wished he could see their faces when they learned of their mistake. All that toasting, congratulating, and backslapping would quickly turn to fear, denial, and finger pointing. A lot of new faces would be showing up in Siberia in the next couple of weeks.

Amused at the thought of all those state officials going to prison, it suddenly dawned on him that he, too, might be going to prison. Jack Johnson was AWOL, maybe even wanted for desertion. What if the only two people who knew what he had been doing for the last eight years were dead? He might be listed as a spy, with no way to prove otherwise. He remembered reading about an army officer on a secret mission for President Lincoln. Two days after President Lincoln was assassinated the officer was captured and unable to prove his innocence, was hung by his own troops. It could happen to him. He could be shot by a firing squad for treason. To compound his problems, numerous KGB agents in the United States would be watching, listening, and reporting. Did they have orders to kill if he reneged? Of course they did. He began to realize he had problems. Yes indeed, he had lots of problems. Hell, he didn't even know what Gatorade was.

NO PLACE TO GO

The crowd was large, and everybody shouted questions at the same time. Security was having a hard time keeping everyone at what they considered a safe distance. But for Jack Johnson it was merely routine, another show and another con job. Every major TV network was there with their video cameras, all vying for the best position. Photographers from all the newspapers and magazines were clicking shutters continually. Jack was beginning to enjoy the charade, a moment in the limelight. Having already decided to go along with the Soviets' plan until he could figure out what to do, he delivered a short speech and continued to answer questions as his attendants wheeled his gurney toward the helicopter that would deliver him to the Bethesda Naval Hospital. "Yes, he was treated well in the Soviet Union." "Yes, he received excellent medical treatment."

Another crowd of reporters was waiting by the helipad outside the hospital. He made another short speech and again answered questions as his gurney was loaded into another ambulance for the short trip to the hospital. "Yes, Soviet hospitals were clean and well equipped." "Yes, doctors were exceedingly skilled." "Yes, the staff was very competent and conscientious." Max wondered if anybody believed his lies. He figured the hate-America crowd and Communist sympathizers would believe it simply because they wanted it to be true; it didn't matter. What did matter was that the KGB section bosses who cooked up the harebrained scheme would believe he was still on the team and carrying out their instructions to the letter.

After the doctors poked and probed until they were satisfied, the lab technicians drew all the blood they wanted, and the X-ray technicians took pictures from every possible angle, he was put to bed, given a sedative, and was once again dreaming.

Henri Tosi had finished dinner and was enjoying a cup of coffee as he watched the six o'clock news.

Their lead story, the return of Ambassador David Harte, began with lots of commentary and speculation before cutting to the video, taped earlier at Andrews Air Force Base.

Suddenly the coffee cup fell from Henri Tosi's hand. He leaned forward in his chair, eyes glued to the television set, oblivious of the hot coffee burning his skin. He turned up the volume and continued to stare in disbelief. Yes, there it was again. It was impossible, but he heard it clearly and distinctly. Ambassador David Aaron Harte had spoken a code known to only one other man in the world besides himself, a code worked out in Budapest nearly nine years ago by two friends while sipping cappuccino made in a hundred-year-old porcelain espresso machine in Gerbeaud's, after which Jack Johnson had walked out across Worosmarty Ter, turned right toward the Danube and disappeared.

Still watching the TV, he picked up a phone and punched out a number, a series of clicks followed by a single short tone. At the sound of the tone he punched out another series of numbers. The man on the other end answered with a single word.

"Langley."

"Connect me with the watch commander." The voice on the other end asked for an identification authenticator. Henri complied. There was silence; neither party spoke as the young man fed the information into his computer. Smiling at the astonished and anxious expression he knew would be present on the young man's face when he viewed the computer readout and realized he was speaking with the DDO, Henri waited patiently. In a matter of seconds the voice came back crisp and clear. "Yes sir, one moment, sir."

Five seconds later another voice answered. Henri spoke briefly with the second voice and hung up without waiting for a reply.

He wasn't aware of the blistered skin underneath his coffee-soaked clothing yet—even the pain, when he bent to retrieve the fallen cup, did not penetrate his train of thought. Placing the coffee cup on the breakfast bar he continued into the dressing area of his bathroom, removing his shirt as he walked. Sitting on a valet chair he removed the rest of his clothing, tossed everything into a hamper and pulled on a bathrobe as he walked toward the kitchen. With a fresh cup of coffee in hand, he returned to his chair opposite the television set, picked up the remote control unit and started tuning through channels on his satellite receiver, searching for another news broadcast.

Although Harte was mentioned in the news from time to time he was normally pretty low profile. Henri had never met the ambassador and knew very little about him. With bandages on his head and face it was difficult to tell anything about his features, yet there was something vaguely familiar about the man. He did know, however, that in his speech at Andrews, and again at the Bethesda Naval Hospital was a clear cry for help from an old friend he had never expected to see again. They had become the best of friends in the five years they worked as a team in Europe, one the teacher, one the student. The student had disappeared behind the Iron Curtain—very few ever made the return trip.

The telephone rang. Henri lifted the receiver to his ear and spoke once, listened intently to the voice on the other end, passed on more instructions, and hung up. He wouldn't get much sleep tonight.

The hospital corridors were busy at seven in the morning. He found the room he wanted, presented his identification to the two men sitting outside, took a deep breath, exhaled slowly, opened the door, and walked inside. The man on the bed, clad in standard blue hospital pajamas, still slept, his breathing slow, even, and rhythmic. Henri walked carefully from one side of the bed to the other and back again. The size and weight were right, about two hundred pounds, a little heavier than he remembered. With bandages covering most of his face it was difficult to tell, but if fingerprints didn't lie, this was his old friend. Henri pulled up a chair and sat down.

He thought about those five years and about the friendship that had evolved. They were more than friends—they were the best of friends. He thought also of the wealth of information Jack had gotten out of the Soviet Union. Puzzling, though, was the fact that no information had been received from Jack in nearly a year. The flow had ended abruptly. Henri had assumed his friend was dead, identified as a spy and executed in secrecy. But if Jack was alive, several developments of major importance were about to unfold.

At the moment the whereabouts and well-being of the real David Harte was not one of the developments concerning him, but rather the implication that someone in the chain stretching from Langley to Moscow and back was about to sell out his country to the Communists. This person was collecting information, tactics, routing procedures, and, most importantly, names. When that person decided to "go over" he or she, no doubt, had evidence in place to incriminate Jack, evident by the fact that he was alive. Even without useful information to send the CIA, Jack would still have sent situation codes. But if Jack Johnson was passing himself off as David Harte this meant there were other plans in the works which could mean a lot of surprises for people in high places.

No movement betrayed consciousness before the eyes opened to stare across the space of three feet into the face of Henri Tosi. Unable to speak because of the lump swelling up in his throat, his eyes closed again, to reopen several seconds later, moist and reddened. He heaved a sigh and calmly said, "You remembered."

"Yeah, I remembered," came the reply. The one brief emotional moment had come and gone. "So, how've you been?"

"Couldn't be better," Jack countered. Either man would, without reservation, sacrifice his own life to save the other, yet there was little to suggest the strength of the bond between the two men as the conversation began as casually as when they had left off more than eight years ago. Jack's parting sentiment had been, "See you around."

Henri had replied with an equally offhanded remark, "Yeah, well, don't take any wooden nickels."

The two men reminisced at length, taking their time getting around to the problems at hand. Problem number one, what to do about David Harte, and problem number two, how to ferret out the conspirator. Henri had been considering these problems since two o'clock that morning when information reached him confirming that the fingerprints of the man registered at the Naval Hospital in Bethesda, Maryland, as David Aaron Harte matched those of Sergeant Jackson Jefferson Johnson, wanted by the United States Marines for desertion. The operative had removed fingerprints from the sleeping man in one of the VIP suites at Bethesda and delivered them personally to the FBI for identification. An expert at the FBI matched the prints to Sergeant Johnson, but was told nothing. No entries showed in FBI records. There would be no paper trail—only five people knew the facts.

The amount of time required to trap the conspirator would depend on how long it took to get an operative in place inside the embassy in Moscow. Couriers were no longer used or needed for getting information out of Russia. The space age had made life less risky for agents when, on a secret mission, shuttle Colombia had launched two satellites. One of these satellites passed over Moscow at regular intervals, then on the other side of the earth it intersected the orbit of the other satellite. After the two satellites rendezvoused, the second satellite continued on its orbit which took it directly over Haines, Alaska. The satellite passing over Moscow, by design, appeared to be inoperative with no transmissions back to earth, thus the code name, "Dead Man." However, utilizing open-ended receivers, it listened to radio signals as it crossed the Soviet Union and passed this information, by way of a narrow beam at very low power, to its sister satellite each time their orbits intersected. The second satellite then beamed the information down to the listening station in Haines as it passed over Alaska, where it was coded, scrambled, and rerouted through a third satellite to Langley. One very special signal intercepted by Dead

Man, when it passed over Moscow, came from the American embassy. This signal transmitted at very low power—a mere 10 watts—on a vertically transmitted conical beam, less than two tenths of a degree in diameter at the source, with the carrier frequency controlled by a randomly firing oscillator which shifted thousands of times a second, made transmissions virtually undetectable either from adjacent rooftops or from airplanes flying overhead.

For the last two years intelligence gathered by agents in Russia had traveled on this beam to CIA Headquarters in Virginia. Within the last year Jack had reported to only four agents. These four agents were all inside the embassy and had access to incoming reports from everyone working for the CIA inside the Soviet Union. Many of those agents were Soviet citizens as well as members of the military and state officials. It was imperative to place an operative, unknown and unannounced, in the embassy before the conspirator could cut his deal with the Communists. Failure would result in total devastation of the CIA intelligence-gathering network behind the Iron Curtain. Agents throughout the Eastern Bloc would be at the mercy of the KGB. Torture and death, not mercy, were the watchwords of the *Komitet Cosudarstvinnoi Bezopasnosti.*

Getting up from his chair, Henri said, "I have to take care of a few things, shouldn't take over three or four hours. I'll stop back by about lunchtime and we'll work out this little problem of yours."

He reached the door before Jack inquired, "What's Gatorade?"

Henri laughed, "I'll send you some."

David Harte would die in a fiery automobile accident in which a John Doe from the city morgue would burn beyond recognition; his dental work would be the only thing to identify the ambassador. It would be simple enough—a traffic-related fatality occurred in the D.C. area on an average of once a week. A little plastic surgery, a new identity, and Jack could, maybe for the first time ever, get on with his life—a life of his own, not a life totally immersed in and dedicated to the service of his country.

Henri thought about his own life. In thirty years he had never gone fishing, been on a picnic, nor had a birthday party. He wondered what life was like for people who worked five days a week, went home to a wife and kids, mowed the lawn on Saturdays, and watched ball games with friends...

"That will be four eighty-five, sir." The girl at the drive-through window jolted Henri back to reality. He reached for his order, placed it on the seat beside him, counted out the money, and handed it to the girl. Driving away, he wondered how agents had kept from starving before fast-food restaurants.

It was almost noon when he reached the hospital. The same two men sitting outside the door nodded in recognition as Henri approached. One motioned towards the door indicating identification wasn't necessary.

Jack, watching the midday news on a small bedside television, looked up and waved Henri into the room. "Am I, David Harte, really this popular or is there nothing worth reporting today?"

"Oh, you're a popular guy all right," Henri answered, as he pushed two chairs together, placed his package on one and sat down in the other. "You should see all the reporters hanging around outside. If the doctor didn't have you quarantined—I thought it might be better to have the public thinking you picked up something contagious on your trip—you'd have a regular parade through here." He pulled a Big Mac out of his bag and tossed it over to Jack.

"I'll bet you haven't seen one of these lately." Jack gave out a low whistle.

"You've got that right. You wouldn't believe how popular Mc-Donald's is in Moscow. With a room full of these and a truck load of Levis you could be the richest man in the Soviet Union by the end of the day. Would you believe the waiting time to get into McDonald's in Moscow is six hours? You wouldn't happen to have any of those skinny little fried taters in that sack, would you?"

Henri pulled out a container of French fries and passed them to Jack, then pulled out another Big Mac and took a bite as he unfolded the morning newspaper, intending to pass it over to Jack.

"I see you made the front page." Jack switched off the television and reached for the paper, but Henri pulled the paper back as one of the headlines caught his eye. He read intently for about thirty seconds, then exclaimed, "This is it."

"This is what?" asked Jack.

"This is your escape hatch. I had figured on arranging a traffic accident, but this is better. Fewer complications."

The article speculated that an upcoming trip, scheduled months in advance, might be canceled or postponed. Because of the unfortunate accident in the Soviet Union, the article explained, the ambassador might need an extended period of recuperation. The pending trip was scheduled for the following Monday, less than a week away.

"This is perfect. Do you think you can pull off three or four more speeches for the press?"

"A piece of cake. What do you have in mind?"

Henri grabbed another Big Mac and headed for the door. "I'll tell you later, but first I have to arrange a few things."

It had been six days since Henri left Jack's hospital room. The two men now sat, with a cup of coffee, in front of the television, waiting for the evening news. Henri's den was not rustic, with lots of dark wood and overstuffed brown leather furniture. Much to the contrary, the den as well as the rest of his apartment was ultra modern with clean lines designed to be comfortable and serviceable. Four chairs, separated by small tables that fanned out in front of a large-screen TV, were good examples. Each chair reclined and molded to the body at the touch of a button. Considerable space separated this minitheater from the computers, telephones, recording equipment, and various other electronic gadgets located on or above the built-in desk that ran the length of the opposite wall. Except for a wet bar, two desk chairs, and a world globe six feet in diameter, no other furniture existed. The two walls adjacent to the desk were lined with books from floor to ceiling. Those along one wall covered every aspect of the cold war. The remaining shelves were filled with reference books, history books, and books on constitutional law.

Henri had not collected an array of paraphernalia during his assignments around the world as most people do. The only memento to be found, the Medal of Merit, still in its case, rested out of sight in a desk drawer. Henri's one vice was the luxury of his home, a vice he could well afford. His job paid well and he had invested every cent. There had been little opportunity to spend anything until recently, when time in service, dedication, and hard work had moved him up in the ranks to a position requiring him to spend most of his time at Langley.

Having spent too much time in hostile and substandard environments, he welcomed the chance to give up the excitement of travel and the thrill of danger to the young and able. He had paid his dues and was ready for some quiet and comfort in his life.

He had first considered an estate around McLean, not too far from CIA headquarters, but, settled for a high-rise condominium overlooking the Potomac off Rock Creek Parkway in southwest D.C. near George Washington University.

The less-filling-versus-great-taste beer commercial ended and the newscaster came on with the lead story. Only hours after being released from Bethesda Naval Hospital, where he had been recuperating from injuries sustained in an automobile accident while touring the Soviet Union, Ambassador David Harte had flown to the Middle East. The U.N. ambassador was to mediate a new round of peace talks beginning tomorrow in Beirut. Shortly after arriving, Ambassador Harte was abducted from his hotel room. A splinter group of the PLO claimed responsibility for the kidnapping. No demands had yet been received. An analysis of details surrounding the kidnapping was followed by a review of the ill-fated trip to the Soviet Union.

Henri got up from his chair, walked over to the bar, picked up a Waterford decanter and poured a finger of Rhemy Martin into each of two brandy snifters. He returned to his chair with the two snifters and passed one to his friend.

"Thanks. It's been a long time since I've seen any of this stuff."

Henri raised his snifter and said, "Well, here's to the demise of David Harte and the birth of Max Kayne."

"To Max Kayne." Maxwell Alexander Kayne. Jack liked his new name. It was a name with class. Yeah, he liked it just fine. Something he liked even more was the opportunity to break free of the past. He knew he would never be completely free of the past, but he would no longer have to worry about the problems of previous identities. He had been given a new beginning complete with name, social security number, birth certificate, driver's license, bank account, an apartment of his own, and in a few weeks a new face as well. Yeah, he liked it more with each passing minute.

Swirling the cognac he asked, "Did you know that you can't smell or taste vodka?" It was a statement rather than a question. He lifted the snifter as he leaned forward, breathing in the bouquet, and then slowly tilted his head back, allowing the liquid to spill into his mouth, savoring the fine flavor for several seconds before letting the brandy trickle down his throat.

"After eight years of Russian vodka I'd forgotten an elixir like this existed." Treating his taste buds once again, he leaned back in the recliner and asked, "How long has it been since that night in General Boaden's office?"

"Fourteen years." Henri answered.

"That was the first time I ever tasted brandy."

"Yeah, you were pretty green in more ways than one, but you were eager. You sure impressed the general."

"Where is General Boaden?"

"With the Joint Chiefs of Staff, he's the Army's top gun." Max didn't hear Henri's answer. All his attention was focused on the television, and he leaned forward, pointed toward an air force colonel discussing the future role of the military in the space shuttle program at Vandenberg.

"Who is that man?"

"Howard Tolinger," Henri answered.

"The same Howard Kent Tolinger who sold the Soviets detailed locations of our long-range missiles?"

"Yep, a major then, but the same man. He also sold them NORAD computer access codes."

"Why isn't he in prison?"

"Does the name Alger Hiss mean anything to you?"

"Sure, convicted spy, somewhere around 1950, I think."

"You've got part of it right. He was a spy and he was convicted in November of 1949 and served three years and eight months in federal prison for two counts of perjury, but was not found guilty of spying, even though he was guilty as hell. With the exception of the Rosenbergs, it took another thirty-five years to actually convict someone for selling or giving away our national secrets. To convict Tolinger would have exposed some of our own agents in very sensitive positions, so we repaired the damage as best we could without tipping our hand to the air force. We weren't even sure we could get a conviction."

"Why didn't the air force kick him out of the service?"

"We didn't tell the air force."

"You didn't tell them?" Max couldn't believe what he was hearing.

"I know it's hard for you to accept, but you aren't aware of some of the attitudes in the country—neither the CIA, the FBI, nor the military have been very popular in the last decade. When you were in Vietnam there were people marching on the capital claiming we were persecuting the North Vietnamese. While you were behind the Iron Curtain these same people were saying the Communists mean us no harm and we should disarm. Since the Communists wanted peace they, too, would disarm and we could all live happily ever after. A lot of politicians trying to get elected, or in many cases reelected—the country be damned—were speaking out along the same lines and some were even meeting with Ho Chi Minh. Hell, we had celebrities going to Hanoi, marching with the Viet Cong and calling for American soldiers to lay down their arms."

Henri was getting a bit sarcastic, but he felt a need to awaken Max to some of the attitudes in the country. Max was visibly shaken.

"Are you telling me I've wasted my life, shamed my parents and friends who think I'm a traitor, disgraced the Corps, given up eight years of my life to help preserve the freedom of my country and nobody gives a damn?"

"A lot of people care. There are countless citizens as well as historians, international traders, and government officials who know and full well understand the only way to a lasting peace is to maintain a strong defense. Unfortunately, not everyone agrees. Some of our own citizens and politicians work against peace by trying to subvert our own freedoms; they keep cutting funding for espionage and some even go so far as to suggest we hand our sovereignty over to the United

Nations. At the moment, the laws favor those who would rob us of our freedom and hinders those who work to preserve it. But things are looking up. We have a new leader and the country is experiencing a resurgence of patriotism. For the time being, however, all we can do is hang tight, play by the rules, and hope for the best."

Deep emotion contorted Max Kayne's face. He spoke softly, but with open contempt for all those who sought to destroy his country and steal his heritage.

"Maybe we should stop playing by the rules."

Henri admitted he had entertained the same thought more than once, but logic had always won out over emotion. He was a team player and the team always played by the rules. He went ahead to explain how just one such act by a single agent could jeopardize the very existence of the entire agency.

"I'm no longer working for the Company. I'm just Joe Citizen, a guy nobody ever heard about. What could anyone say if I break the rules?"

"They would say you broke the law and, if caught, should and would be punished just like any other criminal."

"Well, it's a hell of a way to fight—just stand around with your hands in your pockets while the other guy punches away."

"Hey, come on, lighten up, you've earned the right to enjoy life for a while. Once you spend some time in that health resort in Los Angeles, get some of that West Coast sunshine, and meet a few of those California women, you'll be able to just kick back and forget all about everything."

"Yeah, right, I've already forgotten." Max wouldn't forget, but he didn't want to argue with an old friend. Old friend, hell— Henri was his only friend.

Early the following morning the two men parted company at Dulles Airport, and Max boarded a plane for California.

A lot of cosmetic surgery took place in Los Angeles. Nobody ever grew old in Southern California—at least no one able to afford the price of a face-lift and various other body maintenance programs provided by the luxurious spas and health resorts flourishing in the well-to-do neighborhoods. Several such resorts around LA catered to movie stars and other celebrities demanding discretion. One such resort was Siempre Primavera.

Max stepped from the limousine that had been waiting for him at the airport, mounted a couple of steps and walked across a spacious patio toward large double doors where a young man in his early twenties, smartly dressed in a tuxedo, held one of the doors open as he approached. Max passed through the door and continued across another forty feet of terra cotta tile to a reception area, where another young man in a tuxedo asked, "May I help you, sir?"

"I have an appointment with Doctor Gammons."

"Yes sir, your name please?"

"Mike Kayde."

The young man checked the reservation list, picked up the phone, punched a couple of numbers, waited a few seconds and stated, "Mr. Kayde is here."

Replacing the telephone receiver he replied, "Someone will be with you in a moment, sir. Would you care to wait in our refreshment bar?"

"Thanks."

The attendant directed Max to an area with several tables covered with white linen tablecloths and set with sterling silver, fine china, and linen napkins. A fruit and juice bar was set up to one side; Max chose a glass of apple juice and sat down at the nearest table.

"Mr. Michael Justin Kayde?" Max placed his half-empty glass on the table, got up and turned to face a very attractive young woman with short, blonde hair and a bright smile, wearing a leotard that fit her shapely, tanned body like a second skin.

"Yes."

"Hi, I'm Heather. I'll show you to your cottage." Max followed her as she wiggled through two large rooms with various arrangements of overstuffed furniture, across a large covered patio, around a swimming pool, along a walkway, and turned onto another walkway that led to the door of a nice-size cottage. Opening the door and standing to one side she said, "I'm sure you will enjoy your stay with us, Mr. Kayde."

Max walked into a comfortably sized room with more overstuffed furniture. "If you follow me, please, I'll show you around."

Heather walked past a bar at the opposite end of the room and continued through a sliding glass door onto a small, completely private patio. The usual patio furniture, an umbrella table with chairs, and a chaise lounge were placed strategically around two sides of a Jacuzzi. On the opposite side of the Jacuzzi, near another sliding glass door that led to a bathroom and dressing area stood something resembling a hospital examination table. To the left a third sliding glass door opened into the bedroom. The rooms connected in a sort of horseshoe around the patio in a modern-day version of Old California.

Flowers, trees, and shrubs surrounded every building, concealing one from another, and masking the size of the resort. Siempre Primavera was a health resort where the well-heeled came to lose a few pounds and rejuvenate in a pampered environment with a little surgical assistance if so desired, and of course, all in the strictest confidence.

Max followed Heather as she wiggled back across the patio and into the living room. She opened the door, then turned and said, "I'll tell Doctor Gammons you're here. If you want or need anything just ask for me; I will personally take care of all your needs while you're staying with us."

Max gave Heather one of those, do-you-mean-what-I'm-hoping-you-mean looks when he asked, "All my needs?"

"All your needs," she repeated with raised eyebrows and a devious grin, then closed the door and was gone.

Doctor Gammons was the first person over thirty he had met since arriving at Siempre Primavera. Well, after all, he surmised, you did expect to see a health resort run by the young and fit, not the out-of-shape middle-aged. After a brief consultation he followed another shapely leotard-clad young lady to a studio where she photographed him from several angles. After the photo session he followed her to an examination room, where she recorded his weight, measurements, and vital signs. He was then led back to Doctor Gammons' office.

A dozen eight-by-ten close-ups of his face, shot at different angles with little scribbles, arrows, and shaded areas on them were neatly laid out on a drafting table. After half an hour Max and the doctor agreed on the changes. Doctor Gammons liked to refer to them as enhancements. The doctor would straighten and reduce his nose as well as fill in a crease at the bridge of his nose, remove his double chin and remove some cartilage from his chin to create a cleft. His hairline would be changed. His ears would no longer stick out like saucers. The doctor insisted that several other enhancements were also necessary if the surgery was to be successful. He assured Max that none of his old friends would recognize him and he would be more than happy with the results. Looking at a sketch the doctor perceived to be the final result, Max agreed that his appearance not only would be incredibly different, but immensely improved as well.

Surgery was scheduled for the following morning, after which he would rehabilitate three weeks at Siempre Primavera while incisions healed and all telltale signs of surgery disappeared. Doctor Gammons encouraged Max to take advantage of the resort's services and programs during rehabilitation. Max immediately thought of one amenity of which he hoped to take full advantage.

The young lady in the outer office took charge again, explaining among other things, that all pictures and records would be given him at the end of his stay. As a first-time guest he would be required to pay in advance, and everyone was required to sign a waiver of liability. Max signed the waiver, paid in cash, and received a receipt.

Heather was waiting to escort him back to his cottage. His measurements had provided her with the last details she needed to furnish his cottage with everything he would need during his stay, including clothes. Guests were all required to dress the same, shirts and shorts for men, and leotards for women. Warm-up suits were optional. Running shoes were the required footwear.

"Dinner will be served here on the patio in an hour. We have just enough time for me to give you a massage." She led him to the examination table, now covered with a soft pad. A serving cart with towels and various ointments stood nearby.

Max lay, naked and face down, on the table while Heather's fingers worked magic up and down his back. He was fully relaxed, with his eyes closed, almost asleep, when he heard the pumps in the Jacuzzi come to life. He opened his eyes just in time to see Heather remove her leotard and step into the water. No question about it, she was blonde. Dumb questions raced through his mind. "How long before dinner? What had she said, an hour? How much time has passed?" Then, smiling, he whispered to himself, "Hell, what difference does it make anyway." He slipped off the table and into the hot aerated water.

The limousine pulled away and headed for the airport. With the exception of a couple of hairline scars that would eventually disappear, his memories would be the only evidence he ever visited Siempre Primavera—all pictures and documents had been shredded. Looking back for one last glimpse, although he knew it unlikely, he found himself thinking that one day he might return for a tune-up. According to Heather, the clinic had bent the rules to give him a reservation at short notice, reservations were filed a year in advance except for regular clients, and at two grand a day it was unlikely he would ever become a regular client. Counting surgery, he'd shelled out nearly a hundred thousand dollars. He had collected eight years' back pay with interest, but at this rate he would be broke in a matter of months—there was no back pay; unbeknownst to Max, Henri Tosi had arranged a onetime compensation from the CIA's black-ops account, Henri also arranged to have Heather help clear his mind of any cobwebs and dust from the past that might have remained.

Well, tomorrow he would worry about finances, and whether or not he might be destitute in his old age. Yes, there would be plenty of time to think about adjusting to mainstream America, but today he just wanted to enjoy his first day of freedom. To enjoy the first day in the life of Maxwell Alexander Kayne. Today, he had nothing to do but everything and no place to go but everywhere.

SEVEN-MINUTE WATER

It was a typical Southern California day when the sunshine made everything sparkle. The kind of day that made you feel good just to be alive. Max had never been more alive and never felt better. He had put Siempre Primavera's exercise equipment, weight room, and running track to good use and was back to his normal 185 pounds; his reflexes were quick and his mind sharp. Yes, it was a great day and it was, indeed, good to be alive.

Max watched the Naval Hospital slip past his window as the 727 flew low over Balboa Park before it swooped down into the heart of the city for a landing. He had celebrated his twenty-first birthday at Balboa Naval Hospital while recovering from wounds received at Khe Sanh. When delivered by "Dust Off" to the Evac Hospital at Qui Nhon he had not been expected to live. He'd recovered enough to be moved to Yokosuka via Saigon and after a month was flown back to "the world." Two years later he was in Europe working for the Central Intelligence Agency.

As he rode down Harbor Drive past the tuna fleet tied up along the embarcadero he sat back and watched the pleasure boats on Glorietta Bay. He remembered when, as a young marine, he had taken a similar ride from the same airport to Camp Pendleton. From his first glimpse of the Pacific Ocean he had fallen in love with Southern California and especially laid-back San Diego. Now he hardly recognized the city. It had changed beyond belief. He wondered if the open, easygoing lifestyle had changed as well.

The taxi driver dropped Max in front of an ultramodern high-rise with an impressive entrance. After several minutes he finally convinced security to open the door. Once inside he was escorted into an office where he produced enough identification to satisfy everyone, after which he received a copy of his lease, a copy of the house rules, and a list of services and telephone numbers, plus a handful of other papers and documents. Two plastic cards with magnetic coding, he was told, served as keys to his condo and all other security locks in the building, including the elevators, parking garage, fitness center, and the various recreational areas.

A cute little redhead named Sherry escorted him to his apartment. He thought about the last young lady to show him to his quarters and took a second look at his sexy little escort and wondered, "Twice in a row? Nah, not a chance."

The elevator stopped on the eighteenth floor and they stepped out into a foyer with a lot of marble, terrazzo, and potted plants. He followed Sherry to the left along a wide passageway to the last door and had a second opportunity to use his plastic key, the elevator being the first.

Once inside, he followed Sherry through the apartment as she explained some of the gadgetry. Back at the entryway she instructed him on the use of the television monitor, how to view guests and which button allowed them to enter if he wished to receive them. The guest would then be escorted to his apartment by security. Convinced he understood everything, she asked, "Any questions, Mr. Kayne?"

He thought for a few seconds. What the hell, he'd give it a shot. "What time do you get off duty?"

She walked to the door, turned, and smiled brightly. "Have a good day, Mr. Kayne."

Before he could respond she was gone. Max shrugged and mumbled to himself, "Well, nothing ventured nothing gained."

What to do first? He wanted a car, he needed clothes, he wanted to see a movie, to walk on the beach, to sit in the park and just watch people. The list was endless. Also, he needed to furnish and decorate his apartment.

Henri had done well by him, arranging a two-year lease with the option to buy. Max was pleased with his condominium, although he liked referring to it as an apartment. Its eighteenth-floor corner location provided a fantastic view. West across Coronado and North Island was Point Loma, to the north he could see Mission Bay, and south across the Silver Strand the Coronado Islands were visible. Yeah, he was going to like being back in San Diego.

Time passed rapidly. He found the car be wanted, a 1967 Ferrari 330 Spider, not flashy like the popular 308, but small, quick, and fun to drive. Sherry had helped him choose furniture and decorate his apartment. She also influenced him in the selection of his wardrobe. Max had been attracted to Sherry from the beginning and persisted until she finally agreed to a dinner date, and within a few weeks they became good friends and romantically involved.

Six months and nearly two hundred thousand dollars later serious thoughts concerning employment and what to do with the rest of his life floated through his consciousness from time to time. He had first thought the money he'd received for the last eight years with the CIA would be enough. He would just live off the interest. But he had already been dipping into the capital rather substantially. And, too, logic told him inflation would continually reduce his buying power until for all practical purposes, he would be broke.

He had taken a course in bartending, gotten a real estate license, and completed a couple of courses in computer programming. It wasn't that he couldn't get a job—he didn't want a job. You can't live on the edge all your adult life and then in your midthirties settle into a nine-to-five job. He had been formulating a plan in the back of his mind for some time now, although up front he tried to deny its existence. But the very fact that he was taking another advanced computer programming course, had spent a considerable amount of money on equipment, had designed and loaded up highly technical and complicated programs told him it was time to admit the truth and get on with his plan.

Max had kept in touch with Henri and with some wrangling had persuaded him to provide access codes for the CIA, FBI, and DEA computers. Max had programmed his computer to interface with Henri's via modem and to accept and store the codes automatically as they were updated in Henri's computer.

Getting into other computers wasn't very difficult providing you'd done a little research and had the right equipment and the proper codes. But getting into another computer wasn't enough. The computer's program might ask for any number of authenticators at any given time. You also needed safeguards of your own—otherwise, while you were busy hacking away at a computer's memory banks, that very same system might be sorting through the data in your own memory banks, identifying you and your interests. Max felt comfortable with his system. He had spent over six months setting it up and so far it was working beautifully.

Max had been compiling data on KGB activity in the United States with cross-reference to name, code name, present or last known location, dates, associates, U.S. citizens contacted, areas of expertise. He could not believe how openly the KGB operated throughout the country. Maybe Americans didn't believe Khrushchev was serious when he said to them, "Your grandchildren will live under communism."

Well, Max knew Khrushchev was serious and believed world domination was still the Communists' goal. America needed a deterrent for the three hundred thousand KGB agents who operated throughout the world openly and without fear of prosecution. The judicial system was certainly no deterrent. Anyone visiting the United States with a diplomatic passport was exempt from prosecution and there was always an overabundance of attorneys with an allegiance to money rather than country to protect the others. Someone needed to answer the Kremlin in terms they understood and respected. Max figured there was no one better for the task. He had been schooled and trained by the best, the Marines, the CIA, the SIS, the GRU, and the KGB. Perhaps destiny had led him from that day in the nation's capital when he had resolved to help determine the future course of America to this very day and the only decision possible. He would work outside the law, becoming a fugitive himself. If caught, he might be executed by the very system he was trying to preserve. What the hell, it was better than tending bar and a lot less boring than selling real estate.

The conspirator had not been found in the embassy in Moscow. This left two other possibilities—CIA Headquarters at Langley, and the listening station in Alaska. A simple plan was devised. Messages with Jack Johnson's old code name, Spider, were sent at specific times along with routine traffic. Spider was the code name given Jack Johnson at the very beginning of his association with the CIA because of his involvement in road racing during his assignment in Europe and his passion for open-top Italian sports cars. The coded messages did not arrive at Langley.

The operation near Haines in Alaska's Southeast panhandle was well disguised. A few miles out of town a small, obscure military base used as a supply depot for the Aleutian campaign during World War II had been closed down in the early sixties. A minimal contingent had remained to secure and maintain the base.

In the midseventies, two men brought a construction crew to Eagle Point and promptly took up residence in one of the central buildings in the compound. Crates of equipment arrived and were moved into the building occupied by the newcomers. All the windows were painted black, the locks were changed, and two diesel generators were set up in hush houses near the building occupied by the strangers and their equipment—the security contingent was not privy to what went on inside the building. A year later, with the installation complete and all the equipment operating properly, the construction crew departed. The two remaining men lived and worked inside the building, supposedly tracking weather patterns developing in the Gulf of Alaska. Everyone around Haines believed the three large, newly erected satellite dishes near the building to belong to the National Weather Service. No one ever suspected that from this small, out-of-the-way military base the CIA operated a vital link to a U.S. spy network in the Soviet Union.

Max, for reasons unknown even to himself, had been gathering information on Howard Tolinger. Possibly it was because he had personally handled material Tolinger had turned over to the KGB, or perhaps he suspected that the colonel, having betrayed his country once, would do it again or that just maybe he had never stopped selling his country's secrets. Whatever the reason, it seemed to have paid off.

———

A month after Colonel Tolinger had been transferred to Vandenberg Air Force Base and assigned to the SLC Six project, John and Evone Gilbird bought and moved into a house on Surf Road in Lompoc, California, near Vandenberg Air Force Base. The Gilbirds also purchased a bankrupt janitorial service on the outskirts of Lompoc. This had been a real stroke of luck. John and Evone Gilbird had been in "cold storage" since they had immigrated into the United States in 1968.

When the Soviet Union, along with Warsaw Pact allies, invaded Czechoslovakia and set up a Communist-controlled government, purges followed—a Stalinist practice that had become standard in the Eastern bloc. A practice that worked very well—simply arrest and kill anyone and everyone who opposes or disagrees with Communist ideals. During these purges many Czechoslovakians fled their homeland and migrated to the West. Among them were numerous KGB agents using birth certificates and other records of Czech citizens, who were either dead or in prison, to obtain passports. In this manner agents Sergey Gorsky and Marina Maslov, members of the Foreign Intelligence Directorate, became Jan and Marja Gottwolk, refugees fleeing the Communist takeover of their native Czechoslovakia.

After arriving in the United States they legally changed their names to John and Evone Gilbird and eventually became naturalized Americans. Fortunately, a high-ranking party member from the Main Directorate of Archives and Reports defected to the West a few years later and as a gesture of good faith identified, for the CIA, some fifty KGB agents in cold storage in the United States. Jan and Marja Gottwolk were two of the agents identified.

Agents in cold storage sometimes waited decades before receiving an assignment. The Kremlin did not call one of these agents out of the "freezer" except for a mission of the utmost importance to the Soviet Union. Then and only then would they risk disclosing their true identity; in the meantime, they would live as model citizens. Although many of these cold storage agents were known to the CIA, the agency could do nothing until they were caught in the act of spying or otherwise breaking the law—under the guise of civil rights, the ACLU was always there to defend anyone engaged in spying against America.

———

It wasn't that he didn't want to trust Sherry—she had become a major part of his life—but his past had made him suspicious of all women, especially those with whom he became close. So it had been merely coincidental that Gilbird's name showed up on his computer screen. He was searching PSA's reservation list to confirm Sherry was actually en route to San Francisco—to visit her father, or so she had said—when Gilbird's reservation from Los Angeles to Juneau, Alaska caught his attention. Max Kayne's gut feeling told him John Gilbird had a very important assignment.

Immediately after seeing Gilbird's name on the reservation list Max had double checked the KGB agent's itinerary then called PSA and Alaska Airlines and reserved seating on the same flights. The fact that the PSA flight Gilbird would board in Los Angeles originated at Lindberg Field in San Diego worked in Max's favor. Max was relieved to learn that Sherry had a confirmed reservation on a direct flight from San Diego to San Francisco which left an hour earlier than the one he would be taking. He would make sure he did not arrive at the airport until her flight had departed—if she didn't know he was flying to Juneau there would be nothing to explain.

The "Fasten Seat Belt" sign went off and a voice came over the PA system.

"Good morning. Welcome to Pacific Southwest Airlines flight 104. We will be serving complimentary coffee in just a few minutes. If you would like a cup, please lower your serving tray and the flight attendant will be with you shortly." Max lowered his tray and watched a guy pushing a serving cart up the aisle. The name tag on his vest read, "Shawn, Flight Attendant."

"Cream and sugar, sir?"

"Just cream." Shawn placed a Styrofoam cup, three quarters full of coffee, and a small packet of nondairy creamer on the tray in front of Max, "Have a nice flight, sir."

Yeah, thanks." Max took a swallow of coffee and wondered, what had become of all the cute little girls wearing pretty smiles, miniskirts, and name tags declaring them to be stewardesses that he remembered from the sixties.

The captain announced their arrival at Los Angeles International and instructed passengers booked through to Seattle to remain on board the aircraft. All other passengers were to deplane at this time.

The flight from San Diego took only thirty-five minutes while the unloading and loading of passengers took almost an hour.

Max watched the new arrivals file through the hatch, passing over some quickly, completely disregarding many, scrutinizing others more closely, and studying a few in detail. By the time they were taxiing into position for take-off he was fairly certain he had identified John Gilbird. He was about five feet ten inches tall, around fifty years old, and a little on the pudgy side at approximately one hundred-ninety pounds. Before they made connections for Juneau he would make sure.

It was twenty minutes before noon when the passengers finally began making their way up the ramp into the terminal at SEA-TAC. Max kept a half-dozen people between himself and the man he suspected to be John Gilbird. As the man approached the Alaska Airlines check-in counter Max stopped, feigning interest in a Northwestern Native Art exhibit. The man spent only a few minutes at the counter. After receiving his boarding pass he headed straight for the waiting area.

A woman with a little girl in tow approached the counter and began searching through her purse. Not finding whatever she was looking for she dumped the contents of her purse on the counter and put things back in her purse one at a time. Max made his way over and waited while the woman stuffed everything back inside her purse. She then frantically started going through her luggage.

"May I help you, sir?" Max stepped around the woman, who was still searching through her suitcase, and handed his ticket to the attendant at the counter. The man took the ticket and punched his computer keyboard a few times.

"Smoking or nonsmoking, sir?"

"Nonsmoking." The man punched the keyboard a couple more times and the printer spat out a boarding pass.

"You'll be boarding in about forty-five minutes at gate five."

"Thanks. Say, I'm flying up with a business associate—can you tell me if he's checked in yet?"

"What's his name?"

"John Gilbird." The attendant typed the name on his computer keyboard, waited about ten seconds, punched in some more information and without looking up, said, "Your friend checked in less than ten minutes ago."

"Thanks again, I appreciate your help."

The woman had given up her search and was trying to get everything back in her suitcase while yelling at the little girl. The little girl had started to cry. Max felt sorry for the kid but didn't want to attract attention to himself by offering assistance. He turned back to the attendant at the check-in counter and asked, "What's their problem?"

"The lady claims to have purchased round-trip fares in Juneau and has misplaced their return tickets."

"How much will it cost them for first class?" The attendant consulted his computer,

"Three hundred eighty-seven dollars." Max placed four one-hundred-dollar bills on the counter. "Make sure they get to Juneau. Handle it any way you want, just don't mention my name." The man smiled and nodded, "I'll take care of it, sir. You have a good trip."

Max knew very little about Alaska and nothing whatsoever about Juneau, except that it was the state capital. Knowing he would be at a disadvantage if he ended up playing cat and mouse in a place he knew absolutely nothing about, he found the gift shop and purchased a book on Southeast Alaska, with lots of maps and pictures. He would read it on the flight and whatever he learned in the next couple of hours would have to suffice.

Descending into a cloud bank that seemed endless Max began to wonder if they were going to fly straight into the ground. At 400 feet they broke through underneath and were lined up perfectly with the runway. As the passengers deplaned, Max, not wanting to lose Gilbird in the crowd, followed only a few yards behind. Carrying an overnight-sized suitcase and a shoulder bag, Gilbird bypassed the baggage claim area, hurried outside and headed straight toward a line of waiting taxicabs. A light rain was falling, not unexpected for a region averaging over a hundred inches of precipitation a year. A gusting wind carried not only a chill but the hint of snow as well. Max already suspected—from reading the book purchased at SEA-TAC, and now he knew for sure—he didn't have the proper clothing.

He hung back until Gilbird's taxi pulled away from the curb before hailing the next cab in line. The driver held the door open and Max, welcoming the opportunity to get out of the rain, which was coming down harder now, jumped into the back seat. The driver slammed the door, slipped in behind the wheel and asked, "Where to, Mister?"

"See that taxi just pulling into the traffic?" Max continued without waiting for an answer. "I want you to follow it, but don't let them know your intentions."

"Hey, what is this, some kind of cops-and-robbers game?"

Max had assembled a few props for such an occasion. Henri was obviously aware of his friend's intentions to impersonate various government officials and might not have approved, but had delivered, without requiring an explanation, the various blank identification cards requested. A Polaroid camera with the correct color background and a ninety-five-cent lamination kit from the five and dime store produced very authentic looking identification.

Pulling an official Government Issue ID case from his pocket and making sure the card he wanted was behind the plastic window, he flipped it open under the cabbie's nose.

You could get someone's attention and probably impress most people by showing any type of official law enforcement ID, but if you really wanted cooperation while scaring the hell out of them, you told them that you're from the IRS. "I'm with the Internal Revenue Service and I would appreciate your help."

The driver took a good long look, swallowed a couple of times and said, "Sure thing, Mister."

"Okay, don't lose this guy and I'll double your fee, and if you assure me you aren't going to start talking about how you've been tailing some guy for the IRS, I'll add another hundred bucks."

"Mister, there are three things I do well, drive a cab, follow instructions, and mind my own business."

"Hey, you're just the guy I'm looking for. What's your name?"

"Bernie."

They followed Gilbird downtown. When his taxi stopped in front of the Alaska Marine Highway ticket office Bernie continued past, made a U-turn in the middle of the next block, and parked on the opposite side of the street near the intersection.

"I get the feeling you've done this sort of thing before." Bernie chuckled, but didn't reply.

Gilbird jumped out of the taxi, holding the suitcase over his head to shield his face from the rain and sprinted for the ticket office doorway.

"Is the other driver a friend of yours?"

"Yeah, I know him."

"Do you think you can find out where he's going from here?"

"I'll see what I can do."

Bernie picked up his microphone, "Yo, Chuck, what's up?"

Chuck's voice came over the radio loud and clear. "Not much, just waiting around for some guy. How about you?"

"Same thing. What's your next stop?"

"Don't know."

"It's worth a six-pack if you let me know."

"See what I can do. What's happening, man?"

Bernie lowered his voice as though trying to keep a fare, sitting in the back seat, from overhearing, "Jealous wife."

"See what I can do," Chuck repeated.

A few minutes later John Gilbird dashed out and threw himself into the back seat of the taxi. As soon as the door closed a loud click came over the radio followed by Gilbird's voice. Chuck was holding the microphone key open so the entire conversation could be heard over the radio.

"Take me to the ferry terminal."

"Which one, Auke Bay or Juneau?" Chuck asked.

"I don't know. She just said the ferry leaves from downtown." The radio went dead.

"Okay, we got it, do we follow him?" Bernie asked.

"Not yet." Max replied.

For several minutes Max and Bernie talked about the things you always talk about when you're trying to pass the time, they talked about the weather, entertainment, and the economy. After about five minutes Max got out of the cab and walked into the Alaska Marine Highway ticket office.

A woman of about thirty-five, a little on the chubby side, looked up from the paperback romance she was reading, and asked, "Can I help you?"

"I was supposed to meet a friend here, but I'm a little late. You wouldn't happen to know if a man has been in here by the name of John Gilbird?"

The woman typed something on her computer keyboard and checked the monitor. "You just missed him; he was in about five minutes ago and purchased passage to Seattle."

"Well, I guess he decided not to wait around for me; how much to Seattle?"

"Passage from Juneau to Seattle will be eighty-five dollars. However, there are no staterooms available; you'll have to sleep either in the lounge or in the solarium."

"Well, that's okay; I can bunk with my buddy. What's the number of his stateroom?" She consulted her computer again. "He's in stateroom 26, on the main deck."

Max handed over a C-note and waited while the lady typed the necessary information into the computer. Punching one last key she turned and waited for the printer to serve up the appropriate paperwork.

"Okay, Mr. Anderson, you have confirmed passage on the *Matanuska* from Juneau to Seattle departing from the downtown terminal at five twenty this afternoon. I suggest you board at least an hour before sailing."

"Thank you." With ticket in hand Max returned to the taxi and explained the problem of berthing to Bernie and asked his advice.

"Well, personally I like the solarium. You get a great view, lots of fresh air, and unlike the lounge, once you've staked out your territory it's yours for the rest of the trip. And besides all that you meet a better class of people." Bernie gave Max one of those smiles difficult to interpret. Max couldn't tell whether or not Bernie was serious, but when he added, "The tourists all ride up front and the locals hang out in the solarium," Max had the feeling Bernie was just having some fun with a cheechako.

"Of course you're going to need some clothes and equipment, otherwise you'll get cold and maybe a little wet if this rain keeps up."

"I'm already cold and wet."

Bernie laughed. "Well, we can fix that if you don't mind spending a few bucks."

"I'm putting myself completely in your hands."

At the Alaskan Nugget Outfitter Bernie suggested several items, including thermal underwear, heavy wool socks, a wool shirt, and a pair of wool pants, a Gore-Tex parka, down vest, rain pants, a pair of black rubber boots he called Juneau sneakers, a sleeping bag, and a rainproof backpack. In the dressing room Max stripped off his wet clothes, slipped into his new duds, stuffed the wet clothing into a heavy plastic bag and placed them in the bottom of his backpack. When Max walked out of the dressing room Bernie looked him up and down, shook his head and smiled, "Well, you won't pass for a sourdough but you're going to stay warm and dry. Where to now?"

"Back to the airport."

Max picked up his suitcase, which was still making the round-trip to nowhere on the conveyer belt, and walked to the nearest telephone.

The phone rang twice before Henri answered. The conversation lasted only a couple of minutes. When Max hung up the receiver he stood looking at the instrument the way a cat sometimes stares at a blank wall, as though watching something on the other side. He stood motionless, eyes narrowed, lips tight, mouth pulled back at the corners, watching some scene unfold somewhere in the recesses of his mind.

"Excuse me, are you finished with your call?" an elderly lady asked.

"Yeah, sure." The spell broken, he picked up his suitcase and headed toward the waiting taxi.

"Where to now, Mister?"

"I've got a ferry to catch." Max replied, between clenched teeth.

It wasn't the words of the barely audible response that made the cabbie uneasy, but rather something cold and calculating inferred by the voice itself that sent a chill creeping up his spine. When Bernie glanced in the rearview mirror the face he saw looking back at him did nothing to relieve his anxiety.

"Are you okay, Mister?"

Max was immediately aware, by the uneasiness in Bernie's voice and the concern expressed by the question, he had made a mistake. He had let his emotions show. It wouldn't happen again. Luckily, it made little difference at this particular time, Bernie was no threat, but now he might not be as willing to assist.

Max was suddenly aware of another problem. During the last couple of hours a strange sort of friendship had developed between the two and it troubled him that Bernie now had misgivings. A sure sign he was losing his edge. He could not afford to be concerned about other people's feelings. Nevertheless, he felt compelled to try and restore the relationship, even if it was a relationship built on lies.

"Yeah, I'm okay, I'm just tired." He hesitated, then continued, "Tired of everything, tired of following people to hell and back, of never getting a good night's sleep or a home-cooked meal, tired of never knowing where my next assignment will be. Sometimes I just want to flush it all."

"I hear you, man." The serious tone of Bernie's voice conveyed his understanding.

Well, it looked like the cabbie was more at ease now. Another lie or two should do the trick. Max wondered if anyone ever told the truth. Maybe everybody's life was, in one way or another, a fabrication.

"Do you have a family?" Max asked, his voice now touched with melancholy.

"I've been married three times, but none of them worked out."

"Well, it looks like I may be joining your club. Mine doesn't seem to be working out either." He hesitated again and inhaled deeply and let it out slowly for effect. "Well, that's enough of this crap; I've got to get on with my job. Would you do me one more favor?"

"Sure, what do you need?"

Bernie was back in the fold. "Let's make one more stop at the Alaska Marine Highway ticket office."

"Hey, no problem. And, say man, for what it's worth, I hope things work out for you back home. That sort of thing is hard on a man, I know, I've been there and done that too many times."

"Thanks Bernie, I appreciate it."

The conversation continued, but on a lighter note, and as they eased through the traffic Max transferred the contents of his suitcase to the newly purchased backpack, except for one soft leather case slightly larger than a pack of cigarettes. The leather case he slipped into the pocket of his parka. The plastic bag of wet clothing went into the suitcase. Next, he stripped off the airline routing tags and the identification tag attached earlier at the insistence of the clerk at the baggage check-in counter in San Diego. He removed the identification information tag the manufacturer had felt compelled to provide, from behind the plastic window and filled in the name, Haskel Mitchell, Eagle Point, Haines, Alaska. Insuring the suitcase was locked, he placed it in the front seat as the taxi came to a stop in front of the ticket office.

"Take this inside and tell them you dropped off a passenger at the ferry terminal and you later discovered his suitcase. Ask them to check and see if he's booked on the ferry leaving Juneau today. If he is, find out where he's going and which stateroom he's in. If they're uncooperative, tell them the guy was a big tipper and you're hoping for a reward if you return the suitcase."

"I'll see what I can do."

Bernie was back in a couple of minutes, tossed the suitcase onto the front seat, slipped in under the steering wheel, turned and gave Max a big grin. "Your man is in stateroom 24 on the main deck. He's getting off at Rupert."

"Getting off where?"

"Prince Rupert, British Columbia. The ferry makes one stop in Canada just below Ketchikan. It's the last stop before Seattle."

"Thanks, Bernie."

"Nothing to it, man. I think I'm a natural for this sort of work. Does it pay well?" They both laughed.

"It doesn't pay well enough, but if I ever need a full-time assistant I'll look you up, okay?" Max wondered if the man would have been as willing to help him if he had known the truth.

"It's a deal. Say, I'd better get you on down to the ferry, she's gonna sail in about forty minutes."

Max had discovered earlier, at the Alaskan Nugget, goods and services did not come cheap in Alaska. He was reminded again when Bernie flipped down the flag on the meter; it read $142. He held out four crisp hundred-dollar bills. Bernie shook his head.

"Ah man, you don't have to do that."

"A deal's a deal, okay?"

"Okay, thanks." They shook hands and Max headed for the gangway, where the purser took one copy of his ticket and informed him he would need to show the other copy upon arrival at Seattle. The second copy would also permit him to depart and return to the ship at any port along the way.

He found the solarium all the way aft on the uppermost deck. All deck chairs along the starboard side and forward bulkhead were either occupied or otherwise staked out with the traditional backpack or sleeping bag. The rule of thumb, according to Bernie, was to choose the starboard side going south and the port side coming north. This would provide the best protection from weather since the wind always came out of the Gulf of Alaska. The glass would protect you on the windward side, but the wind and rain would whip in across the solarium's open end aft and make the trip a bit uncomfortable for people on the leeward side. Bernie had passed this bit of information along as though it was a secret shared by only a few. Obviously the secret was out. Max spread out his sleeping bag on a chair midways along the port side, shoved his backpack underneath, and set out to explore the ship.

It didn't require much time to find the two staterooms, 24 and 26. Obviously the day for the exchange of money for state secrets had been chosen well in advance. The fact that Gilbird and Mitchell had side-by-side staterooms was not a coincidence—they had been booked well in advance. On the same deck, forward of the purser's office, he found a sleeping lounge, occupied mostly by older people who preferred the large reclining chairs and the controlled environment to the solarium. One level above the main deck was the forward observation lounge. The majority of passengers seated in the comfortable couches and arm chairs were tourists all set for the scenic cruise down the famous Inside Passage. Further aft was a bar, a game room for kids, a dining room, and a cafeteria. Max had slept only a couple of hours the night before and it seemed like a good opportunity to check out the comforts of his new sleeping bag. However, the aromas drifting out of the cafeteria persuaded him to postpone crawling into his sleeping bag for a little while longer.

Balancing a bowl of chili, a piece of hot apple pie, and a glass of milk on a tray he walked toward the no-smoking section. He was just about to put his tray down when he spotted John Gilbird sitting alone at another table nursing a cup of coffee. On impulse he walked over, placed his tray opposite Gilbird, pulled out a chair and was about to sit down.

"There's no one sitting at the next table," Gilbird snapped.

"I like this one." Max replied as he placed his food on the table opposite Gilbird. After handing the empty tray to a nearby busboy he sat down and began eating.

The KGB agent was quite nervous and fidgeted almost continuously. Max had nearly finished his chili before Gilbird pushed his chair back from the table and stood up.

"Sit down, Comrade Gorsky," Max commanded, in perfect Russian. Startled, the man sat down without hesitation. He tried to remain calm, but was unprepared for anything so profound and stammered out his reply in English. "You have mistaken me for someone else."

"No, Sergey, there is no mix-up," Max continued, still speaking in Russian. "How's Marina?"

"I do not understand." Again, Gilbird spoke in English.

Max did not respond right away. He continued to eat while thinking everything through one last time. He could have waited until Gilbird was alone and least expected trouble, rather than alerting him to some impending danger. That would have been the sensible thing to do, but this had been spur-of-the-moment, brought on by a combination of the chance meeting and the telephone conversation with Henri Tosi. At the moment, emotion ruled his actions and logic was of little concern. Max had already decided the agent's fate, but for the moment he would let the man sweat.

Max had expected Gilbird's flight up the Pacific coast to end in Haines and was puzzled when, arriving in Juneau, he immediately booked passage on the ferry to Seattle. It became quite clear, however, when Henri filled him in on the recent events in Haines.

Since only two men at Eagle Point were privy to data transmitted by Dead Man, the plan to expose the guilty man in Haines was simple. One man at Eagle Point would be relieved of his duties with orders to return to Langley, for a supposedly routine indoctrination before reassignment to another listening station located in Asia. Messages would again be transmitted from Moscow using Jack's code name, Spider. If the messages arrived at Langley, the conspirator had been the one transferred, if they failed to arrive then he would be the one remaining at Eagle Point.

Henri had learned, only a few minutes before Max called, the CIA agent arriving at Eagle Point had found one man still in bed with his throat slashed and the other man missing. Henri had been notified immediately and extra CIA people were presently on their way to Haines.

Max had learned from Bernie that once each week an Alaska State Ferry left Seattle bound for the upper Lynn Canal and stopped at several towns along the Inside Passage. The ferry turned around at Skagway, the northernmost community on the canal, and made the same ports of call on the return trip, arriving in Seattle exactly one week later.

The "Mat," as it was known by Alaskans, was on her return trip to Seattle. The Mat's last stop before Juneau was Haines. Haskel Mitchell in stateroom 24 had killed his coworker earlier that day and was on his way out of the country. Mitchell could not have been alerted to the investigation; the transfer orders were being hand-carried by the newly assigned agent. The timing of events was strictly coincidental. Mitchell had not killed simply to cover his tracks. The crime would have been discovered when routine security inquiry codes went unanswered. He killed in order to buy enough time to make his deal with Gilbird and get out of the country. A few extra hours was all he needed. Sailing time for the Mat, including port calls, was about thirty-six hours from Haines to Prince Rupert. He needed only two days to meet with Gilbird, get paid for his pilfered information, and disappear through Canada.

Max continued to eat and consider his choices. He could call Henri and report everything he knew about Mitchell and Gilbird. Mitchell would be arrested—then what? The State Department could not make public the fact that what everyone believed to be a weather station at Eagle Point, Alaska was actually an intelligence-gathering station, operated by the Central Intelligence Agency. A deal would be struck and therefore, no trial and no conviction, and in return for silence a murderer and traitor would be allowed to go free. Gilbird would be deported as persona non grata and whatever the KGB was involved with at Vandenberg would continue undetected. Max knew he had no choice. It was time to stand up for what he believed in although he would become a fugitive and before he was finished would most likely head the FBI's most wanted list.

John Gilbird sat watching the stranger, who spoke his native language and knew his Russian name, waiting for him to speak again. But the stranger did not speak again; he only stared across the table and continued eating. Gilbird felt the muscles in his face twitch; his fists were so tight his fingernails were cutting into his palms, and he knew he was going to become sick. The minutes seemed like hours. He wanted to run, but he feared the consequences. He wrestled with his emotions as long as he could before summoning every ounce of strength and composure he had left in his body and asked, "Who are you?"

He had intended the question to sound demanding, but his voice broke and it became nothing more than a plea from a frightened man.

"My name is not important." Max spoke to the man in English for the first time. Lowering his voice almost to a whisper, forcing the man to lean closer in order to hear, "We cannot talk here; let's go to your cabin."

"I don't have a room, they were all taken." He knew all too well what happened to agents who made mistakes. When a superior called unexpectedly there was always reason for concern, and the meeting usually ended unpleasantly for the subordinate. He did not want to be alone with this stranger but what other choice was there? Again he had the urge to flee, but there was nowhere to run. For a moment he considered finding the ship's captain, confessing everything, and asking for political asylum. He liked America; he had a much better life here than he had ever had in the Soviet Union. Several times, in the last couple of years, he had considered going to Immigration and asking for asylum, but his life kept getting more complicated and he had never found the courage to take the first, crucial step. Maybe it wasn't too late—what if he killed the stranger? Why not? He had lots of money with him; he could change his name and just disappear. He was jolted back to reality when the stranger leaned close to his face and growled, "You're in stateroom 26 on the main deck, now let's go."

John Gilbird's eyes narrowed. He stood and inhaled deeply, and then slowly expelled the air from his lungs. His shoulders rose slightly as he filled his lungs then fell into a relaxed position as he exhaled. He had come to a decision. There was no tension in his voice when he replied, "Okay, let's go."

Max had watched the man struggle with his emotions and knew the questions with which he labored. He followed the man's thinking almost thought for thought and was especially alert as they entered the stateroom. He knew there was danger, but this was where he wanted to be, alone with Gilbird in his stateroom.

John Gilbird took plenty of time with the lock, removing the key with his left hand. Although he'd been in deep cover for over a decade his training was still there, automatically recalled by the situation at hand. Gilbird knew it was now or never—there would be no second chance.

Max stayed close behind Gilbird as they entered the room. He saw Gilbird's left hand toss the stateroom key onto the bed, a ploy to divert his attention, watched the KGB agent slip his right hand in and out of his pocket with lightning speed, he saw the glint of steel, heard the spring lock the blade into place, watched the man plant his right foot in order to pivot back to his left and thrust the knife upwards into the soft tissues of the unsuspecting man who followed him blindly into the room. The KGB agent, no matter how fast, was too slow. At the very instant Gilbird attempted to plant his foot, Max grabbed him by the seat of the trousers with his right hand, lifting him to an off-balance position. At the same time his left hand seized Gilbird by the hair pushing his head down and using his own weight and the KGB agent's forward motion, ran him headfirst into the steel bulkhead opposite the door. Max released his grip on the unconscious man and let him fall to the deck. There was nothing to indicate anyone had seen them enter the room or heard any suspicious noises; there was no one in the passageway outside when Max closed and locked the door.

He removed the small leather case from his pocket, knelt and placed it on the floor beside the motionless figure. Max opened the case and carefully removed a hypodermic syringe. He attached a needle and pushed the needle through the top of a small rubber stopped vial containing a clear liquid, drew a measured amount into the syringe, and replaced the vial in its niche inside the leather case alongside several other identical-looking vials. He pulled up Gilbird's pant leg, and jammed the needle deep into his calf, slowly forcing liquid out of the syringe into the muscle tissue where it would make its way into the bloodstream. Tonight he would return and bring Gilbird out of the drug-induced sleep, shoot some sodium-amytal with benzedrine into his veins and see what he could learn about KGB involvement at Vandenberg.

With the syringe back in its case and safely in his pocket he rolled Gilbird over onto his back and started searching through his pockets. A wallet was the only item of interest; he would check it later. Next he turned his efforts toward locating the suitcase he had seen Gilbird carrying when he boarded the plane in Los Angeles and which he was still carrying when he hailed a taxi at the airport. It didn't take long to find. Max looked around for something to open the locks and spotted the switchblade Gilbird had planned on using to open up his vital organs. He retrieved the knife and used it to pry open the locks.

Neatly taped bundles of fifty-dollar bills filled the suitcase. Each bundle contained one hundred fifty-dollar bills, there were two hundred such bundles. Well, as the saying went, one man's loss was another man's gain and his one-man crusade against the KGB was sure to be expensive; it seemed only fair to let the bad guys pick up the tab. At that moment Max wished Gilbird had brought hundred-dollar bills, since they would have taken up less space in his backpack and would have been easier to stuff in his parka, but he knew the KGB had a theory that hundred-dollar bills attracted too much attention and always used fifties.

There were too many bundles to fit into the large pockets of his parka. The black plastic bag lining the trash can, by the cabin's small writing table, would serve to carry the cash to the solarium. Max stuffed the money inside, then twisted and tied a knot in the top of the bag. After returning the empty suitcase to its original hiding place he picked up the black plastic bag and opened the cabin door. Using the key Gilbird had tossed on the bed Max locked the door, and then walked toward the ladder leading to the upper decks.

Max stopped in front of stateroom 24 and raised his hand to knock, hesitated, lowered his hand, and moved on down the passageway. Mitchell would wait. A ladder led to an open deck aft of the cafeteria. He walked to the fantail, leaned his back against the railing and breathed deeply, filling his lungs with the fresh air blowing crisp and invigorating across the open deck. Another minute or two passed before he walked a dozen paces and climbed a ladder that opened directly onto the solarium.

The ship's whistle sounded and the traditional announcement came over the address system. "The *Matanuska* will sail in five minutes; all visitors ashore."

The rain had stopped and the clouds were lifting to reveal numerous glaciers hanging in the high valleys below the snow-covered peaks towering over Juneau. The capital city seemed to be clinging desperately to the lower slopes of the mountains. The mountains seemed determined to push it into the water. In time the mountains would surely win.

Passengers, taking advantage of a break in the weather, gathered in small groups along the ship's railings on the open deck aft of the solarium watching the last of the trucks, autos, and recreation vehicles being driven onto the car deck below. Line handlers stood by to cast off hawsers securing the big blue and white ship to the pier. They were about to get underway.

Max made his way through and around the other chairs until he located the one he had staked out for himself. Pulling his backpack out from under the chair, he removed the items near the top and stuffed the plastic bag down toward the bottom, then replaced the removed items, secured the backpack and shoved it back underneath the chair. After removing his parka and placing it on top of his backpack he adjusted the chair to a horizontal position, and then unzipped his sleeping bag. Sitting on the chair, he removed his Juneau sneakers, also known as Ketchikan tennis shoes, and placed them alongside the backpack. As he swung his feet up and pushed them down into the sleeping bag, the ship's speakers blared, "Stand by to cast off all lines," followed a few seconds later by the command, "Cast off all lines."

The solarium on the big Alaska State Ferry, open to the rear with glass overhead and on both sides, offered an unobstructed view. Whereas a person traveling the Inside Passage for the first time might stand in awe, Maxwell Kayne, settling into his lounge chair, was aware of the majesty surrounding him, for a moment only, as he reminded himself he was not here to enjoy the beauty of this vast land—he was here to kill.

The *Matanuska* slipped her mooring, eased out into Gastineau Channel and slowly moved off into the semidarkness as alpenglow, playing along 6,000-foot peaks above Juneau, signaled an end to this late October day. In the Lower Forty-eight the sun was still high in the western sky, but Alaska's Panhandle days were growing shorter; winter was fast approaching. Already nights were below freezing along Lynn Canal; snow, now down to 1,000 feet, gave off an eerie glow as evening faded, giving way to the night.

Radiant heaters overhead, glowing red, kept the chill out of the solarium and with a stretch of the imagination you might even consider it warm, except when the wind, carrying an icy hint of the impending winter, whipped in across the stern. Passengers here, however, preferred fresh air to the stuffy closed-in observation deck or sleeping lounge, and dressed accordingly; Max Kayne was not unprepared. Pulling the drawstring on his mummy-style sleeping bag until only his face was left uncovered, he welcomed the chance to sleep. In the fleeting seconds before sleep came, he thought about the past, about the events that had brought him to this space and time.

As sleep took control of his body, unconsciousness took control of his thoughts, and he drifted back into the past, some of which he had forgotten, some of which he would never forget.

The pulsating sensation on his wrist stopped. He lay motionless, eyes closed, still breathing slowly and evenly as if in a dead sleep. Thirty seconds passed and the pulsating came again, lasting for another ten seconds. Cautiously he moved his hand to the watch on his left wrist and touched one of the tiny push-button switches. The pulsating did not recur. Max opened his eyes only slightly at first and then they popped open wide as he bolted upright. His pulse was racing, the color drained from his face, and beads of perspiration formed on his forehead.

As he became aware of his surroundings he relaxed, color returned to his face, his pulse returned to normal, and the panic racing through his body only moments before was swept away with a sigh as he sat marveling once again at the beautiful and mysterious aurora borealis dancing across the northern sky. For one terrifying moment he feared he had awakened from a dream and was still in Moscow. On countless nights and for hours on end he had gazed out across the Russian steppes watching the northern lights, but now for the very first time he watched them from the sanctuary of the free world.

Something nudged his consciousness and he remembered the reason for setting his wrist alarm. When he touched a certain button on his watch the numerals 1:21 glowed red for five seconds and were then automatically extinguished.

Easing out of his sleeping bag, he reached underneath the chair and retrieved his Juneau sneakers. After slipping his feet into the black rubber boots he knelt down and felt around inside the pockets of his parka until he located the small leather case, dropped it into his shirt pocket and buttoned down the flap. All the chairs were now occupied with people snuggled into various-colored sleeping bags. Two free-standing tents had sprung up in the after section of the solarium near the unprotected area. Nothing moved as everyone appeared to be asleep. The ship's stacks and the unbroken rhythm of the huge screws cutting through the water were the only sounds to be heard.

Well, it was time to bring Gilbird out of his drug-induced sleep and with the help of a little truth serum find out what he was involved in at Vandenberg. When Max climbed down to the fantail, the cafeteria was dark, just as he suspected it would be at this time of night, and he reached stateroom 26 without seeing or being seen by anyone. The key turned easily and the door opened quietly.

After stepping inside he closed and locked the door. As he reached for the light switch he realized something was wrong. When he flicked the switch, light flooded the room and he knew exactly what was wrong. He found himself looking into the business end of a short-barreled .357 magnum. Many would have panicked at the sight of a big mean-looking guy sticking a gun in their face, but Max had been there before, many times. Pretending to be Gilbird he asked, "So, you must be Haskel Mitchell?"

Max reasoned no one other than Mitchell was likely to be in Gilbird's room. A key had probably been left at a prearranged drop, and now Mitchell was waiting in the room, wondering who the unconscious guy was and why Gilbird hadn't shown up with the money. Max continued without waiting for an answer, "I understand you have something you want to sell me."

When there was no response from the stranger, Max changed his tone to infer a hint of concern, but was sarcastic when he said, "Well, maybe I was wrong, perhaps you have nothing to sell and you intend to rob me instead?"

The man was unmoved; the gun remained steady and trained dead center on Max Kayne's chest. Feigning impatience, Max snapped, "Look, Mitchell, I've got a problem here. If you want to get your money put the cannon away and give me a hand."

Finally, without moving or lowering the gun the man asked, "Who's the guy on the floor? What's wrong with him?"

Mitchell was a big man about six feet four inches tall and well over two hundred pounds. Max knew he couldn't make any mistakes with Haskel Mitchell. A company man turned traitor and killer would be suspicious of everyone and everything. He was not a man to be taken lightly. Max knew also that he could forget about the sodium-amytal with Benzedrine. Whatever secrets Gilbird might have divulged while under the influence of truth serum he would take to his cold and watery grave. "I don't know," Max lied. "I came back from the cafeteria this evening and found this guy filling his pockets with money. I banged him on the head, loaded him up with ketamine hydrochloride, and stayed away until I thought it was safe to drag him topside and dump him overboard."

"Do you still have the money?" Mitchell asked.

"Yeah, I've still got the money. It's stashed in a locker in one of the showers. Do you have the material you promised?"

"Everything is in my room," Mitchell replied.

"Okay, good. Help me get this guy up to the fantail and over the side and then we can get down to business."

"Why should I help you?" Mitchell was beginning to come around.

"Because neither one of us can afford to have someone find this guy. I don't know about you, but I don't want him following me around when he wakes up." Mitchell seemed convinced; he lowered the hammer on the big revolver and slipped it into a shoulder holster.

"Check the passageway," Max instructed, and without waiting for Mitchell to react, grabbed Gilbird's arms and started dragging him toward the door.

"Looks okay," Mitchell reported. Max continued dragging the unconscious man through the door and out into the passageway. Mitchell closed the door and took hold of Gilbird's feet. They paused at the top of the ladder. The cafeteria was still dark and the fantail deserted. Without further hesitation they carried Gilbird across the open deck and swung him up and over the railing.

"Seven-minute water," Mitchell remarked, as he stood looking down at the ship's wake some fifty feet below.

"Seven minutes until what?" Max inquired.

"Seven minutes until you can't move your arms or legs," Mitchell explained. "In thirty-four-degree water it takes about seven minutes."

"Well it's reassuring to know you won't be able to swim ashore."

Mitchell reacted quick as a cat, but even then he was too slow. He had been leaning against the railing, but straightened up hauling out the heavy-caliber revolver all in one quick motion. Max had noted earlier that the .357 magnum was single-action and knew the hammer must be manually cocked each time the gun was fired. As Mitchell concentrated on getting the gun out of the holster, pulling the hammer back, and bringing the weapon to bear, Max shifted his weight forward and at the same time his right hand, held flat with the fingers together and the thumb pulled back, shot upwards. In one smooth motion Max caught Mitchell in the Adam's apple with the inside edge of his hand, crushing the windpipe; he continued the motion by rotating his upper body and stepping into Mitchell, transferring the weight of his body through his rotating shoulder into his elbow as it came up crashing into Mitchell's solar plexus. As Mitchell slumped forward, a chopping right hand came down like a hammer on the top of his shoulder, shattering the man's collarbone.

The gun skittered along the metal deck as Mitchell fell forward, clutching his crushed windpipe with his left hand. He tried to cushion the fall with his right hand, as his legs, unable to support the weight of his body, gave way and he pitched forward, but the broken collarbone wouldn't let his right arm respond and his face crashed against the steel deck. The broken windpipe prevented him from disgorging the liquid welling up from his stomach, a result of the blow to his solar plexus, and he was drowning in his own vomit.

Max quickly searched through Mitchell's pockets until he found the key to stateroom 24 and slipped it into his own pocket. Then, grabbing a handful of hair, he yanked Mitchell to his knees and snarled into the face of the doomed man, "That's for the guy you left at Eagle Point with his throat cut."

He dragged Mitchell to his feet and slammed him into the railing. Unable to stand he grabbed the railing with his left hand and frantically held on as Max reached down and grabbed the helpless man by the ankles, lifting him up and flipping him over the railing. Mitchell managed to hold on to the railing with his left hand, the useless right arm hung limply at his side.

Max retrieved the pistol and walked back to where Mitchell was dangled over the side of the ship and still clinging desperately to the railing with his one good hand. Looking down into the panic-stricken face staring up at him, Max spoke softly but the tone of his voice conveyed his contempt for the man, "Just so you'll know before you die, my code name is Spider."

Mitchell's eyes opened wide, pleading, and he tried to speak. There was no doubt that he knew who was sending him to his death.

The heavy revolver slammed down, crushing the knuckles of Mitchell's left hand. There was no other sound as the fingers released their grip on the railing; unable to scream, Haskel Mitchell plummeted silently into the seven-minute water fifty feet below. Max half-whispered, "And that's for me."

He tossed the gun over the side and stood looking at the dark waters below for a few seconds before turning toward the ladder leading to the solarium. As he looked up someone moved back away from the railing on the deck above. He hesitated for only a moment before taking the ladder two steps at a time. It had been a moment too long. No one was in sight and nothing moved in the solarium. He walked to the railing where he had glimpsed the shadowy figure, turned, and stood surveying the sleeping passengers. There was no place to hide—perhaps it had been an illusion? Yet, something told him he had, indeed, seen someone. Possibly it was the aroma he detected as he approached the spot where the person had stood watching him dump the two spies overboard, an aroma he couldn't place at the moment but was familiar with just the same. Well, he would concern himself with that later, but now it was time to take a look in stateroom 24.

It was all there, names, codes, information on Dead Man, and much more, a suitcase full. Mitchell had obviously been planning this day for years. There were copies of pilfered documents from duty stations before he was assigned to Eagle Point. Most likely, he had been selling his country's secrets for a long time while setting the stage for the big payoff—well he'd got his big payoff. Among Mitchell's personal stuff was a passport in the name of Charles Randell Climer, along with an airline ticket from Prince Rupert to Montreal. Had all gone as planned, he would have disappeared without a trace. There was no way of knowing the damage that would have been done had all this material fallen into the hands of the KGB. He only knew lots of people in the Eastern bloc would have died. Well, he had done his job. Whatever the problems were now belonged to Henri.

Max moved everything belonging to Mitchell, along with the suitcase full of classified material, into stateroom 26. This would give Henri's people plenty of time to board the Mat, since Gilbird had booked his room all the way to Seattle. After wiping his fingerprints from everything he had touched in the two rooms he locked the door and headed for the solarium and his sleeping bag.

By the time he reached the fantail, lights of Petersburg were glowing on the horizon. He tossed both stateroom keys over the side and leaned against the railing watching the rapidly approaching lights as the big ship steadily closed the distance. The cold wind blowing across the open deck sent a shiver through his body. But it wasn't the chill of the icy winds gusting in his face that caused this involuntary reaction—it was the memories of eight long winters of watching blizzards sweeping down out of the Russian wastelands freezing everything in their path.

He checked his watch; it read 2:35. It was time to get some sleep. There was nothing to be done until they reached Wrangell.

The phone rang once and was followed by a series of tones, then started ringing again. Max knew Henri was not home and the call had been automatically routed to another location. Henri answered with a single word, "Tosi."

Henri sounded tired. Max guessed he had probably gone without rest since learning of the circumstances in Haines.

"Have you ever heard of the *Matanuska*?" Max asked; there was no need to identify himself.

"Yeah, I believe it's the name of a glacier somewhere near Anchorage, Alaska."

"You've got the right ball park but the wrong game. This *Mata-*

nuska is going to dock at pier 52 in Seattle early Friday morning. I believe you will find something very interesting in stateroom number 26. The room is registered to John Gilbird and may have been shared by Haskel Mitchell."

"Yes, it does, indeed, sound interesting. How can I learn more about the *Matanuska*?" Henri inquired.

"The Alaska Marine Highway office in Juneau might be of some help." Max replied. Henri would never ask and Max had no reason to volunteer an accounting of his own involvement. The conversation lasted no longer than a couple of minutes.

He made two more phone calls, one to Ketchikan, and one to Juneau. It was still dark when he walked out of the small ferry terminal in Wrangell and climbed the gangway back onto the Mat.

Max knew back in Washington, where the sun had been shining for at least six hours, wheels were already being set in motion and he wondered if he had given himself enough time. Perhaps it would have been wiser to wait until he reached Ketchikan before calling Henri. Oh well, what was done was done.

The smell of sizzling bacon and fresh-brewed coffee beckoned from the cafeteria. A good hot breakfast was just what he needed. After finishing an order of bacon, eggs, hash browns, and a stack of pancakes, he sat savoring a third cup of coffee and speculating on what might await him at Vandenberg.

The first rays of sunshine lit up snow-capped peaks of the aptly named Coast Mountains and began reaching down the slopes into the canal. He watched Prince of Wales Island slide past the starboard side as the *Matanuska* continued her journey southward. His thoughts, however, were not on the magnificent panorama that lay before him, but on another exquisite beauty with dazzling-green eyes and flaming-red hair, 3,000 miles away.

As the Mat eased up against the dock a voice came over the public address system instructing passengers wanting to disembark at Ketchikan to proceed to the car deck. Max stood up, reached underneath the chair and pulled out his backpack, swung it onto his shoulders, and adjusted the straps. For no particular reason he took one long last look around the solarium, noting that another tent had been erected. Walking toward the ladder he suddenly stopped, turned, and stared at the tents. No, not just one, but two tents had been added. Last night there had been two brown tents; now there was one brown, one green, and one orange. Someone had got off at either Petersburg or Wrangell. He was unable to explain why he found this seemingly unimportant fact disquieting. Max was among the first passengers to disembark. He crossed the ferry terminal parking lot past the lines of cars, trucks, and recreation vehicles waiting to be driven on board, destined either for Prince Rupert or Seattle and walked across the street toward a ten-year-old pick-up truck with large, faded lettering on the door that read, "Lynn Air Charters." Underneath, in smaller lettering was printed, "Fly-in Fishing, Scenic Fjord and Glacier Flights."

Max approached the young man leaning against the front of the truck and asked, "Is your name Willis?"

"Yep, Jake Willis, people just call me J.W. You the guy wants to go to Juneau?"

"Yeah, when can we leave?"

"The quicker the better. The weather is closing in and if we don't get airborne pretty quick we may not get out at all today. Throw your stuff in the back and we can get started."

Max was beginning to think he might have been a bit hasty in contracting with J.W. by telephone. The kid didn't look to be a day over twenty and the bit about the weather wasn't very comforting either. The book he'd read during the flight from Seattle had a chapter on Alaskan bush pilots and the number of crashes that occurred each year. It also mentioned many of these people were not licensed to fly. He wondered if J. W. was one of those unlicensed pilots. He was just about to pay the kid for his trouble and book the next northbound ferry when a taxi sped past and screeched to a stop in front of the ramp leading down to the ferry. One look at the man getting out of the taxi and Max knew he was stuck with J.W. no matter what. The man didn't bother with a ticket; he showed the purser his credentials and hurried on board.

Max smiled to himself, yes, indeed, he had cut it close. He had forgotten about the new CIA man in Haines when he phoned Henri from Wrangell. Henri had simply called Eagle Point, briefed the guy on what he had just learned about the *Matanuska*, and had him charter a plane from Haines to Ketchikan. Max threw his backpack in the truck bed, turned to the kid and said, "Well, what're we waiting for? Let's go."

J.W. and his plane looked to be about the same age. A single-engine Piper mounted on two long, skinny pontoons J.W. called floats did nothing to bolster his confidence in either the plane or the kid.

"Why the multicolored paint job?"

"Oh, I didn't choose the colors. Whenever I need something I get it from a guy up by the airport who sells parts and runs what you might call an airplane junkyard. Whatever color he's got is the color you get, but it's a lot cheaper than buying new parts," J.W. explained, as he untied the lines holding the tiny float plane to a rotting dock that bobbed up and down on oil drums as the water rose and fell. Max was once again having second thoughts about J.W. and his airplane, but following instructions, he climbed into the right seat and donned the headset hanging on the yoke in front of him.

J.W. stood on one of the floats and held onto a short line looped around a cleat bolted to the dock as he tossed the other lines into the airplane, then let go the line he was holding onto and climbed into the left seat. The engine coughed once, and then roared to life.

"How many airplanes does Lynn Air Charters operate?" Max inquired. The young man looked over and smiled. "You're looking at the entire fleet."

Max barely had time to strap himself in before J.W. added power and they were skimming across the water.

J.W. positioned his headset, flipped a couple of switches, and then asked, "Can you hear me okay?"

Max answered, "Yep, loud and clear."

"Everything looks okay," the young aviator declared as he made a quick check of his instruments and pulled back on the yoke. "With the ceiling this low we're going to have to stay over water all the way to Juneau."

"Okay, you're the flier. I'm just along for the ride." Max was hopeful, but it crossed his mind that it just might be his last. He noticed the line J.W. had been holding onto before he entered the plane was trailing back from the wing. He didn't ask any questions about the line; he wasn't sure he wanted to know the answer.

They climbed out to 1,500 feet but were forced to descend to 1,200 to stay below the clouds. The farther north they got the faster the weather closed in. By the time they cleared Wrangell Narrows they were down to 400 feet. Before they reached Juneau they were flying only fifty feet above the water.

The little plane touched down heading straight into a dock just north of the Alaska Marine Highway pier. Another ferry, the *Taku*, was tied up where Max had boarded the *Matanuska*. A cruise ship was tied up south of the *Taku*.

J.W. kept the power on until they were within a hundred feet of the dock. When he finally pulled the throttle back they stopped abruptly alongside the floating platform. J.W. cut the engine, stepped out onto the float, and quickly climbed onto the dock. He reached up and grabbed hold of the line hanging down from the wing and then flipped the line over a cleat and secured it with a half hitch. "Okay, you can climb out now, but watch your step.'

Max grabbed his backpack on the way out and joined J.W. on the dock. They stood on the dock talking about the weather and what it was like flying in these conditions as Max handed the kid four one-hundred-dollar bills.

"Keep the change, you've earned every nickel." The contract, made verbally over the telephone, was for three hundred and twenty dollars.

"Thanks. Well, I'd better get started if I'm going to get back to Ketchikan today."

"You can't be serious? You're not going back out in this weather?"

"It should open up a bit once I get a little ways south," J.W. explained, as he untied the half hitch and handed the line to Max before stepping onto the float. "Hold on to this for me until I get her started up again."

"No problem, and thanks for the ride. It's certainly been interesting."

"Anytime," J.W. yelled back as he climbed into the cockpit.

When the engine caught Max dropped the line and watched it trail in the water. As the plane picked up speed the line hung straight out behind the wing. The Piper had barely cleared the dock when J.W. opened the throttle and a few seconds later he was at full power. Max adjusted the straps on his backpack as he watched the tiny bush plane lift off and turn south, flying only a few feet above the water. He raised his hand in a salute to the daring young pilot and speculated that perhaps there was such a thing as reincarnation, and that conceivably he'd flown with Eielson.

It had already started to rain before Max reached the head of the pier and he was relieved to spot a taxi stand on the opposite side of the street. He crossed the street and headed directly for the two taxis parked by the curb.

"Where to, Mister?" The driver of the first taxi in line asked, holding open the rear door.

"The airport," Max replied, as he slipped off the backpack, tossed it across to the opposite side of the back seat and climbed inside out of the rain.

The rain began more like a mist than actual rain, but turned into a drizzle by the time they reached the airport. Max went straight to the check-in counter and inquired about his reservation. Everything was in order. He paid for his ticket and received a boarding pass.

The weather was looking more ominous by the minute. The rain was now mixed with snow. According to the attendant at the check-in counter the airport was closed to inbound traffic, but was still open to all scheduled departures. Max knew less visibility was required for taking off than landing—once airborne you were controlled by radar so a lack of visibility wasn't a problem. However, he was still concerned that the weather would continue to deteriorate and the airport would be closed to all traffic, in and out.

Near the lobby entrance he found the gift shop and purchased a canvas carry-on bag and a towel. He found the men's room empty and wasted little time in transferring the plastic bag full of money from his backpack to the carry-on bag. Next he removed a fresh set of clothes from his backpack and hung them on hooks beside the mirror above the lavatory. He removed a pair of loafers and placed them beside the carry-on bag. The last item removed from the backpack was a leather travel case. By following steps demonstrated by the guy at the Alaskan Nugget Max quickly zipped the straps of the internal frame backpack into specially designed compartments and after completing a few simple adjustments the backpack looked like a piece of softsider luggage. Without hesitation he stripped off all his clothes and stuffed them into the backpack with the exception of the rubber boots. Wetting one end of the towel and using soap from his travel kit he took a quick sponge bath. After drying off with the other end of the towel he wrapped it around his waist like a sarong, lathered his face and shaved off the two-day-old stubble. He finished shaving and splashed water on his face to wash off the soap and used the towel to dry his face and hands before dropping it onto the floor. Standing on the towel he put on clean pants, slipped on fresh socks, and stepped into his loafers. A couple of minutes later he had finished rubbing a protective moisturizing cream into his clean-shaven face, brushed his teeth, combed his hair, and concluded with the proverbial Marine Shower (deodorant and cologne). Finished with the travel kit he slipped it inside the backpack, tucked a new shirt into his trousers, knotted his tie, pulled on his jacket, dropped the towel in a trash can, picked up the two bags, and took one last look at his Juneau sneakers before turning toward the door.

Ten minutes ago Maxwell Kayne could have passed for a local. Now, standing at the baggage check-in counter he looked like an out-of-town business executive in a hurry to get back to his home office.

"We are on our final approach into San Diego, the time is 9:38 and the temperature is a comfortable 73 degrees. Please secure your service trays, bring your seats to a full upright position and fasten your seat belts."

The flight attendant, named Tiffany, replaced the microphone and began walking along the aisle, asking those not yet strapped in to please comply. She wore pants with a matching jacket, a ruffled shirt, and a knit tie knotted with a half Windsor. Her hair was shaved on the sides like a Marine recruit in basic training. The remaining hair was combed up and forward in what he understood was "punk." Why didn't girls want to look like girls? Oh well, what the hell, who was he to tell people how to dress.

Looking out at the lights of San Diego twinkling in the distance his thoughts were suddenly filled with flashing-green eyes, flaming-red hair, silk dresses, and French perfume. Yes, just one glance and you knew Sherry was a girl; she was more than a girl, she was a woman. A woman he liked and enjoyed—yet there were things about her that made him feel uneasy at times, things that didn't fit. Like her ability to fire a perfect score on the police firing range. The skill she displayed standing in a samurai circle. The fact that she spoke seven languages and had degrees from two notably distinguished universities, yet worked as a security guard in a high-rise condominium. The wheels slammed against the runway, jarring his thoughts and returning him to matters at hand.

The taxi ride from the airport to Chalter Tower had taken only fifteen minutes. It was good to be home. He was unaware of the smile on his face as he recalled his previous thought. "It was good to be home." For the first time in almost twenty years he had a place to call home. It was a nice feeling.

Max pushed the door closed and immediately froze. His senses told him someone was in his apartment. He eased the two bags to the floor, slipped off his loafers, then stood motionless for several seconds before carefully and without making a sound crossing the terrazzo entryway. When he felt the carpet under his feet he moved quickly but quietly toward the light glowing faintly from the area of the master bedroom. As he approached the bedroom Max could see, even with the lights dimmed, a lace nightgown laid out neatly on the satin sheets already turned down on his king-size bed. When the sound of splashing water reached his ears a smile slowly crossed his face as he envisioned Sherry soaking in a tub full of bubbles only a few feet away.

Without turning on a light Max removed the wallet from his inside coat pocket as he entered his dressing room and tossed it onto a vanity that ran the entire length of the room along one wall and was puzzled by the resultant clinking of glass. He switched on a light and found a lady's make-up kit with bottles of various shapes and sizes scattered over the dressing table. He picked up a small bottle that lay on its side and sniffed the contents, instantly recognizing the delicate flowers with the undertone of musk as the scent custom-blended for Sherry and shipped to her at an exorbitant expense from a small but exclusive perfumery in Paris.

At the same instant that light flooded the dressing area, reflected off the mirrored walls and into the bathroom beyond, the splashing stopped. Moments later water in the bathtub erupted followed by the sound of bare feet striking marble tile. A heartbeat later, wet, soft, warm, and covered with soap bubbles she was in his arms.

LIES, LIES, AND MORE LIES

Max guided the Ferrari to a stop opposite Lompoc's Central Post Office, killed the ignition, and punched the elapsed time clock. It read 3:56. The trip meter stood at 251. The drive from San Diego had taken just under four hours, considerably less time than he had expected. He considered putting the top up but one look at the blue sky and bright sunshine convinced him otherwise.

He walked back to the intersection of Mission and Los Osos, turned left and continued for another block and a half before crossing the street and entering an office with large black and gold lettering on a plate glass window that read:

"Real Estate, Sales and Rentals." A well-dressed middle-aged lady seated behind a desk facing the door looked up from behind a newspaper and asked, "May I help you?"

"I have an appointment with Mr. Dickerson.'

"Are you Mr. Alexander?"

"Yes, Raymond Alexander."

In a single movement she put the newspaper aside, pushed the chair back from the desk, stood up, and motioned for Max to follow as she turned toward the rear of the office. "This way, please."

Max followed the lady through the room past four unoccupied desks toward one of two doors set into the rear wall. She opened the door without knocking and ushered Max into a small but comfortable office. After introductions the receptionist, whose name was Helen, promptly departed and, Max surmised, returned to her newspaper.

Ed Dickerson, a man of about sixty-five, had a pleasant smile and a firm handshake, and after the proper amount of meaningless chitchat he got down to business. "Mr. Alexander, I have only one property in the area in which you expressed an interest. However, should you find it unsatisfactory I have several other rentals in very nice neighborhoods. We can take a look at one or all and start right now, if it's convenient."

Twenty minutes later, Ed stopped his five-year-old Buick in a parking lot at the end of the road, overlooking the Pacific Ocean. He pointed to the north, "The property I'm going to show you is up the coast a ways."

Without further comment he turned the Buick around and drove back along Costa Vista for about a mile before turning onto a narrow, twisting, road that crossed the Santa Ynez River and wound its way through a dense grove of eucalyptus. "There isn't much privately owned land in this area. It's mostly owned by the military, the railroad, or the Department of Parks and Recreation."

Dickerson kept up a continuous monologue on local history covering everything from the time of Spanish land grants and the days of the grand ranchos up to and including a step-by-step development of the space launch complex at Vandenberg.

The trees gave way suddenly to the rugged Pacific coast, barren except for chaparral and an occasional Monterrey cypress. A few houses were scattered along the cliffs at the ocean's edge. Surf Road was appropriately named; ocean swells crashed against sea stacks just offshore and turned to white spray and foam before rushing on to crash again on the rocks two hundred feet below.

They continued driving for five or six miles until the road ended near a 12-foot chain link fence topped with the traditional strands of barbed wire. A large sign proclaimed everything beyond to be military property and warned against trespassing.

"Thought I'd give you the full twenty-five-cent tour," Dickerson remarked, as he turned the car in a tight one-eighty and drove back along the road for about an eighth of a mile before turning into a driveway leading to a modest, single-story house built perilously close, Max thought, to the cliff's edge.

As he unlocked the front door, Ed explained the house would be available for two years, complete with furnishings, while the owners, an Air Force family, completed their last overseas assignment before retiring from service. Max walked from room to room making polite comments about the interior as he listened to terms and conditions of the lease when in, fact, the only thing that interested him was the house at the end of the road. There was no need to check the address; he'd spotted the house long before they had reached the turnaround near the chain link fence. At least half a dozen antennas could be seen attached to the house, and two of a dish type that resembled satellite television antennas were erected in the backyard. Max needed only a cursory check to determine the dish-type antennas were definitely not used for television reception. He wondered what electronic eavesdropping equipment was inside the house.

The roar of a powerful rocket motor interrupted his thoughts. As the sound waves intensified and the windows, cabinet doors, and several other things in the house started vibrating Dickerson motioned for Max to follow him outside. On a rear patio they watched an intercontinental ballistic missile climb up through the blue California sky until only the vapor trail was visible. Max also watched the two satellite dish antennas tracking the missile as it angled out across the Pacific Ocean towards the Hawaiian Islands.

Max could only guess at the number of people aboard Russian ships and submarines tracking the ICBM and recording data from its telemetry as it headed toward its target somewhere off Kwajalein, five thousand miles downrange. He was surprised that the KGB, by using a land-based tracking station, would risk blowing the cover of agents who had been in the freezer for almost twenty years when a submarine twelve miles off the coast or a trawler fifty miles out could do the same thing just as easily and would probably be lots better equipped.

"That's a Minuteman," Dickerson volunteered, answering the unasked question. "The air force test silos are about eight miles up the coast. Two or three times a year they pull one of the older missiles out of a silo in Montana, Wyoming, or Colorado, and sometimes even Alaska and bring them down here to find out how well they work.

"In a month or two they'll start testing the MX Peacekeeper, and the first shuttle launch from California is scheduled for next February." Ed pointed to the south. "The Atlantis will launch from SLC six"—Dickerson pronounced it *slick six*—"and will land over here on the mesa." He pointed again, indicating the area above the Minuteman test silos.

With a broad grin he added, "Don't worry, you'll get used to the noise."

Max wiped the grin from Dickerson's face, replying in cold earnest as he looked dead into the man's eyes, "Noise? Hell, that's not noise. That's just a sound of freedom."

Back at Dickerson's office Max plunked down the first and last month's rent plus a rather large security deposit, signed the two-year lease required by the owners, received a receipt from Helen, and departed. He would be able to move in anytime after the first of the month. Max still could not believe things were working out so well; the house was perfect—everything was perfect. How long would his luck hold?

Traffic through Los Angeles moved fairly well, even for afternoon rush hour. Still, by the time Max turned off Interstate 5 onto the Pacific Coast Highway just below San Clemente the sun was already sinking into the ocean behind Catalina Island. He nosed the Ferrari into a pullout overlooking Trestle Beach, shut off the engine, and sat back enjoying the panorama while memories of almost half a lifetime ago flowed through his mind. It was here, as a young marine, he had learned to surf.

In those days you could ride your board all day and see maybe a dozen other surfers. Looking now he could count half that many on one wave, all trying to catch a hot one before they lost the light. A lot of years had passed since he last *hot-dogged* on a *smoker* or *shot a curl*. Could he still do it?

California sunsets were more spectacular than he remembered. A giant red ball slowly sank below the horizon and the sky became a kaleidoscope of crimson and gold. As he sat looking out over the Pacific his thoughts took him back to key events and people that had shaped his life since those carefree and innocent times; when after a day of surfing he would lie in the warm sand on Trestle Beach and watch the sun sink into the Pacific. He had escaped reality often by returning, in his mind, to Trestle Beach when there was a need to hide his emotions, his pain, his fears. This was his *quiet place,* where no one could touch him and nothing could harm him.

He was unaware of how long he sat looking down on the ocean, reliving the past, but now, driving back along the PCH his thoughts were filled with the present and the one thing that made it all worthwhile. And she was waiting, only forty minutes away. As the sunset faded into dusk, the blissful memories and fantasies of the past were giving way to the pleasures and delights of present-day reality. Sherry was opening up a new world for him, a world he wanted and needed, but a world he feared as well. He was familiar with the old expression relating to love as an unknown where fools rush in and angels fear to tread. There had been other women, but now for the first time he knew he was just another fool. Yes—he was in love.

Max poured himself a cup of coffee and sat down at the breakfast bar. A note in Sherry's handwriting leaned against a glass dome covering a bran muffin, a cup of yogurt, and a small bowl of fresh strawberries. The note read: "Had to leave early, didn't want to wake you, be home for lunch. Love, S."

He pondered her use of the word *home* as he removed the glass cover and looked at his breakfast. What he really wanted was bacon and eggs with hash brown potatoes and toast with butter and marmalade. He ate the fruit and yogurt but couldn't resist adding cream cheese to the bran muffin—Sherry had tossed the butter months ago and replaced it with a tasteless low-cholesterol spread.

With a fresh cup of coffee in hand he studied the contents of John Gilbird's wallet. For the past week he had been unable to find anything to connect the KGB agent to Tolinger or Vandenberg and there was no reason to suspect anything would change today. However, the wallet was a place to start. Perhaps he had overlooked something—one way or another he had to make something happen. So far, everything he had turned up showed Gilbird to have been a pillar of the community with a successful business, a nice house, a respectable wife, and a substantial bank account. He paid taxes, voted, served on jury duty, and was a deacon in the church. Something very important to the Soviets was going down; the Kremlin would not otherwise risk losing an agent buried this deep. Two items looked promising: one, a permit to operate a business in Santa Barbara County, and the second, an expired credit card with a telephone number written in the space provided for the cardholder's signature.

Using a cordless telephone he dialed the number listed on the operating permit. On the fifth ring a female voice answered. "Spic and Span janitorial, can you hold?"

Reaching for his coffee cup he wondered why no one ever waited for an answer before hitting the hold button. A few seconds later the voice came back. "Can I help you?"

"I'd like to speak to John Gilbird, please."

"I'm sorry, sir, Mr. Gilbird is on vacation."

"When is he due to return?"

"I don't know, sir. He left unexpectedly and didn't leave a number where he can be reached."

"Well, that leaves me with a problem. Mr. Gilbird applied for a very large insurance policy about a month ago. When he failed to keep the appointment for his required physical and didn't reschedule another appointment the insurance company got a little uptight and hired me to look into the matter. You see, when a very large policy with double indemnity for accidental death is paid up for two years on the day of application, and the applicant fails to keep a required appointment and cannot be located, the company executives get a little squirrelly and start imagining all sorts of things like a possibly failing business and maybe suicide among other things. So, they've hired me to relieve their anxieties and in order to do that I need to either talk to Mr. Gilbird or take a look at your books." Max hesitated for a moment for effect, before asking, "You do see my problem?"

"Yes sir, I do. But I can't authorize you to look at our books. You'll need to see Mr. Bell."

"Well okay. May I speak with him, please?"

"I'm sorry, sir, the janitorial business is strictly nighttime and weekends. I'm normally the only one here during the day; you should call tonight about nine and talk to Mr. Bell."

"Okay, I'll do that. Thanks for your help." Well, the stage was set for his appearance at Spic and Span janitorial.

The number on the credit card had the same Lompoc exchange; he surmised the area code would also be the same. The phone rang only twice and expecting someone to answer he almost missed the beep of a telephone answering machine. Normally, answering machines had a recorded excuse from someone for not personally answering and the tone was a signal for you to leave a message for the person who was too inconsiderate to answer in the first place. However, there was no message, just a tone signaling the caller to either leave his message or dial in the correct code to receive a message. This was a good vehicle for exchanging information while remaining anonymous. The phone was probably set up in an empty apartment under a phony name with little chance of being traced to anyone. However, with time and a little more information he might be able to turn up something useful. But for the moment, it would wait. Right now, there were other things needing his attention.

He finished his coffee, put Gilbird's wallet away, cleaned off the breakfast bar, turned Sherry's note over and wrote, "Sorry about lunch. Had to go out, Max."

Ten minutes later, riding the elevator to the lobby, he reflected on Sherry's note and his own response. Why hadn't he signed the note with love, as she had done? He didn't know. He wanted to, but just couldn't bring himself to actually write the words. Maybe it was because he had never known and couldn't identify with love. Most women in his past were now faceless and nameless, associated only with a place, a time, or an event. Some he was unable to recall by the time he sobered up the following morning, but others haunted his memories and were most likely responsible for his present insecurity and distrust. Peggy Jean, the class tease, was only a childhood sweetheart. Nui was a girl merely trying to get out of Southeast Asia any way she could. Jeanne—ah yes, he would probably never forget Jeanne, although she was nothing more than an assignment and a ticket to the Communist camp. With Lara, a member of the Bolshoi Theater Ballet, he had by association achieved a certain refinement for which he would be forever grateful. There were many beautiful memories of Lara. At times she could almost make him forget he was a prisoner behind the Iron Curtain. Yes, at times he could put it out of his mind, but he never forgot, not even in the most intimate of moments. She was a Party member and he knew she would report him if he ever, even for a second, let his cover slip. She would report him to the KGB, not necessarily out of loyalty to the Party, but out of fear. Women in his life had always been women he could never fully trust. Perhaps he couldn't tell Sherry he loved her because her being a woman was reason enough for suspicion. She had told him very little about herself. Neither had questioned the other about their past life. However, he had done a little investigating and found she had never paid into social security or filed an income tax return. She had moved into an apartment in La Jolla exactly two weeks before he arrived in San Diego. Her California driver's license was issued one day after she paid cash for a new Porsche Carrera Targa. A week later she started work as a security guard at Chalter Tower. It had to be coincidence. Even if the KGB knew he had double-crossed them and was living in San Diego they couldn't possibly have gotten an agent, not even one out of cold storage, in place on such short notice. Still, he was unable to put it out of his mind. The elevator door opened, disrupting his thoughts. As he stepped out into the lobby he was thinking of other things. Sherry and the past were pushed to the back of his mind.

The trolley ran from downtown San Diego to the San Ysidro-Tijuana border crossing, making about fifteen stops along the way. Max got off at the first stop in National City. He had no trouble spotting the '57 Chevrolet with a chopped top, a flame paint job and its suspension lowered until it appeared to be only about two inches off the ground. As he approached, a young Chicano slid off the fender, took a few steps forward, extended his hand, and stated, "Hey man, everything's ready."

Max shook his hand, replying, "Great! Let's take a look."

Max had realized some months back that running around in a twenty-year-old Ferrari with the original Italian racing-red paint job was no way to keep a low profile. He started considering options. But any car with enough power to run at the speeds he desired stuck out like the proverbial sore thumb. He remembered a friend from Nam always talking about car clubs—locally known as Low Riders—around San Diego, especially the South Bay area. The only thing Carlos cared about was cars. He talked cars, dreamed cars, and would spend hours telling anyone willing to listen about all the things guys back home could do with engines, transmissions, suspension systems, and so forth. If you showed too much interest he would break out the latest pictures his brother had sent and start explaining every detail. Carlos had been blown away at Khe Sanh three weeks before his DEROS—an acronym for Date Eligible for Rotation from Overseas; in Nam they'd referred to DEROS as date eligible for rotating back to the world.

Max had located his friend's family in Chula Vista. They were very proud of Carlos. His medals, along with the flag that had draped his casket, hung protected by glass on their living room wall, surrounded by numerous photos he had sent home.

Max stared long and hard at the snapshot of a young Marine corporal wearing Vietnamese love beads and a Montagnard bracelet; the ace of spades from a deck of cards was stuck onto the front of his helmet and "Make Love, Not War," was painted on one side. He knew that painted on the other side of the helmet were the words "I'm short." The name "Jack Johnson" was written in the margin underneath. A month after the picture was taken Jack Johnson was in the EVAC Hospital at Saigon and Carlos was on his way home in a body bag.

They had talked at length about Carlos and Nam before Max eased the conversation around to car clubs. Carlos' younger brother, Jorge, was president of the Gatos Frios, but now they were more than just a car club. The "Cool Cats" owned an auto repair shop where they taught complete engine overhaul, transmission rebuilding, and front-end repair among other things, to street kids interested in cars. Another section of their shop housed a complete body repair and paint shop. The club was very successful at getting kids off the street and into well-paying jobs. When Max hinted he would like to own a car with a lot of muscle, Jorge, eager to help a friend of his late brother, even though he had no recollection of Carlos ever writing home about a John Cato, assured him Los Gatos Frios could build exactly the car he wanted. And so, the planning had begun.

At the trolley station parking lot exit the pavement dipped, then rose sharply to street level. Max was wondering how the Chevy with such low-slung suspension would negotiate the dip and get up to the street without dragging off the rear bumper. As though reading his mind Jorge touched a switch on the dash and the rear end of the car lifted up about two feet. When they reached the street Jorge touched the switch again and the car settled back to within a few inches of the pavement.

"That was pretty slick. I didn't know '57 Chevys came with that option."

Jorge laughed and to further impress Max, he touched another switch and the front of the car rose up until they could barely see over the hood. He touched the first switch again and rear came back up and now the entire car was about two feet off the ground.

Max had heard Carlos talk about cars like this, but had never actually seen a low rider before.

"That's amazing."

At the intersection Jorge manipulated the switches in such a manner to make the Chevy actually hop up and down.

"How do you do that?"

Jorge laughed and exclaimed. "Hydraulics, man."

In the short distance between the trolley station and the Gatos

Frios repair shop Jorge amused himself as he continued to astonish Max with the novelties built into the '57 Chevy.

"There she is, man!"

Excitement was evident in Jorge's voice and pride showed on his face as he braked to a stop behind the repair shop and said, "Don't let her looks fool you, man; she'll blow the doors off anything on the road."

Max took one look at the faded brown paint of the old Pontiac TransAm and exclaimed, "That's exactly what I had in mind. She's perfect."

Jorge took the better part of an hour pointing out all the different switches that had been added to the Pontiac's control panel as he explained what they did and demonstrated how they worked.

Jorge then handed Max the keys and said, "The title is in the glove box."

Jorge slipped the envelope Max handed him into his pocket without checking its contents and they shook hands, for what both men knew would be the last time. "Take care of her, man; she's one of a kind."

Later, when Jorge counted the money inside the envelope he found more than four times the amount he expected.

Back at Chalter Tower, Max left the Pontiac in guest parking and walked to the elevator that would take him from the underground garage to his eighteenth-floor apartment. As he was about to step into the elevator he stopped, frozen, eyes glued to the newspaper in the vending machine by the elevator door. He swore out loud as he jammed coins into the machine and ripped out the afternoon edition of the San Diego Union-Tribune. The headlines read, "Crew killed in shuttle disaster."

Scanning the paper as the elevator whisked him skyward he learned the Challenger had exploded two minutes after lift-off killing the crew of seven.

Inside his apartment he switched on the television and watched in disbelief as the Challenger lifted off and later exploded like a giant fireworks display. Every major television network had a special news crew interviewing NASA officials, prime contractor executives, congressmen, or anyone willing to speculate on what might have caused the shuttle to explode. For a moment Max thought his eyes were deceiving him when an interview began with Colonel Howard Kent Tolinger. As he touched the record button on his VCR questions raced through his brain. Why was Tolinger at the Cape? Was the colonel somehow responsible for the Challenger's fate and death of her crew? Max tried to memorize every detail about the man standing next to Tolinger as he listened to the colonel theorize on the possible effects this catastrophe might have on Atlantis, scheduled to be launched on its maiden voyage in less than a year from the new space launch facility at Vandenberg. Every five minutes or so the station would cut away from the interview to show the Challenger lifting off the launch pad and exploding—the media sought out and reveled in negativity.

Interviews and speculation continued, sabotage had not been ruled out; however, comments along these lines were made very carefully. If sabotage was proven or even suspected it would be highly unlikely the general public would ever know. To admit someone or some group had penetrated National Aeronautics and Space Administration security would panic a large sector of the population. Americans read about and saw the results of terrorist acts on television every day, although few had experienced it firsthand. To suddenly realize sabotage of such magnitude had occurred within our own country and to know the saboteurs had circumvented NASA's complex security systems would have every citizen wondering where and when they would strike next. This realization could and probably would change the way people conducted their lives and in so doing might disrupt the entire economy. Max wasn't about to panic, but he wasn't going to write it off as an accident, not just yet anyway.

Max could deceive and evade the truth as easily and as naturally as he breathed. Without this ability he would never have survived the last decade. Now, for the first time, his emotions betrayed him. The lie stuck in his throat, his tongue became thick and his voice lacked the usual control and confidence. It wasn't the untruth he spoke that caused him to inadvertently glance away, it was the shadow sweeping away the lights that always sparkled and danced in her sea-green eyes. The pain evident on her face and in her voice told him she knew he had lied. Damn! Why had she asked? She had never inquired before. Now, out of the clear blue and in rapid succession, she had fired a dozen questions at him all beginning with where, when, or why. He knew it was a bust—he wanted to tell her the truth, but the truth was out of the question. Well, there was nothing to do except follow through with the lie, stick to his story and hope for the best. It wasn't supposed to happen this way.

He had expected during dinner at their favorite restaurant, overlooking Glorietta Bay, he would mention that he would be out of town for a few days and they would go through the I'll-miss-you routine, have a lovely dinner, and a beautiful evening together, and all would end well. This, however, was not the way things were shaping up and he already knew the evening would end badly.

———

Max watched a shiny red Corvette continuously switching back and forth from one lane to the other, passing one or two cars at a time as it slowly inched its way through traffic. On Highway 101 you could drive from Los Angeles to San Jose at freeway speeds without seeing a single traffic light except for Santa Barbara, where the maximum speed limit was thirty miles per hour, regulated by a series of traffic lights. Over a distance of eight or ten miles the traffic crawled along at a snail's pace, trying everyone's patience to the point where sometimes obscenities, fist shaking, and other well-known gestures with a certain digit of the hand were exchanged between motorists. It was not uncommon for a driver to change lanes and pull directly in front of another vehicle, forcing the other driver to either yield or risk a damaged fender.

Two cars in front of Max continued through the intersection after the light turned red, drawing blasts from horns of waiting cross traffic. Max braked to a stop in the right-hand lane, and watched the Corvette, now just three cars back, move over into a "Right Turn Only" lane and pull up alongside. Although a sign hung underneath the traffic light and a 6-by-8-foot sign was posted against an ice-plant-covered embankment across the intersection opposite the right turn lane that read "No Right Turn on Red," Max knew the driver of the Vette had no intentions of turning right and was not simply obeying the law as he waited for the light to change. Although the right turn lane did not continue on the opposite side of the intersection Max knew the kid intended to jackrabbit when the light turned green and pull in front of him before they reached the other side of the intersection. Max was in no hurry and had already tried the Pontiac for speed on Interstate 5 between Oceanside and the Immigration and Naturalization Service check station and had no doubts about its power. But still, here was a chance to see how his machine measured up pitted against a real muscle car. Naw, he'd let the Vette jump ahead, he wasn't going to do anything dumb. If the guy in the Vette wanted to do something stupid Max had no intention of standing in his way.

The two guys in the sleek-looking sports car were about twenty years old. Max guessed them to be students at the University of California at Santa Barbara. They looked over at the old TransAm with its faded paint and laughed at some comment made by the passenger. The driver took a long pull on a beer before passing it across to his friend, who finished it and tossed the bottle onto the curb where it shattered. The Corvette eased forward until its front wheels were even with the Pontiac's front bumper.

"Ah, what the hell," Max said, to no one in particular. "Let's go for it."

The passenger twisted the cap off another bottle of beer as the duo looked at Max and continued to laugh, no doubt sharing another joke about his Pontiac and how they were going to blow his doors off. Had they been more alert, they would have noticed the old car they were laughing at was undergoing changes that might have raised a question or two and maybe even caused some alarm.

They would have heard the hydraulic pump kick in and noticed a lowering of the front end as the suspension was tightened. They would have observed the rear elevate as the entire car was raked into a ground-effects configuration. And had they been paying attention, they would have noticed the air induction door open up in the center of the hood to scoop in extra air to the low-profile, belt-driven Latham supercharger that forced air into the carburetor.

Max had his left foot on the brakes, while his right foot applied gentle pressure to the accelerator in order to keep the power train tight. The entire car shuddered as the powerful engine was held in check.

Max watched the Corvette rather than the traffic signal, knowing the driver might try and jump the light and leave him sitting at the starting line waiting for the green.

The Corvette torqued ever so slightly as the driver opened the throttle and the Vette had barely moved when Max released the brake and slammed down the accelerator. A nanosecond later the two cars reached the middle of the intersection and were dead even. The kid driving the Vette, wide-eyed in disbelief and with no place to go as his lane ended, slammed on the brakes and plowed into the embankment, sending splintered boards and chunks of ice plant into the air.

This had been the last traffic light and the thirty-miles-per-hour speed limit ended. Max adjusted his speed to the traffic, reset all the toggle switches to their original position and watched the Pontiac return to its normal configuration. That had been a foolish thing to do and he knew it, but he was still uptight from his last few hours with Sherry and it served more as a release for built-up tension than as an opportunity to check out the capabilities of his car. Even so, a smile slowly touched his lips as he thought about the surprised look on the faces of the two guys in the Corvette.

For the next half hour he recalled the thrills of European road racing and of the reckless life he had lived. The life of a dedicated, hard-working marine interwoven with fast cars, spies and counterspies, the CIA and KGB, free love and all-night parties. He wondered if in some weird sort of way he'd had a death wish, or perhaps he was just trying to forget Nam. He knew he would never forget Nam.

By the time he reached Lompoc, a city of 30,000 billing itself "Flower seed capital of the world," his thoughts were free of ghosts from the past. Sherry, too, for the moment had been buried somewhere deep in the recesses of his mind. He parked a block and a half from Ed Dickerson's office and in the opposite direction from the spot where he'd parked the Ferrari on his first visit to Lompoc.

"Mr. Dickerson is meeting a very important client at the airport in Santa Maria," explained his secretary. "It was something that came up unexpectedly and could not be scheduled at a more convenient time. He asked me to apologize for his absence. However, I assure you everything is exactly as you requested."

Max attached his signature, "Raymond Alexander," in the appropriate places, said good-bye to Helen and left the real estate office with copies of the signed documents, a set of keys, and the control unit for the automatic garage door opener. Following the route introduced to him by Dickerson, Max pulled into a service station, filled his gas tank, and purchased a street map of Lompoc and the surrounding area, including Vandenberg Air Force Base. At a nearby supermarket he loaded a dozen bags of groceries onto the back seat of the Pontiac. Thirty minutes later he activated the garage door opener, backed his car into the garage, put the gear select lever in Park, and killed the ignition. At the rear of the garage by a door that opened into a hallway, he touched a button on the wall and watched the garage door close back to its original position.

After walking through the house to insure no one was inside, he returned to his car, carried the groceries into the kitchen and put them away. Returning again to the garage, he transferred several pieces of luggage from the trunk compartment of the Pontiac to the master bedroom. Half an hour later his clothes either hung in the closet or lay folded neatly in bureau drawers. Three large bags stood unopened in the bottom of the closet. Two smaller bags rested unopened on the dresser.

The sun was still a good twenty degrees above the Pacific Ocean when Max stepped out of the shower. He finished drying off, dropped the towel into a clothes hamper, walked to the bed, pulled down the covers, climbed in and was asleep almost immediately.

Max awoke without moving or opening his eyes. He continued the slow, even breathing pattern of a person sleeping. Perfected over many years, it gave him the opportunity to evaluate conditions in the room without alerting anyone that might have been in the house—it could be most unpleasant waking up with an uninvited guest in the room. Minutes later, satisfied he was alone, Max opened his eyes, stretched, and got out of bed. There was little need for such caution at present, but it was a practiced habit and had saved his life on at least two occasions.

Turning on a light by the bed he selected a pair of dark gray sweat pants and matching sweatshirt, a pair of heavy socks and jogging shoes. He was in no particular hurry and dressed leisurely and when finished walked to the kitchen and slid a glass door back along its track, allowing the fresh ocean breeze and the sound of pounding surf to fill the room. The house, built in the shape of a horseshoe, provided virtually every room access to a patio that extended thirty feet beyond the house to a four-foot wall overlooking a sheer cliff and the crashing surf two hundred feet below. He removed several packages and containers from the refrigerator, constructed a couple of sandwiches, picked up a bag of chips and a carton of milk, and carried everything to a table on the patio near the wall overlooking the cliff.

A gibbous moon painted a path across the Pacific to the water's edge below and flooded the surrounding countryside.

Max sat bathed by the moonlight enjoying the tranquility. He ate in silence, his thoughts wandering. Slowly loneliness crept into his consciousness as be remembered, too, many similar experiences of the past; a lovely setting and no one to share, no one to care. He found himself wishing Sherry was there with him, wishing also he could be sure she was the person he knew her to be, nothing more, and nothing less.

His thoughts of Sherry and the past were swept away by a sudden glow on the horizon as a very large rocket motor lifted a missile into the night sky. He watched the big rocket's trailing exhaust flames cut through the darkness for perhaps thirty seconds before the sound waves reached him. A few seconds later the sky lit up like the Fourth of July. Max sat frozen even after the sound of the explosion shattered the night. For several minutes pieces of the flaming missile continued to trace eerie patterns in the night sky as they plummeted earthward. He watched in awe for some time before his senses returned. Remembering the day he'd been here with Ed Dickerson and had watched the antennas at Gilbird's track a Minuteman downrange, he turned his attention to the house at the end of the road. In the bright moonlight it was easy to see both dishes were looking down the coast only a few degrees above the horizon.

Could the Gilbird group have transmitted a destruct signal? Not likely, even with the necessary codes and the correct frequency they would first have had to knock out Vandenberg's main transmitter and the backup transmitter as well. It was not unlikely that the air force would also have an airborne command center with yet another backup transmitter. Even if they could transmit a destruct signal, why would they? Too many questions and no answers. He sure wanted to look inside the Gilbird house, but this certainly was not the right time.

He finished eating in front of the television, watching the eleven-o'clock news on a local station. The camera crew at the launch site viewing area had sent the entire sequence back to the station, where it had been recorded and was now being sent out over the network into virtually every home in the country. The network employed the same technique as it had with the Challenger, showing the liftoff and explosion over and over as they explained why the missile, a Titan, had been destroyed by the air force approximately two minutes into its flight. Apparently the second stage had failed and the decision was made to destroy the missile rather than have it crash in an unde-termined area. An air force spokesman, when asked, admitted there were similarities between the Titan failure tonight and the failure of a Titan that had to be destroyed shortly after launch less than a week ago at Cape Canaveral. The interview continued with questions about two Minuteman missiles which had failed in pretty much the same way and had to be destroyed shortly after liftoff. The spokesman was hesitant to compare the Minuteman failures with the Titan's, but did admit there had been a rash of failures in the air force, as well as at NASA, within the last few months. When asked about the possibility of sabotage, he stated nothing had been found to indicate sabotage. Max had no hard evidence, only gut instinct, but he was willing to bet the farm that sabotage was in play, and it all tied into Gilbird and Tolinger. It was time to go to work and he knew exactly where he was going to begin. But first he would take a few precautions.

He was counting on the *Illegal Rezidentura* being overconfident and lax in their security, and probably, if Henri was right about the country's attitude, there was little need for them to be concerned. After all, it had been luck that led him to the group even though he had been keeping an eye on Tolinger. Had he not been searching through the passenger lists in airline computers, trying to confirm Sherry's itinerary, he would never have stumbled onto the name John Gilbird. Earlier, he had assumed Tolinger was selling out his country because of greed or possibly because he was being blackmailed. But now it appeared the colonel was very important to the Kremlin and was controlling at least two groups of Illegal Rezidentura. Only an officer of the KGB would be trusted to control or even know two groups in such deep cover and sensitive operations. If this was true, standard KGB procedures had been thrown out the window. In normal KGB operations members of the group would know only their controller and not one another.

The Gilbird group seemed to be working as a team, as was evident by the telephone recorder, and appeared to be actively engaged in sabotage, again not standard procedure for a group in such deep cover. The Challenger disaster followed by a Titan failure indicated a group at Cape Canaveral was also working together and engaged in sabotage. The failures of two separate Minuteman missiles followed by the Titan tonight indicated the two groups were working together and toward the same goal. But what could that goal be—to destroy the American shuttle fleet? Not likely. The loss of Challenger would produce a higher level of quality control and tighter security throughout the entire shuttle program. It would be unrealistic to believe a second shuttle launch could be sabotaged even by someone working in a supersensitive position.

A delay in the Atlantis launch at Vandenberg would be a more probable and realistic goal. This would do two things: It would give the Soviets more time to develop their own shuttle system while at the same time delaying America's development and deployment of SDI. The Soviets were working on their own Star Wars system and by all credible sources, were already far ahead of the United States. The Soviets had already successfully tested a ground-based laser, powered by a small nuclear explosion, capable of destroying incoming aircraft, missiles, and possibly orbiting satellites. The nuclear-pumped laser system would soon be ready for deployment in strategic locations throughout the Soviet Union. According to reports, they were well ahead in space-based lasers as well, with the only problem being their lack of a deployment vehicle. However, with their own shuttle fleet under construction and a first launch scheduled for early '89 or possibly late '88, this problem was close to being solved. Any delay by the United States to deploy SDI would give the Soviets badly needed time to get their own space transport system operational. If the Soviets could, through sabotage and propaganda, keep the American Space Transport System grounded for two or three years, they could have their own shuttle fleet delivering Soviet Star Wars systems into orbit, leaving the United States playing catch-up just like in the early days of space exploration when the USSR launched Sputnik.

Taking everything into account, it seemed highly probable they would even be willing to risk exposing some exceptionally valuable agents, even some working in sensitive DOD positions, in an all-out effort to keep America's shuttle fleet grounded. But, even if they were willing to lose some agents in some desperate plan, why would they take an unnecessary chance with a simple tracking station in a house in a residential area next to an air force base? Maybe it was more than just a tracking station. Max continued thinking about the recent rash of accidents and failures involving all branches of the military as well as NASA. Did this mean the KGB had agents throughout the Defense Department? He believed this was exactly what it meant. Could these agents be engaged in a coordinated effort toward a single goal? He was afraid the unequivocal answer was yes! As these and other questions and likely answers flashed through his mind the picture began to take focus.

He remembered during the sixties when Soviet Bears were making flights, on an almost daily basis, past the American fleet and in particular the newest aircraft carriers. At least a couple of times a week you would see a picture in the newspaper of the world's largest bomber flying past one of our aircraft carriers. And before long the whispers had started. "Aircraft carriers are vulnerable because of their size and speed."

This whisper was probably started and most certainly kept alive by KGB agents working at the Russian Embassy in Washington and at the United Nations headquarters in New York, in an attempt to manipulate public opinion. The media, always looking for a chance to undermine American prestige, picked up on the whispers and ran editorials and related stories proclaiming the aircraft carriers' day was past and declaring them a waste of money and manpower. Many U.S. citizens were convinced by these stories and truly believed the carriers had outlived their usefulness while some legislators, eager to jump on the bandwagon, were referring to them as dinosaurs, comparing them to the slow-moving battle ships of World War II, which had been removed from service because they could not keep up with the newer and faster ships in the fleet.

The Soviets, of course, would have liked nothing better than to have America pull her carriers from service and reduce the size of her fleet, but they were actually taking aerial photographs to aid them in building their own supercarrier presently under construction at the Naval ship-building and repair facilities in Murmansk. But during that time the Soviets learned something much more valuable to them than the configuration of the flight deck of an aircraft carrier. They learned just how easily U.S. public opinion could be manipulated and it now appeared they were putting that knowledge to work. Every day now, you heard someone in the news expounding some reason why SDI couldn't work. Or you heard how American weaponry was getting so sophisticated no one could operate it, or they lacked the training to keep it maintained. The media were always interviewing someone who recommended America stop building high-tech weapons and put all our efforts and resources into conventional weapons. The very first statement out of the Kremlin after the Challenger disaster was, "The Americans cannot be trusted with high-tech."

A surprising number of people were already agreeing with this line of thinking. If the KGB was, indeed, behind all these failures and if their propaganda machine was in high gear, it might take only one more really big accident to turn the tide in the way the average citizen viewed national defense policies.

Max suddenly became aware of dryness in his mouth and a knot tightening in his stomach. Was his imagination running wild or was the KGB about to create a catastrophe so great America would put SDI as well as other high-tech weapons on hold indefinitely? If he had learned only one thing while in Moscow it was to never underestimate Soviet ambitions no matter how outrageous or farfetched they might appear. He had only to look at the lofty scheme they had hatched involving Jack Johnson and Ambassador Harte. During his years as an officer in the KGB he had come to know that within the Kremlin inner sanctum the unthinkable was considered achievable. Well, speculation was one thing, facts were another, and he had an uneasy feeling time was running out.

Max turned down the volume on the television, and headed for the bedroom. He figured if anyone came snooping and heard the TV they might figure someone was inside and be hesitant to break into the house. From a bag in his closet he removed two magnetic anomaly detectors with built-in transmitters. He marveled at their size. Twenty years ago you would have needed a truck just to carry them around. Today they were no larger than a cigar and contained batteries with enough power reserve for three months.

In strategic positions beside the road he used a small tubelike tool to remove two plugs of earth and dropped a MAD into each of the holes. He removed just enough sod from the plugs to fill the holes to the original level. When he finished, a small brown antenna about one millimeter in diameter and approximately ten millimeters in height was the only thing visible through the sage grass growing sparsely beside the road. Only a well-trained eye, lucky enough to focus on that particular spot would detect his handiwork. The video camera was a bit harder to conceal. A Monterrey cypress about thirty yards off the road, directly across from his house, proved satisfactory. Back inside the house he removed the rest of the equipment from the bags in the closet. The setup, although sophisticated, was quite simple. The magnetic anomaly detectors were sensitive to any change in the earth's magnetic field; a vehicle, having a flux field of its own, traveling along the road would disturb the earth's magnetic field. The

MAD would detect this change and cause the related transmitter to send a burst of RF energy to the receiver in the cypress, which would trigger the video camera. A transmitter would send the picture to the receiver in the house, which in turn would pass it along to the video recorder. When the car passed the second MAD the same thing would happen, but this time the receiver in the cypress would shut the video camera off. No matter which way the vehicle was traveling, the first signal from a MAD would activate the system and a second signal from the other MAD would deactivate it. With this setup he would be able to monitor traffic and visitors to the Gilbird house. Also, the system would automatically activate every two minutes and record for a period of five seconds; this would provide him a reasonably good chance of getting a picture of anyone entering his property. Since the video recorder only recorded when it received a signal from the transmitter across the road, Max would need to change the tape only every couple of days.

Satisfied everything worked, Max chose a few items from another piece of luggage and arranged them in a fanny pack, then pulled on a pair of black jogging shorts over his sweat pants, strapped on the fanny pack, and left the house by way of the patio.

He ran almost effortlessly along Surf Road with long strides that rapidly ate up the distance, but slowed to a walk when he reached the eucalyptus grove. In the open chaparral, moonlight made it easy to see the road, but in the trees it was more difficult, and he didn't want to step in a hole and turn or maybe break an ankle. Also, he was concerned about stepping on a rattlesnake lying on the warm pavement. The blacktop soaked up the sun's rays during the day, becoming very warm, and at night the Southern California red diamondback rattler liked to lie on the warm pavement.

It took almost an hour to reach his destination, a ground-level junction box where telephone services for Surf Road connected with the main line running along the highway. He had spotted the junction box the day Dickerson showed him the property. He was about to rotate the fanny pack around his middle to have better access to the zippered pockets when headlights from a car winding its way through the eucalyptus grove flickered through the trees. He walked back up the road and crossed over to the other side, stepping off to the inside of a wide sweeping curve and picked his way through the trees before dropping to the ground. He wondered why anyone would be leaving home at such a late hour.

As the car approached, its headlights lit up the woods to the outside of the curve, but very little light filtered through the trees on the inside of the curve where Max lay hidden. Even so, he didn't move or look in the direction of the road until the vehicle had passed. What he had assumed was a car turned out to be a Dodge Maxivan. Through a small pair of Bausch and Lomb, custom-compact binoculars, designed to specifications of the National Audubon Society, he checked and made a mental note of the license plate. He took his time returning to the junction box. Rotating the fanny pack he removed a Swiss army knife from one of the compartments, opened one of the screwdriver blades and began removing the cover of the junction box. Once inside the J-box he played the high intensity beam of a Mini-Maglite over the list of house numbers taped to the back of the cover plate until he found Gilbird's address. Locating corresponding terminals listed opposite the address he carefully connected the thin leads of a trans-mitter, no larger than a quarter—another miracle of the microchip—to the appropriate terminals. After hooking up the wires he activated the transmitter, removed a protective strip from adhesive on the tiny device, attached it to the underside of the junction box, and replaced the cover. Unless a telephone technician had some reason to look inside or underneath the J-box, it was highly unlikely anyone would discover his bug. The miniature transmitter had a range of only a few hundred yards, however, and would need a more powerful repeater transmitter to boost the signal enough to be picked up by the receiver in his house, more than six miles away. A dead eucalyptus tree about 200 feet away served the purpose well. Fifteen minutes later he was finished and on his way back through the woods.

He walked slowly and carefully until the eucalyptus gave way to chaparral. Dawn was already breaking and with light gathering in the eastern sky, Max could see well enough to run the rest of the way home, arriving just before the sun broke above the horizon. Follow-ing warm-down exercises and a shower Max began fixing himself breakfast while watching the morning news. The local news was a repeat of last night's except for one added bit of information—the Titan had been carrying a classified military payload. Max doubted the payload had anything to do with the missile's blowing up. The national network was already into its anti-high-tech routine as they interviewed a left-leaning politician and a low-ranking official from the Soviet embassy.

When his breakfast was ready he placed it on a serving tray, turned off the TV, and carried the tray outside. It was still cool on the patio but he liked the fresh air and the smell of the ocean. Soon the sun's rays would knock down the chill and the Santa Ana winds would pick up again, making it appear almost like summer. He smiled briefly, thinking of how Sherry would lecture him on the evils of bacon and eggs, on cholesterol, clogged arteries, and so on. He missed Sherry, but he put her out of his mind and returned his thoughts to the events of last night and his theory of one final disaster, a disaster of such magnitude it might very well write an end to American space exploration in this century. It would surely sound a death knell for the Strategic Defense Initiative and possibly, somewhere in the not too distant future, an end to the free world.

He ate slowly, studying the Gilbird house, wondering what was inside. He had to get inside, but not today. He had other things to do today.

Highway 1 turned south just outside of Lompoc and through a series of switchbacks climbed rapidly out of the Santa Ynez valley onto the coastal range, connecting with Highway 101 about twenty miles north of Santa Barbara. A scenic pullout on one of the switchbacks gave a commanding view of Lompoc and the valley below, but Max wasn't interested in the panorama. His only interest was in the fact that the pullout was above Highway 246, which ran between Lompoc and Buellton, and was directly opposite the Spic and Span janitorial compound. Spic and Span was five hundred feet below and a half mile away just across Highway 246.

A warehouse with a loading dock across the front and back, along with a half dozen metal sheds and a couple of Quonset huts scattered about to the rear of the warehouse made up the bulk of Gilbird's operation. Except for the front of the warehouse, a ten-foot chain link fence topped with barbed wire encompassed the premises. Guard dogs were visible inside the enclosure. It had the look of a prison or a military complex rather than a private business. Max had already decided the best way in was through the front door. He lowered his binoculars as a silver-gray Ford Tempo turned off Highway 246 onto a dirt road and continued a tenth of a mile to the end of the road, where it stopped by Spic and Span's front loading dock. Peering through the binoculars again he watched a woman get out of the car, climb six steps to the loading dock, unlock a door and disappear inside the warehouse. Ten minutes later he parked the Pontiac beside the Tempo, got out, climbed the steps, and stood for a moment in front of the door the woman had disappeared through only minutes earlier. A sign above the door read Office.

Inside a rather cramped office he found a couch to his left, on the right a desk, and in the wall directly opposite the door he had entered was another door marked Private. An overweight woman of about thirty sat behind the desk eating a cinnamon roll and drinking coffee. A portable radio on the desk was tuned to a local country western station. The woman put down her mug of coffee, moved the cinnamon roll to one side, turned down the radio, gave him a tired smile and asked, "Can I help you?" She tried to sound enthusiastic but her heart just wasn't it.

"My name is Jeff Price. I have an appointment with a Mr. Oscar Bell."

"I'm sorry, Mr. Bell won't be in until six this evening."

"Well, he personally told me to meet him here at nine o'clock."

"I'm sure you must have misunderstood him, sir. There are never more than two or three people here during the day. Everyone works at night. Mr. Bell works ten to twelve hours every night and I'm sure he would not have agreed to meet with you at nine o'clock in the morning."

Max already knew all this; he was just setting her up for his next move. His plan was to bluff his way inside and poke around as much as he possibly could. "Well, if we could just call him and—"

The woman interrupted him, displaying some annoyance at his persistence. "Mr. Bell does not like to be disturbed at home!"

"Well, if you could just give me his number—"

She interrupted again. "I can't give out employees' home phone numbers." The woman was obviously getting tired of the conversation and appeared eager to get back to her cinnamon roll and coffee. Max figured now was the time to go into the second part of his act.

"Look lady, I'm sorry if I seem a bit anxious. But I'm a one-man detective agency and I'm having a very hard time making it, okay? I'm working for a very big insurance company and this is the first job they've given me. If I can turn in a clear and speedy report there's an excellent chance they'll give me more work, and I sure can use the work. Actually, I need the work. I need the work very badly."

He paused, as though collecting his thoughts, giving her time to consider his plight, before continuing despairingly. "As I explained to you on the telephone, Mr. Gilbird failed to show up for a required physical, and without a physical the company will not issue a new life insurance policy. However, in this case Mr. Gilbird assured the company representative that he would keep the appointment for the physical, so the local agent took it upon himself to write the policy, which is legal and binding even though the agent went against company policy. Since no one seems to know why Mr. Gilbird failed to keep the appointment, or of his whereabouts, the company is somewhat concerned. Well, more than concerned. I would say they're in a bit of a panic. I suspect some heads will roll before all this is cleared up. So if you could just let me take a look at your books I can tell them everything is okay and when your boss gets back from his vacation he can make another appointment for a physical and everybody will be happy—especially me, since I'll

receive a fat fee for my efforts and will be able to catch up on my bills and stay in business for a couple more weeks." Max hesitated for a few seconds, then with a look of desperation and a voice that pleaded said, "I'll be in and out in just a few minutes; no one will ever know I was here."

Max wasn't sure if his emotional plea was having any effect. The woman seemed moved, but appeared to be more interested in her cinnamon roll than his problems. He continued to plead, "Lady, this job might mean the difference between keeping my business or closing my office and going to work for another agency."

Max wasn't sure whether his story or the lure of her cinnamon roll did the trick, but she pulled open a drawer, removed a ring of keys and said, "I'll show you where the records are kept."

Max followed the woman through the door designated Private into what was apparently the employees' lounge. Two tables were lined up in the center of the long, somewhat narrow room. Several chairs were scattered about on either side of the tables. A counter with a deep sink, a coffeemaker, a toaster, and a microwave, with a refrigerator at one end and vending machines at the other end lined one wall. The entire opposite side of the room opened into the warehouse. At this time, however, a steel mesh curtain, similar to the ones used by merchants in shopping malls to secure their spaces at night, prohibited access to the warehouse. The mesh curtain also prevented two very large Doberman pinschers from entering the lounge.

The woman continued straight across the lounge until she reached a door with a large sign that read, Supervisor. She selected a key from the ring, unlocked the door, and swung it open. Max followed her into an office of comfortable size with two desks, each equipped as to be expected in a supervisor's office—a telephone, in and out baskets and several stacks of papers. Two filing cabinets stood in each corner behind the desks and clipboards, numbered 1 through 30, hung in three neat rows of ten each along the wall. On the same wall a couple of dozen sets of keys with numbered tags hung on corresponding pegs. As in the lounge, the wall opposite the desks opened into the warehouse with the same type of steel mesh curtain separating Max and the woman from the Dobermans as they sat dutifully on the other side of the mesh curtain, watching their every move. No signs gave any indication of what might be behind yet another door at the opposite end of the room.

The woman unlocked one of the filing cabinets, pulled open three drawers and said, "Our tax returns are here, our accounts due are in this one, and you will find accounts receivable in this one." She pointed to each drawer in turn.

"What's behind that door?" Max asked, nodding in the direction of the unmarked door.

"I don't know, I've never been inside. It's Mr. Gilbird's office." She volunteered the information without being asked. "But I'm sure you'll find everything you need in these files. I have to go back up front now." She started to leave, and then asked anxiously, "You won't be long?"

"No, I'll be only ten or fifteen minutes," Max assured her.

Max pulled a few pages from the records in the filing cabinets and slipped them into his attaché case before turning his attention to the unmarked door the secretary had indicated was Gilbird's office. The lock had been difficult and took the better part of five minutes to open although he had the latest lock-picking device—Max wondered if he was just out of practice or if they were building better locks.

Max opened the door and was surprised to find the lights had been left on, whether on purpose or by accident he didn't know, nor did it matter. He stepped into a plush and spacious office with 14-foot-high ceilings. A large desk stood in each corner, all neat and uncluttered. One glance and he knew his suspicions were right. Centered on the wall opposite the door was a 10-by-12-foot world map, an area drawn in and crosshatched, on the map, extending from the California coast to Kwajalein; he guessed it to be the Pacific Missile Test Range. Several other areas in the Pacific were also outlined and labeled. The wall to the right of the door had an equally large U.S. road map, with every military base labeled and color coded. Several major cities along the California coast had been circled; Max surmised the numbers written alongside the circled cities represented the populations of each city. The color-coded latitudinal and longitudinal notations starting just above Los Angeles and continuing down the coast into Mexico were puzzling; however, Max did not have the time to give the notations lengthy consideration. A chalkboard, wiped clean, hung on the wall left of the door. Each desk had its own computer terminal complete with monitor and printer. He didn't know much about the janitorial business, but he did know that the computer mainframe standing against the wall adjacent to the door with a heavy-duty modem capable of handling a large number of incoming or outgoing calls all at the same time, could easily handle the needs of every business in town with room to spare. A bank of military-looking transceivers standing beside the computer was of considerable interest to Max, but first things first; he would check out the transceivers later. A copy machine and a fax phone sat on a table on the other side of the door.

Forgetting access codes was one of those things that a majority of computer operators feared and it seemed to be common practice to write down personal access codes, just in case their memory failed

them, and hide them somewhere in their desk. It took only a couple of minutes to locate a list of access codes and corresponding files along with telephone numbers for the modem. This was all he needed. Unless the codes were changed, he could use any computer with a modem to search through the files in Gilbird's computer at a more convenient time.

There was no corresponding ring, but a light blinking on the telephone, signaling an incoming call, caught his attention. He waited until the blinking was replaced by a continuous glow, indicating the girl up front had answered, before easing the receiver off the cradle and lifting it to his ear. The woman was trying to explain about the mix-up with his appointment when a voice on the other end, using a sufficient number of superlatives, declared the girl to be an idiot and instructed her, in no uncertain terms, to do whatever was necessary to insure that Mr. Jeff Price would be present when he arrived, adding the threatening phrase, "If you know what's good for you."

Max had no way of knowing how far away Bell lived, but he had no intention of being around when he arrived. The woman didn't concern him. He had no reason to hide his activities from her or worry about when she would come back to find out what he was doing. Of course, if he had suspected her of being one of Gilbird's people, he would have felt differently. He replaced the telephone receiver, opened his attaché case and took out a microcassette tape recorder.

Most touch-tone telephones had a system for automatically dialing prerecorded numbers. Max pressed a button to select a line different from the one Bell had used to call the woman's office, then laid the receiver on the tape recorder so that the earpiece was directly above the built-in microphone and switched the tape recorder to record mode. Next he punched the redial button on the phone and recorded the series of tones as the telephone automatically dialed the last number called. He momentarily held down the button on the telephone cradle so as to disconnect the outgoing call, and then touched a button on the phone labeled Memory and the buttons 0 and 1. A different series of tones were recorded. Again he momentarily held down the button on the receiver cradle before touching the buttons marked 0 and 2 and recorded the tones. Using the same procedure Max continued recording until he had the tones for all the pre-recorded numbers on tape. Later he could use the tones to dial from another phone or he could convert them to the actual numbers and use a reverse directory to find the addresses; hopefully, something useful would turn up.

He was placing the tape recorder back inside his attaché case when the woman opened the door leading to the lounge. She stopped dead in her tracks as she looked through the first office at Max walking out of Gilbird's office. As he approached her she asked in a shaky voice, "How did you get in there?"

She recovered quickly as she obviously remembered that she was supposed to keep him around, not chase him off, so she answered her own question. "I guess it must have been unlocked." Max knew she was well aware that the door was always locked, even when occupied.

She was still a bit shaken, but was managing fairly well. "Are you finding everything you need? I have some time now—can I help you with anything or assist you in any way?"

"No, thank you. I have all I need. Everything looks okay, I'll send in my findings this afternoon and I'm sure the insurance company will be very happy with my report." There was no reason to tip her off to the fact that he had eavesdropped on her telephone conversation. He headed for the door where she stood.

"Are you sure? I could make copies of any documents you might want to include in your report."

She obviously wasn't aware he had listened in on Bell's phone call. She had only taken a couple of steps into the room and now stepped backward in an attempt to keep Max from opening the door.

"I was kind of hoping you might stay around awhile." Her voice had taken on a seductive tone, her eyes fluttered, and her tongue flicked out to moisten her lips. Max figured Bell must have scared the hell out of her because she sure was doing her best to detain him.

"It gets kind of lonely around here." She took one step toward him, but, still blocking the door, added, "If you know what I mean." She brought her hands up to cup her breasts and gave them a little squeeze. Desperation was beginning to show in her face and she was having a difficult time keeping her voice from breaking.

"I could lock the front door; no one would disturb us." Max felt sorry for the woman.

"Thanks, but I have to go."

"Please, you can't leave, you have to stay." She was pleading now.

"I'm very sorry, but I can't." He took her by the shoulders, moved her aside, opened the door, and walked out into the lounge. She ran after him, catching up just as he entered her office. "You lied to me!" she yelled.

He continued walking through her office and onto the loading dock. She followed, clutching at his arm. "You lied to me, and now I'm going to lose my job!"

She started to cry. "I need this job," she sobbed.

"Damn!" Max swore under his breath. He knew he should walk away and never think about her again. It was frightening that he should consider anything other than walking away; the fact that the woman was telling the truth wasn't the problem. Yes, he had lied to her and played on her emotions—probably the reason his ploy had worked so well was that she really did need her job and was sympathetic to a fellow human being in the same boat. But so what—he had more to worry about than some naïve broad. In his world the weak died young and he wasn't ready to die just yet. He wanted to walk away, but couldn't. She was right; he had lied to her and jeopardized her job, and maybe even her life. Of course, there was always a chance she was one of Gilbird's agents, and the tears were just an act, but he didn't think so. She appeared to be frightened half to death. If she was acting she was one of the best he'd ever encountered.

"How long before they arrive?" She kept right on crying, seemingly oblivious to the question. Max grabbed her by the shoulders and shook her, repeating the question. "How long before they arrive?"

The crying stopped; she seemed a total blank for a moment or two. "Ten minutes, maybe more, maybe less," she replied after looking at her watch. Then she volunteered, "Mr. Bell lives in Vandenberg Village. It's a twenty to thirty minutes drive, depending on traffic."

"Damn!" Max swore again, mumbling under his breath, and then said, talking to himself, "Ah, what the hell."

Then he spoke directly to the woman, "Okay lady, I know I got you into trouble and against my better judgment I'm going to try to get you out of whatever danger you may be in right now, but you've got to trust me, okay?"

"I, I, I don't know," she stammered.

"Alright, I'm going to tell you something I shouldn't and you had better make up your mind fast. Otherwise, I'm out of here."

Looking straight into her eyes he said. "Gilbird is dead." He let her think about what he had said for a moment or two, and then repeated it for effect and slipping in a lie he figured would do the trick unless she was either stupid or crazy or both. "Gilbird is dead and I think Bell killed him."

For good measure he flipped open a leather-bound ID case exposing an FBI identification card and badge and let her take a good look at it. She sucked in her breath; her skin suddenly became clammy and turned a ghostly white. Max thought she was going to collapse; he grabbed her by the shoulders and shook her hard. As she recovered her senses he snapped, "Well, what'll it be?"

She could barely speak. "What do you want me to do?" she asked in a shaken, almost inaudible, voice.

"Do you have a family in town?"

"No, I have a boyfriend, but he moved out two days ago and took all my money when I told him I was pregnant. That's why I need this job so badly. My rent is due next week and my car payment is already a month overdue."

"Damn!" He swore under his breath again, and asked without thinking, "How did you get your life so screwed up, lady?"

She started to cry again. Well, at least she had no ties in the area, which was good. Max grabbed her by the shoulders again and forced her to look him in the face, then asked, "Is there someplace at least a 1,000 miles from here where you could start a new life, if you had the money?"

She wiped her eyes with her sleeve and answered, "I have a sister in Coos Bay."

"When I say a new start, I mean one without relatives or friends."

She thought for several seconds, then said. "I used to visit my aunt in Atlanta when I was a teenager. I haven't been back since she died about twelve years ago. Is Atlanta okay?"

"Atlanta sounds good, but don't call or write anyone in Lompoc or tell anyone you lived here and don't ever mention Spic and Span Janitorial. Don't visit or write any relatives or old friends for at least a couple of years, okay?"

"Okay." She seemed even more frightened than before; he certainly hoped so, since scaring the hell out of her was exactly what he was trying to do. Well, she certainly seemed willing, at this point, to do whatever he suggested.

The paranoia plaguing agents who spent too much time on the other side of the wall crept into his thinking as he wondered if maybe she was too willing. Recognizing the symptoms, he dismissed the question. He knew this was in itself dangerous. One day he might attribute a logical question to paranoia and it would cost him his life.

"One question first."

"Okay."

"Why did you call Bell?" He knew she hadn't called, but he just wanted to hear her respond to the question.

"I didn't. He called me, wanted to know who was in Mr. Gilbird's office."

"I guess I must have tripped an alarm. We probably have less time than you think, so let's *di di mau.*"

"Let's what?" He didn't bother to explain; she wouldn't understand anyway. Hell, you had to have been there.

"Take your car to the shopping center just past the post office and park near Safeway, then walk back to the post office and wait for me inside. Don't leave with anyone no matter what they tell you. If they insist, yell your head off. Do not, and I repeat, do not, go home, don't stop to see anyone, and don't call anybody."

She hurried down the steps and opened the door to the Tempo before realizing she didn't have her keys or purse. She ran back up the steps, through the door into her former office, and was back in a flash with her purse. "What are you going to do?" she asked in a worried voice as she fumbled through her purse for the keys to her car.

Max knew she was wondering what to do if he failed to show up as promised. "Don't worry, I'll be there. I just want to check on one more thing."

She wasted no time getting her car started. He waited until she made the turn onto the highway before walking down the steps to the TransAM.

He reached the pullout above Highway 246 before anyone arrived at the warehouse; at least no vehicles were parked beside the loading dock. He parked the Pontiac, got out, unlocked the trunk, snapped open the locks on a small suitcase with padded compartments and removed a portable tape player and headset, resembling those used by walkers, joggers, and cyclists. He closed the suitcase and trunk compartment a couple of seconds before a Camero IROC Z28 made a fast turn onto the dirt road leading to Spic and Span Janitorial and slid to a stop beside the loading dock. Two guys piled out of the "Z" and took the steps two at a time, ran across the dock and into the warehouse. Less than a minute passed before a late-model Cadillac pulled in behind the Camero. A man got out and hurried into the warehouse.

Returning to the driver's seat, Max put the headset over his ears before plugging it into what was actually a receiver with a built-in tape recorder, pulled out the antenna, flipped on the power switch, and adjusted the gain control until a soft audible hiss came steadily through the headset. A few seconds later when the sound of a door bursting open came over the radio he switched on the recorder.

"Goddammit, they're both gone!" This was the same voice Max had heard on the telephone when he eavesdropped in Gilbird's office.

"Who was the guy and what did he want?" a second voice inquired.

"I don't know," declared the first voice. "He passed himself off as an insurance investigator. Claimed John took out a large insurance policy and wanted to look at the records."

"Where is John, anyway?" the second voice asked.

"I don't know, but it's about time we had some answers and I intend to get some tonight. I'm going to stay around here and see if anything is missing. In the meantime, you two go over to that stupid bitch's apartment and bring her back over here. If she isn't home, wait around until she shows up. I intend to find out what the hell she knows about all this crap." The sound of a door opening and closing came through the headset. Two men came out, jumped into the Camero and headed off toward town.

Max switched off the little receiver/recorder, collapsed its tiny antenna, and placed it along with the headset on the seat beside him.

"Well, isn't that interesting?" Max said out loud, although talking to himself. He had assumed Gilbird was controlling the cell; obviously this was not the case. Someone had sent Gilbird to Juneau. Bell wasn't in charge—he didn't even know where Gilbird had gone, so who could it be? Tolinger? Possibly. If only he could be at that meeting tonight he might find out, but first he had to get the woman safely on her way. Making a U-turn out of the pull-off he glanced at a tree on the opposite side of the road where he had secured a similar receiver/recorder earlier in the morning. The bugs he'd left in Gilbird's office had worked perfectly and would continue to operate for several days before their power cells were spent. In the meantime, the little device he had attached to the tree would record every word. He could retrieve the tape anytime.

The girl was waiting in the post office exactly as he had instructed her to do and she came running out when he turned into the parking lot. Max leaned over and opened the door. She was near panic when she climbed into the passenger seat and asked, "Where have you been? What took you so long?"

Max ignored the questions. He guessed she'd had time to think about her situation.

"What's your name?"

"Claudia Russell. What's yours?"

"Just call me Max."

"I need some clothes and a few other things. Could we stop by my apartment and pack a bag?" Without answering the question, Max picked up the headset and held it out to her. "Put this on, I want you to listen to something." She complied without any further questions. While Claudia was fitting the headset to her ears he rewound the tape. When she had the headset in place he pushed the play function and waited. It was easy to tell when the conversation on the tape ended. Claudia's face lost its color, beads of perspiration broke out on her forehead, and she slumped back in the seat. Max switched off the tape player, reached over and removed the headphones. Neither spoke as he drove out of the parking lot and turned toward the center of town. When he reached Main Street he turned right and followed Highway 1 to 246, and headed for U.S. 101 at Buellton. As they passed the dirt road leading to Spic and Span Claudia looked over at the warehouse and then back at Max. "Who are you?" The question was only a whisper.

"It doesn't matter. Are you okay?" She kept staring at him without answering or moving. He reached over and touched her shoulder. "Claudia, are you okay?" She nodded affirmatively.

"Did you recognize those voices?"

"The first one was Oscar Bell. The other one was a guy everyone calls Jake, I don't know his last name." She was silent for a few seconds, then asked, "Could we stop somewhere for a few minutes? I don't feel well. Whenever I get scared or nervous I get sick."

Max didn't answer. The obvious questions flashed across his thinking. Had she contacted someone before meeting him at the post office? Was she trying to delay leaving the area, hoping for an opportunity to make contact a second time? Once again he dismissed his thoughts and questions as paranoia. A few more seconds of silence passed before she spoke again. "I haven't eaten much in the last couple of days. Could we get some coffee and a sweet roll or something?"

Max thought she was on the verge of crying again. She rolled down the window and leaned her head against the door allowing the wind to blow in her face.

They were approaching Buellton, which consisted of a handful of gas stations and motels that had sprung up around the intersection of Highways 101 and 246. Lompoc was eight miles behind them, less than ten minutes away. Just two miles past the intersection was the Danish community of Solvang with numerous restaurants, shops, and hotels. What had once been just another ethnic community had now become a regular tourist trap on the well-traveled route between San Francisco and Los Angeles. Max was concerned about stopping at a restaurant only ten miles from Spic and Span, but knew the woman wasn't faring well and figured some food might help her feel better while loosing her tongue at the same time. "Alright, we'll stop at Solvang until you feel better."

He drove past the first three restaurants and pulled into a hotel parking lot and guided the TransAM to a stop in front of a doorway with a sign declaring an all-you-can-eat breakfast buffet. He helped Claudia, apparently dazed by the turn of events and a bit wobbly on her feet, up the steps and into the restaurant. Max ate a stack of thin pancakes with spiced apples and sour cream with a side of bacon and drank coffee while he watched Claudia wade through a breakfast that would have made a Northwest lumberjack proud; she made three trips to the buffet table. Color returned to her face and with each bite she became more at ease and seemed quite willing to tell him everything she knew about Spic and Span janitorial, which wasn't much.

She had worked for Spic and Span almost six months, but knew very little about their operation. Almost everything took place at night, and she worked days. Her job consisted of such mundane chores as signing for deliveries, going to the post office, answering the phone and taking messages. Mostly however, she just sat in the outer office and listened to her radio.

She had come to Lompoc from Houston with a guy by the name of Warren Satterfield, an out-of-work carpenter who hoped to get a job in construction. A building boom followed the announcement by the air force of its intent to construct a new space launch facility for the military space transport system on South Vandenberg. The boom had cooled by the time Claudia and Satterfield arrived in Lompoc. He didn't find a job and she continued supporting him and herself as she had done in Houston. She had managed to save a little money but made the mistake of opening a joint checking account with Satterfield.

She seemed relieved to be able to talk with someone about her problems and in doing so was able to supply Max with a few names and descriptions of people associated with Gilbird, including the description of two air force officers. Howard Tolinger fit the description of one of the officers. Bell seemed to be in charge, although Gilbird was listed as owner. Even after working there for six months, today was the first time she had ever seen the inside of Gilbird's office.

Claudia was not the addlebrained person he had first thought her to be, but a fairly intelligent woman with a good middle-class background. Over a period of time she had made several poor choices involving a series of bad situations and simply lost control of her life, and consequently, the courage to try and regain control. Her downhill slide had started when after three years of college she dropped out to take a job with an agency promising travel, glamour, and big bucks. Her parents vehemently disapproved. The altercation with her parents resulted in her leaving home and taking an apartment with a girlfriend. The girlfriend got married and moved out, a boyfriend moved in, and from there it had only gotten worse.

Max promised her the financial support she'd need to give her time to put some order back in her life. In exchange for the financial help, she promised to finish college, take some self-improvement courses, and to join a health club. He warned her that the money would run out and she should give serious consideration to a realistic and attainable career, and forget about glamour.

When they returned to the car, Max counted out thirty thousand dollars from a concealed compartment in the trunk and put it into a thick brown envelope. He handed the money to Claudia as they pulled out of the parking lot, instructing her to put two thousand in her purse before sealing the envelope. Her eyes almost popped out of her head when she saw the thick stack of fifty-dollar bills. Her gratitude seemed genuine as she promised again, this time with a great deal of enthusiasm, to do exactly as she had said she would. Concluding with, "I won't blow it this time!" Max wondered what she would be thinking if she knew the money had come from her dead boss.

He drove her to the Los Angeles International airport, purchased a ticket in the name of Janice Weaver, and waited with her until she boarded. He didn't leave the terminal until her plane began taxiing toward the runway.

As Max drove down Century Boulevard toward Interstate 405 he was tempted to take the southbound ramp. San Diego and the woman of all his dreams and fantasies were less than two hours away. As tempted as he might have been, he turned north, as he knew he must

ONE MORE BAG OF SCUM

It was five thirty in the afternoon when he drove into his garage on Surf Road. Not much to do until tonight. He figured he might as well get some sleep. But first a quick check of his recording equipment. There was nothing of interest on the telephone recorder. The video setup had recorded two vehicles. A clock in the video camera painted the time, to the nearest second, on each frame of the tape and established the time the two vehicles had passed in front of his house. There was nothing new to be learned from the tape about the Dodge Maxivan he had seen driving through the eucalyptus grove early this morning, except to confirm it had left Gilbird's house.

The video of the second vehicle, however, was very interesting. An official air force sedan with two uniformed officers, fitting the description given him by Claudia, had arrived at five minutes past noon, stayed almost an hour and a half, leaving at 1:26. The young lieutenant driving, a very clean-cut looking kid was probably in his midtwenties. Max felt he had seen the lieutenant before, but couldn't recall where or when. The passenger, an older man somewhere around forty-five or fifty, he recognized as Colonel Howard Kent Tolinger.

He reset the equipment and twenty minutes later, after eating a sandwich and taking a shower, he was asleep and dreaming of green eyes, red hair, soft creamy skin, and freckles.

Just before midnight Max braked the TransAM to a stop in front of Pablo's A to Z Janitorial Services, on the outskirts of Santa Maria. A driveway on either side of the office led to a graveled parking lot in back with two Quonset huts and a covered area resembling a large carport with about ten Chevy vans parked underneath. The building had at one time been someone's house. Probably the owner had started a business from his home and as he became more successful built a new house and kept his old residence for his office. The house was small by today's standards, about nine hundred square feet. The interior walls had been replaced by four wooden posts attached to the ridge beam to support the roof, leaving one large room about twenty feet by forty-five feet. The layout of the room was similar to the lounge at Spic and Span with chairs, tables, vending machines, a microwave, and a coffeepot. A three-foot-high partition across one end of the room separated two desks, four filing cabinets, and a table surrounded by half a dozen chairs like the ones in the lounge. On the wall by the door opening out into the rear compound was a sign that read, Restroom Outside.

There was no sign to indicate who was in charge. A sign wasn't necessary; one look at the competent-looking old man, with his desk in position to survey the entire room at a glance, and Max knew he was the man he wanted to talk with. Two younger men sat at one of the tables drinking coffee. All three watched Max with conspicuous curiosity as he entered the room. The old man behind the desk looked up from a ledger and peering over his reading glasses, watched, but did not speak as the stranger walked across the room toward the partition. Max stopped in front of the desk and stood looking at the old man for about five seconds, lending an air of authority and perplexity to his presence before asking, "Are you Pablo Montoya?"

The old man had no intention of being intimidated by a pushy man in a fancy suit. Leaning back in his chair, he took his time looking the stranger up and down before finally answering, "Si."

"Mr. Montoya, I'm with the Internal Revenue Service." Max held out his identification for the old man's inspection and handed him a business card even the expert eye could not have spotted as bogus. The old man looked over the ID and took his time reading the business card before replying, "I pay my taxes, señor."

"I'm sure you do, Mr. Montoya. I'm not here to inquire into the way you conduct your business. I'm here because I need your help, sir."

"And how might an old janitor like me help the almighty IRS?"

Max didn't know if the old man was just being cynical or if he had more reason than most to hold the IRS in contempt. He remembered the vehicles parked out back. They were all relatively new and appeared to be in good condition. At this time of night these vehicles should be out on the job. Based on this and what he had already gleaned from the records at John Gilbird's office he replied, "Mr. Montoya, we have noticed your business has declined over the last couple of years while one of your competitors has increased his business tenfold during the same period. We suspect he has set out to bankrupt his competition and is using unfair trade practices to accomplish his goal. The IRS suspects that Spic and Span is in violation of the Rico Act and we have asked the Justice Department to file charges.

However, the Justice Department kicked it back to us, saying that we don't have enough evidence. And that's why I'm here. I'm trying to gather more evidence against Spic and Span, and I would appreciate your help and cooperation, sir."

Pablo Montoya leaned even further back in his chair as he weighed the cost of collaborating with the IRS. Several seconds later, his decision made, he asked, "Would you like some coffee, señor?"

"Gracias, si."

The old man's face softened a bit as Max replied in his native language. "Manuel, dos cafes, por favor."

Pablo pointed to the chair beside his desk. "Take a load off, young fellow."

Max walked through the open gate in the partition, settled into the chair and waited for Manuel to bring the coffee. When it arrived, he took a sip and found it strong and bitter. It tasted like it had cooked for three days in a pot which hadn't been cleaned for six months. He raised his cup slightly in a salute, even though he found it a vile brew. "Muy bueno."

"No it's not." The old man laughed. "It's terrible; nobody around here knows how to make good coffee." After a pause he added, "But nobody cares either."

They both laughed. "Well, it sure wakes you up." He lifted his cup a bit higher this time.

The old man didn't waste any time on idle conversation. "So you want to know about Spic and Span?"

The old man continued without waiting for an answer. "Well, they have almost put me out of business. I've lost half the contracts I had in Santa Maria and all but two of the contracts at Vandenberg, and I'll probably lose those when they come up for bid. For the last year I bid jobs at cost just to keep my employees in work and still I lose the contracts."

The old man took a sip of coffee, and then added. "They are losing money on every job. I know. I've been a janitor for thirty years. I know!"

Max had no doubt the old man knew the janitorial business and was speaking the truth. He forced down another swallow of coffee before asking, "What about the office buildings in Casmalia and Guadelupe? They show substantial profits on both projects?"

Pablo sneered. "Have you seen Casmalia and Guadelupe?"

Before Max could answer the old man continued. "Guadelupe is a farming town. You could hire local labor to clean every office in town for less than it would cost to drive over and back. Casmalia is an old railroad town with a whopping population of twenty-two people." He took another sip of coffee and waited for the man from the IRS to react.

"Well, Mr. Montoya, Spic and Span paid taxes on over twelve million dollars last year. If what you tell me is true, and I do believe you, where do they get their profit?"

The old man was astonished. "You mean you really don't know?"

"No sir."

"They sell dope. They bring it in through Vandenberg. That's the reason they bid the contracts so low. It gives them easy access to the air base."

Max had never considered the KGB would be running a dope-smuggling operation, but it made sense. Wow! What a sweet deal. The narcotics were flown onto a government installation and unloaded while the air force unwittingly provided them with some of the best security in the world.

The surprised look on his guest's face told Pablo the man knew nothing of the dope-smuggling operation. "I tell the truth, señor. They supply pushers from Ventura all the way up the coast to San Luis Obispo." Max, realizing there was much to be learned from Pablo Montoya, shifted in his chair to a more comfortable position and took another swallow of coffee; it tasted delicious.

It was well after 1 a.m. when Max drove away from A to Z Janitorial. According to Pablo, Bell, a small-time pusher from Oakland, had been recruited to wholesale cocaine, using Spic and Span as a front for the operation. Bell had brought Jake Hatcher, a former Hell's Angel, with him to put the arm on any of their clients that got out of line or caused trouble.

The janitorial business was the perfect cover; with almost free access to Vandenberg they could leave the bulk of the narcotics on the air base, removing only the amounts needed to fill orders by dealers. No one would have reason to suspect a legitimate business, known to have normal night and wee morning operating hours, with service contracts all along the coast, to be dealing in drugs. Pablo knew only because of lifelong friendships, some reaching into areas he was not eager to discuss or proud to acknowledge.

Max could only guess at the percentage of profit Bell was allowed to keep for himself and what he did with his share. But Gilbird, no doubt, used his share to fund espionage.

Since Bell was unaware of Gilbird's whereabouts, it only made sense that his connection with Spic and Span was strictly cocaine and he was ignorant of Gilbird's involvement with the KGB. The questions for Max remained the same; who controlled the Communist cell and what was their objective? The openness with which they were operating, the chances they were taking and the total disregard for practiced methods of the KGB were in themselves scary. This could be one last do-or-die operation for the Communists. President Reagan had been tightening the screws on the Soviets, forcing them to spend over 25 percent of their gross national product on weapons buildup just to stay in the race. The weapons buildup plus the expense of their invasion of Afghanistan was bringing their economy to its knees. The citizens were complaining openly, the Kremlin was beginning to lose control, and cracks were starting to show in the iron curtain. Gorbachev had shown a willingness to engage in disarmament talks, but kept backing away from the table. Possibly he was awaiting the outcome of the KGB operation here at Vandenberg to either make or break. Max still didn't have a clue, just instinct, but his instinct told him whatever was going down was in its final stage and time was running out for any hopes of undermining their plans. He started to perspire although the night was cool and the driver's window on the TransAM was down.

The Pacific Telephone building on Palo Verde Avenue was dark except for floodlights in the rear, where several repair vans were parked, and a single light above the door designated Service Entrance. The door did not open when Max tugged at the handle. A small sign beside the door read "Ring for Entry." Max pushed the button underneath the sign, and waited. Nothing happened. The door still would not open. He was about to push the button again when he heard the dead bolt retract. The door was opened by a short pudgy guy, beginning to go bald, probably in his midforties. The man was startled as Max pushed past him into the standard waiting lounge found anywhere in the country, consisting of a couch and matching chair, a corner table with a lamp, a potted plant and a coffee table with old issues of Time and National Geographic.

"I thought you were Reggie." The man stated nervously.

"Reggie?"

"Yeah, he's been out on a call for three hours. The job should have taken an hour at most. He's probably asleep someplace."

Regaining his composure, he asked. "Who the hell are you and what do you want?"

"I'm Randal Evans. I have a telephone number and I want the address to go along with the number."

"Well, Mr. Evans." The man, clearly irritated by the intrusion, was curt with his reply. "In the morning you go down to the library and look in their reverse directory. It's very simple."

"I can't do that. It's an unlisted number."

"Well, you're wasting your time. People pay extra to keep their names and addresses private. The telephone company won't give out the address of an unlisted number."

"I know the telephone company won't help me, but I thought maybe you might."

Max reached into his pocket and pulled out a roll of fifty-dollar bills and counted off ten bills, and stared at the pudgy little guy without speaking again. The man's eyes were glued to the wad of fifty-dollar bills. Max waited a few seconds and counted off ten more bills and watched for the man's reaction. He swallowed once and glanced nervously at the door. Max surmised the pudgy little guy was hoping Reggie wouldn't pick this particular time to show up. Max counted off another five hundred dollars and put the rest in his pocket. The man still had not spoken. He swallowed hard this time, glancing at the door again. Max waited for about ten seconds then folded the thirty crisp fifty-dollar bills and started to put them in his pocket with the others when the man held out his hand and asked, "What's the number?"

Max pulled a piece of paper from his pocket and handed the number to the man along with the fifteen hundred dollars.

The night air, cool and fresh, felt good against his skin as he stripped off his Italian-made suit and replaced it with a set of black sweats. He traded his Guccis for Nikes and pulled on a pair of black jogging shorts over the sweat pants. Checking to make sure everything had been placed in the trunk, he closed the lid and walked away toward the street, looking back only once at the TransAM.

Half an hour later he stood surveying the Safeway parking lot. Late-night shoppers loaded groceries into their cars and drove away to be replaced by newcomers, creating sparse but continuing traffic to and from the 24-hour supermarket. The silver-gray Tempo was fairly well hidden in the cluster of cars near the store's entrance. He approached the little Ford cautiously, walking completely around the car, looking for any telltale signs of forced entry. After rocking the car from side to side a couple of times he used the key and opened the door, rolled down the driver's window and slammed the door shut. Reaching in through the open window he inserted the ignition key and twisted it to the start position. The starter turned the engine over several times before it caught. It ran rough for a few seconds before smoothing out to a steady purr. Reaching through the window for a second time he turned on the headlights, waited another ten seconds, opened the door and slipped in behind the wheel.

It was twenty minutes later when he turned into the parking lot behind Claudia's apartment building, cut the lights, and killed the engine. Leaving the keys in the ignition he locked the doors and slowly walked away, keeping to the shadows. Convinced no one was watching, he broke into an easy run with deceptively long strides that carried him along the sparsely lighted streets of Lompoc back to his own car, a distance of just over eight miles, in a little under an hour.

Slowing to a walk for the last 200 yards gave his body a chance to warm down and provided an opportunity to pick up on any activity in the hotel parking lot. At three thirty in the morning very few people stirred in Lompoc and nothing moved in the parking lot. Satisfied no one had tampered with his TransAM, he opened the door, slipped into the driver's seat, reached across to the passenger's side, and retrieved a bottle of Gatorade. Drinking half the refreshing beverage before lowering the bottle he sat back looking at the label, remembering the first time he heard the strange-sounding name.

Bright moonlight made it easy to drive the last quarter of a mile with his lights off. A switch on the dash allowed him to disable the brake lights; as a result, no telltale red lights glowed on the rear of the TransAM as he pulled into the turn-out overlooking Spic and Span Janitorial, and parked. The warehouse was lit up like a stadium. A quick check with binoculars revealed an armed guard at the entrance to the storage yard and several cars parked along the front loading dock. Max put away the binoculars, walked across the road and climbed over the fence. About 150 feet up the hill he found the tree with the radio/recorder he had attached to one of the branches almost twenty-four hours ago. There was no green light glowing to indicate the voice-operated keying system was recording. He removed the tape and replaced it with a new cassette and climbed back down the hill to the road.

He drove south for a couple of miles before turning on the headlights and returning the brake light to normal operation. Finding a wide spot in the road he hung a one eighty and drove back into town, and then turned west toward Surf Road.

After a long, hot shower Max put on a fresh set of sweats, walked into the kitchen, and prepared a large breakfast. He ate on the patio in the predawn, listening to the surf below. A fog bank hung off the coast, typical for this time of year, and the air hung heavy with aromas of the sea. Before he realized it, shadowy images of Sherry were drifting through his mind. He closed her out, adjusted the headset, and pushed the play button on the cassette player lying on the table. The first voice was Claudia's—he'd planted the bugs immediately after entering Gilbird's office. After he and Claudia left, the next sound was the door opening followed by the voices of Bell and Hatcher. Following the exchange between Bell and Hatcher, resulting in Hatchers' departure along with the unidentified man, Bell spoke again.

"We've got troubles!" He was obviously speaking to someone on the telephone. Max had not bugged the phone, so only half the conversation had been recorded, but since the VOX triggered the recorder only when sound came in on the radio, there were no breaks in Bell's conversation and no indication of how long the man (or woman) at the other end talked.

"Some guy in here nosing around and asking about John. Says he's an insurance investigator. Yeah. I don't know. I think he's a narc. I don't like it, especially with a shipment late. Yeah. What time? Well, don't worry about me. You just make sure those goddamn dogs aren't around when the stuff is unloaded; they almost screwed it up last time. Yeah, well I'm gonna get to the bottom of it and somebody had better have some answers. See you tonight. Don't sweat it." Anger was evident in Bell's voice and accented by the resultant crash as he replaced the telephone in its cradle. The sound was followed a moment later by the slamming of a door.

There was no way of knowing how much time had elapsed before the door opened again. A woman asked, "How long will it take?"

"About an hour to make a good sweep and another hour to change all the access codes," answered a man with a high-pitched voice.

Well, he could forget about hacking away at Gilbird's computer banks. The new access codes would require too much time to bypass. Besides, his computer was in San Diego and although he wanted an excuse to see Sherry, his instincts told him time was of the essence.

"Just make sure everything is completed by midnight," the woman ordered.

"No sweat. Why midnight?"

"Everything will be explained tonight."

"Well, well, well! Look at this."

"Damn!" Max exclaimed as he banged his fist down against the table. He knew the man had uncovered one of his bugs and it was only a matter of time before he would find the two remaining.

"Okay. No more conversation until you're absolutely certain the room is clean," the woman snapped. And indeed, no other sounds emanated from the little tape player, none at all.

Bell had referred twice to a meeting scheduled for tonight. The woman had indicated everything would be explained after midnight. Midnight, however, had come and gone. Playing Good Samaritan with Claudia had denied him any chance of eavesdropping on the meeting. Chances were, with his bugs destroyed he would have had little chance of doing so anyway. With armed guards, floodlights, barbed wire, attack dogs, and probably trip wires, he stood a better chance of getting caught than he did of getting into a position to listen in on the meeting. It was becoming evident they were not as lax in their security as he had first suspected. Perhaps it would behoove him to be a bit more cautious himself. Keeping this in mind, he spent the better part of an hour viewing the latest video recording of the road in front of his house. Besides his leaving and returning the camera had recorded a woman he assumed to be Evone Gilbird, driving a Chevrolet Caprice station wagon, leaving at 6:11 last evening. She returned, followed by the Dodge Maxivan, at two 2:41 this morning. The van left at 3:56. He had probably missed passing the van on Surf Road by no more than ten minutes. He viewed one section of the video three times before dismissing a moon-cast shadow, recorded five minutes after he departed for A to Z Janitorial, as one of the numerous deer that roamed the coastal chaparral from dusk to dawn.

The telephone tap had recorded three calls, one from a woman, whose voice he'd heard in Gilbird's office just before the bugs went dead, who confirmed the midnight meeting with an unfamiliar male voice—Max surmised the woman's voice belonged to Evone Gilbird.

Max recalled another secret meeting that took place in August 1921, long before he was born. A secret meeting at Bridgman, Michigan when the Communist Party of America (The Third International) adopted a thesis written by J. Lovestone, Executive Secretary, Communist Party of America. Lovestone's Party name was L.C. Wheat. The thesis was a blueprint for infiltrating and controlling every organization in America, including the federal government. Had they succeeded, Max wondered? Did his efforts really matter? Had the Communists already won? Was it just a matter of time before they openly declared victory?

Max cleared his mind and concentrated on the other two calls. They were calls to the number with the recorder; the first call was to receive a prerecorded message, and the second time the caller left a message. He had grossly underestimated their security. The recorder was set up with a voice scrambler. The caller, of course, needed a scrambler to receive the message; the message she left was scrambled as well. The dial tones, however, could not be scrambled without the cooperation of the telephone company. This service required a lot of paperwork and government approval. The Gilbirds were not about to attract attention to themselves by applying to the telephone company for scrambled dial tones. He now had the code to command the recorder to play back its recorded messages, but without knowing the codes manually set into the scrambler he would be unable to decipher the messages, even with a scrambler of his own; without these codes it would sound like gibberish.

Well, he had paid fifteen hundred dollars for the location of the telephone; it was time to cash in on his investment. The address was a surprise—not that it should have been. At least there was a chance he could get a look at the scrambler and check positioning of the coding switches—these were normally sliders, similar to the ones used in telephones to select operating frequencies between the base and remote units. It would then be simple to set up a similar system. But, first, he had to get onto Vandenberg and find building 5001, no easy task considering the air base had an area of nearly 3,500 acres. To make it more complicated, buildings on military installations were numbered in the order in which they were built, with no reference to use or location. Building 843 might be a hospital while ten miles away building 844 could be a storage shed for oil drums. To further confuse things, numbers were recycled when buildings were torn down or otherwise destroyed, so that building 63 might be new and 2,196 could be fifty years old. He would need help. It would have to wait.

The only other chance of uncovering some useful information, at the moment, lay in the dial tones recorded from the phone's automatic dialing system in Gilbird's office. By listening to the tones over and over several times he would be able to correctly identify each digit associated with its corresponding tone. But why bother, when an inexpensive piece of equipment, sold at almost any do-it-yourself electronic store, allowed you to convert the tones directly to numbers? It was just a matter of plugging the handy-dandy device into the tape player's headset jack, stopping the tape at the end of each series of tones, and copying the numbers from the gadget's LEDs. And presto, an hour's work was completed in five minutes.

Over a fresh cup of coffee Max scrutinized the list of the ten numbers before him. He placed a checkmark by Gilbird's home phone number, another by the message phone; the third number he recognized and checked off was Bell's. The fourth number checked off was the last dialed, held in the zero file. It had been placed to the message phone. Three numbers had out-of-state area codes. A check in the directory placed one, a 407 area code, in Florida. Cape Canaveral was in the 407 area. The second was a Nebraska area code, 402. Offutt Air Force Base, headquarters of the Strategic Air Command, was south of Omaha and within this area code. The third was 202, Washington, District of Columbia. This was heavy stuff. Logic told Max he was in over his head and he should call Henri and turn over every scrap of information to the Company. But, contrary to what most people believed, the CIA had limited powers within the United States. They would have to work through the FBI's counterintelligence group. This would take time and possibly any action taken would come too late. The other three numbers were local, but a quick check of his reverse directory proved them to be unlisted. It looked like he would be making another visit to the despicable little man in the telephone maintenance office.

Max held in contempt anyone who, for a price, would compromise information their position required them to safeguard, no matter how unimportant that information might seem. Over the years he had dealt with dozens, maybe even hundreds, of people just like the little man in the dispatch office, and each time he'd had the urge to grab them by the throat and explain integrity to them as he choked the life out of their greedy little bodies. Well, that, too, would have to wait.

The early-morning news was just coming on as Max settled in front of the television. The lead story on the local front focused on a car bomb that had killed an as yet unidentified man in the parking lot behind the Rio Vista Apartments. The explosion had rocked the neighborhood at about six thirty that morning, breaking windows and sending debris flying about the parking lot, damaging several other vehicles, and injuring at least one other person. A TV camera panned the apartment building and the damaged cars in the parking lot before focusing in on Rex Brown, the on-scene reporter. What was left of Claudia's silver gray Tempo, roped off with the familiar yellow tape used by law enforcement, was in the background. Police, along with paramedics were poking around in the wreckage. The reporter glanced at a piece of paper handed him and announced the victim had been identified as Warren Satterfield, an unemployed construction worker from Houston.

Max felt a bead or two of perspiration forming on his forehead. When checking the little Ford for explosives before moving it from the Safeway parking lot to Claudia's apartment he had not been all that concerned about being blown away. The cursory check was merely a routine precaution. Well, he was concerned now. Max knew the bomb had been intended for Claudia and was planted after he left the car at her apartment. Had the Tempo been spotted in the Safeway parking lot and the bomb set earlier, he, rather than Satterfield, might be the morning news. Satterfield had cleaned out Claudia's bank account and was apparently waiting around for a chance to steal her car and blow town. Well, he blew town alright. As far as Max was concerned he got his just reward and society was free of one more bag of scum.

A REAL UGLY GUY

"A lot of buildings aren't shown on this map," Pablo explained as he placed an X on a detailed map of Vandenberg, near the intersection of Fifteenth and California. "These buildings are left over from Camp Cook; the army had a lot of people and equipment here during World War II, but when the air force became a separate service they tore down just about everything and built to suit their own needs and changed the name from Camp Cook to Vandenberg. These are two of the old Camp Cook buildings lucky enough to escape demolition."

Pablo drew two circles on the map and pointed to the first. "This is the theater; the movie will be over at about ten o'clock. We'll start cleaning at that time. When we finish we'll move over to the bowling alley." He pointed to the second circle. "They close at midnight. It takes about two hours to clean each building. That will give you about four and a half hours to find whatever it is you're looking for and get back to either the theater or the bowling alley. If you aren't back by the time we finish, we'll wait if we can, but after we finish cleaning, security comes around and locks the building. Once that happens, we'll have to leave."

"Thanks, but don't worry about hanging around. If I'm not back, leave without me." Max got out of the van and walked across the parking lot toward the base hospital, approximately five hundred yards away.

Once past the hospital, following Pablo's directions he picked his way through a thick woods for a couple of hundred feet until he broke out onto a paved street, he then turned left and walked along the street until he intersected Air Field Road and followed Air Field Road until he found an unnamed dirt road cutting off through the woods. According to Pablo, building 5001 would be off this road on the left just before it intersected California Street.

Thirty minutes later he found two buildings set back off the road, surrounded by eucalyptus and cypress. Numbers 5001 and 5002 were the only buildings in the area, apparently old army housing that had somehow escaped the bulldozer. The rest had all been cleared away. Along the deteriorating streets, with grass and bushes growing up through cracks in the pavement, a few old foundations remained as the only evidence that a residential neighborhood, where hundreds of military families once lived, had ever existed. Both buildings were boarded shut except for the rear doors, which had new locks.

He worked the lock-picking device in and out until he found the right combination. It opened easily and in about half the time he spent on the lock to Gilbird's office. Playing his Mini-Maglite around inside he found the interior of the house to still be in pretty good condition. The roof had not leaked and the hardwood floors still had a shine.

He found the telephone, recorder, and scrambler neatly arranged on shelves inside a locked closet. Using the screwdriver on his Swiss army knife to remove a cover on the underside of the scrambler, he exposed the slider switches. After diagramming the switches' positions and double-checking to insure he had not copied in error, Max replaced the cover plate, made a note as to manufacturer and model number of the unit, arranged everything as be had found it, and locked the closet door.

Shipping crates marked HIGH EXPLOSIVES lined the walls. The metal bands on all crates had been cut and the tops pried open. He lifted one of the heavy wooden tops and peered inside at a shiny yellow metallic cylinder. "Dummy warhead-MX," in two-inch black lettering was painted lengthwise on the cylinder and continued line after line around the entire cylinder. He checked a second crate and then a third. The crates all contained identical cylinders, fifteen in total. This seemed an odd place to store ordnance, even if it was inert. His curiosity piqued, he decided to look inside the other building.

Outside, he waited in the shadows a couple of minutes before moving to the second house. The lock opened more easily this time. Playing his flashlight around, he found the interior to be in even better condition than the first house. More packing crates sat along the walls. These crates, however, marked "Electronic Components," were much smaller than the ones next door. These, too, had been opened. Inside each crate, nestled in Styrofoam, was a small black box with two Cannon plug connectors on one end. The plate underneath the electrical connectors read, "Target-seeking computer." He counted fifteen crates. Another crate housed a larger piece of equipment, with an identification plate that read "MX guidance computer."

In another room he found several empty crates with packing material scattered about, a wooden table about six feet long, and another locked closet. He was much faster opening the lock this time. He didn't need to guess at the contents of the packages of white powdery substance all neatly stacked on the closet shelves. He estimated the wholesale value of what he guessed to be over four hundred kilos of cocaine to be in excess of ten million dollars. Well, this didn't belong to the air force—probably none of this stuff belonged to the air force. But what could Gilbird want with the electronics equipment and fifteen dummy bombs?

He hadn't heard the back door open. The only sound to alert him before the lights came on was the clicking sound on the hardwood floor. When he turned around he found himself eyeball to eyeball with the largest Doberman pinscher he had ever seen. With teeth bared, and without making a sound, the dog waited for a command.

Jake Hatcher stood just inside the door with a .44 Magnum in his right hand. Max momentarily found himself amused as he wondered why everybody carried cannons when a small caliber would kill you just as dead. All you had to do was shoot where you aimed.

Max reasoned he had tripped another alarm. If this was true and Hatcher, not air force security, was answering the alarm, then all the crates did indeed tie into whatever Gilbird and his group were planning. But what were their plans? Did they intend to blow up the MX on its first test launch? This was a possibility—he was sure they had somehow had a hand in the other missile failures. Still, although it would cause a setback in deployment of the Peacekeeper, it would not be the media event he believed the Kremlin was working toward.

"Okay, clasp your hands behind your head and back away from the closet. Do it slowly." Jake, knowing he had the upper hand, was calm and deliberate as he moved toward the closet. Curious to see if the intruder had removed any of the narcotics, he chanced a quick look inside, taking his eyes off Max for only a moment. At the very instant Jake glanced inside the closet Max sprang into the air and with lightning speed his left foot delivered a sharp blow to Jake's right elbow. Jake felt his entire arm go numb as the weapon leapt from his hand. Still in the air, Max rotated his body and delivered a crushing blow to Jake's chin with his right foot. Hatcher landed on his back, Max landed on all fours, and the Doberman landed on Max, going for his throat. Max felt the sharp teeth rip through his flesh as he rammed his left hand into the dog's mouth, barely in time to keep the animal from ripping his jugular veins open. Max managed to throw the dog to one side and spring to his feet. The Doberman landed on his feet at the same time as Max and they raced for the door. Max grabbed the door jamb, stopping his forward motion, and swung around against the wall on the other side of the door. The dog tried to make the turn and attack again, but his weight and forward motion caused him to slip on the hardwood floor. Max had just enough time to jump back into the other room and slam the door shut. He had escaped from the Doberman, but now he was back in the room with Hatcher who was still dazed, but reaching for the big revolver. Max threw himself at the man and grabbed the gun, twisting it away from his face. Jake, in his effort to wrench the gun away from Max, put too much pressure on the trigger. The sound was deafening. The bullet went into the lower chest and out through his left shoulder.

Max rolled the dead man over and went through his pockets, but found nothing of interest. His left hand was a mess. Blood soaked his sleeve to the elbow and trickled from his fingers. Using his Swiss army knife, he cut off the other sleeve, wrapped it around the bleeding hand, and secured it as best he could.

Max was just about to leave before he remembered the dog on the other side of door; he stopped and retrieved the heavy revolver, wondering if anyone had heard the gunshot. Well, either way a second shot wouldn't matter. Halfway back to the door he stuck the gun under his belt, walked to the closet, and removed one of the packages of cocaine. Cutting through the tough plastic he opened up one end and sprinkled the one-thousand-dollar-an-ounce substance over a ten-foot area on the floor in front of the door. Holding the pistol in his right hand he stood behind the door, and pulled it open with his mangled left hand. The Doberman lunged into the room, saw Max and turned to attack, but unable to maneuver on the slippery floor, lost his footing and skidded halfway across the room. Max stepped through the door, and pulled it closed behind him. After wiping his prints from the gun he dropped it inside one of the shipping crates. He sure pitied the next poor sucker to open that door. He hoped it was Tolinger.

Skirting all lighted areas and keeping to the woods whenever possible, he made his way to the bowling alley. Pablo was outside by his van; the crew was finishing up inside. Fifteen minutes later they were passing through Vandenberg's main gate and heading toward Santa Maria. Pablo stopped at an all-night service station and made a phone call. Returning to the van, he said, "We'll stop off and get your hand fixed up a bit."

Pablo dropped the crew at his office and after giving some instructions in Spanish to one of the men, drove off toward the center of Santa Maria. He still hadn't asked any questions about the blood-soaked sleeve, but as he turned toward the ocean on Betaravia Road he remarked, "Looks like you're going to owe me for a new uniform."

"Yeah, I met a real ugly guy with a big, mean dog. The dog did a number on me. I guess he didn't like your logo."

Pablo chuckled. "Sounds like you met up with Jake Hatcher and one of his Doberman pinschers. Did you find what you were looking for?"

"Mr. Montoya, you don't know how much I appreciate your help, but, in the interest of your own safety there are things going on I can't discuss, and I would advise you to forget you ever met me. Your life could already be in jeopardy."

Pablo gave Max one of those I'm-not-as-dumb-as-you-think-I-am smiles and said, "I knew from the beginning you weren't telling me everything, but if I can help shut down Spic and Span I'll take the risk."

Pablo didn't ask any more questions. They stopped in the driveway of a modest ranch house. Max assumed it was Pablo's home. They waited inside the house for perhaps ten minutes before a woman, probably Pablo's wife, wearing a nurse's uniform, arrived. The lady cleaned his hand, stitched the lacerations and applied a clean dressing. She didn't ask any questions, but instructed him to keep the bandage clean and dry and to see a doctor.

Back at Pablo's office, Max removed his pants and stripped off what was left of the blood-soaked shirt, with the big A to Z logo on the back, and dressed in what had become his own uniform, black sweats and running shoes.

As he opened the door of the TransAM, Max thanked Pablo for his help and suggested, "You might want to destroy what's left of that uniform."

"I have an incinerator out back," Pablo replied.

Without further conversation, the two men shook hands, then Max slipped under the wheel and drove away.

The full moon, in a star-studded sky, set everything aglow. With the warm Santa Ana winds one could easily have mistaken this late night in December for a summer's evening in August. Max sat on the patio listening to the surf as he tried to assemble all the data he had compiled, but it was like guessing at the picture in a jigsaw puzzle by looking at the border and a couple of unrelated pieces. The importing and selling of narcotics to finance their operation was another example of the KGB not following standard procedures, indicating, as Max saw it, a do-or-die effort. Sabotaging Atlantis on her maiden voyage had at first seemed the logical target, but now with the entire space program being revamped it would be at least a year before another STS launch. This eliminated another shuttle disaster, since whatever the KGB had in mind would take place in the very near future—of this he was absolutely certain. The MX parts seemed to indicate the KGB and GRU had combined forces and were concentrating on the Peacekeeper. However, destroying another missile, although he was sure the Communists would not pass up the opportunity to do so, was not, in his opinion, representative of the enormous destruction required to turn the entire country against space exploration and SDI research.

Turning public opinion against SDI, he believed, was their goal. If war broke out at this moment between NATO forces and the Warsaw Pact nations, space would play an important but limited role. Satellites presently in orbit, U.S. and Soviet alike, were passive, used only for various means of intelligence gathering, but wars of the future would be fought in space and the USSR now stood ready to deploy a new generation of satellite-based weapons. If they could delay or in some way prevent the United States from developing and deploying a space-based weapons system, they would be able, by the end of the decade, to dictate conditions to the entire Western world without fear of reprisal, since they would have total control of space. Most Americans were not privy to the successes of the Soviets in their quest to dominate the world and few were concerned about, or even contemplated the world ten years hence.

Their timing was perfect. Another disarmament summit was scheduled in two weeks. At the last meeting the Soviets had walked out when President Reagan refused to put SDI on the table. Max was convinced whatever was going down here at Vandenberg would take place before the next meeting and it would be so horrible and the thought of a possible recurrence so terrifying the American public would demand the president include SDI in the disarmament package.

For Max nothing had changed. The questions were still there—the answers were not. The telephone numbers had not provided any new leads. One local number belonged to Tolinger, a second number belonged to a guy named Mitchell Cole, and the third number was Linda Larkin's. The numbers in Florida, Nebraska, and D.C. were set up with telephone recorders. Well, his scrambler should arrive sometime this morning; an electronics supply in L.A. had assured him delivery within twelve hours. Maybe a clue was on the message phone. He felt he was grasping at straws and was about to drown along with everyone else. He would give it one more day. If nothing turned up, he'd call Henri.

He stuck his left hand into a plastic shopping bag, taped the open end tight around his forearm, and showered. He towel-dried, then ripped off the plastic and checked the dressing. The bag had done the trick, the bandage was still dry. His hand was a bit sore and starting to get stiff; he figured the way his luck was running the dog had rabies.

Max lay awake trying to reason why Gilbird's group had stolen MX parts. He could see stealing one of each to send back to the Soviet Union, but why fifteen of each? The more he learned the more puzzling it all became. His mind wandered and his thoughts focused in on Sherry. Recalling the last evening with her he reached for the phone and dialed her number. On the fourth ring her answering machine picked up. Max wondered why she wasn't home at this time of night and dialed again just to hear her voice. The mere sound of her voice, melodious and enchanting, only served to intensify his lonesomeness. Finally, on the third call he left a message. He told her how much he missed her and managed to include the three magic words, "I love you."

He dialed the number at his own apartment, hoping she might be there waiting for him. The phone just kept on ringing.

Whether he awoke in the morning or in the evening, his routine was the same, watching the news over breakfast. No mention of Hatcher this morning, but of greater interest were the fifteen seconds devoted to circumstances surrounding Air Force Lieutenant Mitchell Cole, found dead of a drug overdose early this morning in his car on the eighteenth green of the Vandenberg golf course. He was reported to have had a fight with his girlfriend the night before at the Hitching Post Bar and Grill. He had been drinking heavily, according to the bartender, and left just before closing.

The telephone rang, giving him a start. He hadn't been this jumpy in a long time. He attributed it to a lack of sleep. The caller informed him that a package had arrived at their warehouse with instructions to call immediately upon receipt of the package. The warehouse turned out to be a small room at the bus depot where they held luggage and other parcels shipped via their bus line. On the way back through the lobby he dropped two quarters into a newspaper vending machine and removed the morning edition. Placing the newspaper and package on the front seat, he drove back to his house on Surf Road.

Anxious to know what secrets, if any, the KGB message phone held, he hooked the scrambler into his telephone, set in the codes, and dialed the number. The phone rang but the answering machine did not pick up. He tried the number again—the phone continued to ring. There was little doubt Hatcher's body had been discovered by some of his own people, both buildings cleaned out and the phone abandoned. The recorder had either been set up at new location using another number or they had discontinued the message setup altogether. Things just didn't seem to be going his way, but sooner or later he would surely get a break. It had better be sooner for time was running out.

Max spread the local newspaper on the breakfast bar and sat down, eyes glued to the picture of an air force lieutenant on the front page. He recognized Mitchell Cole as the young man standing beside Tolinger during the television interview after the Challenger's ill-fated flight. Also, Cole was the officer captured on videotape in the official air force sedan with Tolinger on the way to Gilbird's house. With a cup of coffee in hand he sat down and read every detail surrounding Cole's death. The story followed the television broadcast pretty much, but in greater depth. One item of interest—the girlfriend involved in the altercation at the Hitching Post was listed as Linda Larkin. Another interesting bit of information: Cole was the officer in charge of security at the MX buildup and checkout facility at Vandenberg. Of further interest was a statement noting the MX team had completed their final checks and the MX had already been moved to the test silo above Missileman beach. The MX should be ready for launch by the end of the week.

Max still could not understand how so many Soviet agents were working in such sensitive DOD positions, but whether he understood it or not made little difference—he needed to know why all these agents were taking so many chances. He did not believe the efforts would culminate in the blowing up of another ICBM.

Unable to check out any of the new leads until dark, he drove to the airport at Santa Maria and chartered a plane to San Diego. By using his computer to search through the memory banks of the CIA and FBI computers he might get lucky with the names Cole and Larkin. Also, by hacking his way through computer files he might turn up some of Bell's and Hatcher's associates. He denied the decision was in any way influenced by his burning desire to see Sherry.

Sherry wasn't at his apartment and he was relieved in one sense, knowing if she were there and asked the wrong question the lying would begin again. On the other hand, he was disappointed, he wanted to see her, touch her, and hold her.

He spent three hours at his computer without turning up anything on either Cole or Larkin. The drug enforcement agency had Bell and Hatcher linked to a couple dozen people each, but nothing tying them to Gilbird or Tolinger or Vandenberg. Taking a break, he stuck a frozen pizza in the oven and made himself a cappuccino. While waiting for the pizza, he gave in to his emotions and dialed Sherry's apartment in La Jolla. When the answering machine picked up, he listened to her voice and hung up without leaving a message. He called Chalter's security desk and was informed she had taken a two-week leave of absence and had not been at work for five days. Her clothes were still in his closet, but most of the food in the refrigerator was stale. She apparently hadn't been in his apartment in several days. He ate the pizza trying not to think about the implications.

Returning his attention to the computer, he spent an hour and a half before getting past DOD safeguards and into air force personal records. Patience paid off. Mitchell Ray Cole was twenty-seven years old, from San Francisco, graduated from UC Berkeley, and held a top secret security clearance. Linda Marie Larkin was thirty-five years old, a graduate of MIT and like Cole, held a top secret security clearance. Max found it very interesting that Linda Marie had been naturalized in 1974.

Greg Carlton, the pilot whose plane Max had chartered for the day, was watching television in the visitors lounge at Montgomery Field—most pilots of small, privately owned aircraft used either Montgomery in Mira Mesa or Gillespie in El Cajon when flying into San Diego. They were airborne within half an hour, heading northwest. Their flight plan carried them west of Catalina, well out of the heavy commercial traffic around Los Angeles. Carlton continued flying along the Channel Islands until they were over San Miguel, and then turned north towards Point Conception. The Point Conception light was dead ahead and ten miles away when he turned northwest again along the coast. Just past Honda Point Carlton hugged the coast as closely as he could without violating military air space while Max took pictures of the same areas of Vandenberg he had photographed earlier on the way down the coast.

It was well after dark when they landed in Santa Maria and by the time the Photos Finished While You Wait outfit developed his film it was nearly ten o'clock. Thirty minutes later he parked the TransAM across the street from the Hitching Post. Not many cars were parked on the street. For some reason people patronizing bars liked to hide their cars, which probably accounted for bars always having parking areas in the rear.

Half a dozen couples were on the dance floor as a country western band finished their number and announced their first break of the evening. Most of the tables surrounding the dance floor were occupied, but the tables to the rear were mostly empty, as were the stools at the bar. Max chose the stool at the end of the bar farthest from the band. The bartender, in his midforties with ex-military written all over him, asked, "What're you having, man?"

"Whatever's on tap?"

The bartender pushed a frosty mug of cold beer across the bar. "That'll be a buck fifty."

Max folded two fifty dollar bills, placed them on the bar, and pushed them toward the bartender. "The change is yours if you have time to answer a couple of questions."

Without hesitating the bartender replied, "For that kind of money I'll make the time. Ask your questions."

"Do you know the guy they found dead this morning over on the Vandenberg golf course, Mitchell Cole?"

"Sure, I knew him, he was a regular."

"Were you here last night when he had the fight with his girlfriend?"

"I was here last night when he got into it with Linda Larkin, but she wasn't his girlfriend. His girlfriend is sitting at that table over in the corner getting drunk." He nodded toward the back. Max glanced toward the corner and then took a second look. A guy about twenty-two or twenty-three sat alone staring into an empty *rock* glass; Max turned back to face the bartender.

"Are you telling me Cole was..." The bartender answered before Max could finish.

"Yep, queer's a three-dollar bill."

"You wouldn't BS me, would you, buddy?"

"Why would I do that, man? Ask anybody. They came in here all the time, everybody knows." The bartender picked up the two fifties and slipped them into his pocket.

"What's your name?"

"Thomas Durham. Most folks call me Tommy D."

"Well, Tommy D., I've got two more bills identical to the ones you just put in your pocket if you think you might have a little more time later on."

"Hey man, like I said before, for a hundred bucks, I'll make the time."

Max glanced toward the corner table before asking, "What's he drinking?"

The bartender grinned and, with his pinkie dangling back and forth answered in a feminine-sounding voice, "Black Russian."

"Fix me one. Do you get a break later on?"

"Yeah, I'll take a break about fifteen minutes before the band comes back. I'll be out in the kitchen."

Max picked up the Black Russian the bartender placed in front of him and asked, "What's his name?"

The bartender grinned again and replied, "John Glasman."

"Did Cole have a nickname?"

"I don't think so. Everybody called him Mitch."

"Thanks." Max walked over, placed the drink in front of Glasman, pulled out the chair nearest the wall, and sat down. He took a swig of his beer, put the mug on the table, and said, "I'm sorry about Mitch. You okay?"

The guy looked up and started to speak, but thought better of it, returning his gaze to the drink Max had placed on the table.

"Hey, look, you don't know me, but I've known the Cole family for a long time. Mitch called me last night at my home in San Francisco, said he was in some kind of trouble and asked me to drive down, said he would meet me here. The bartender told me what happened, said you two were close. I thought I should talk to you."

"I don't feel like talking to anybody. Who are you, anyway? How do you know Mitch?"

"Like I said, I'm a friend of the family, that's as far as it goes." Max wanted to make sure Glasman knew that Cole, finding himself in trouble, hadn't turned to a former lover for help. If John was willing to talk, Max didn't want him inhibited by jealousy.

"Mitch called, said he was in a lot of trouble and wanted out but was afraid of going to prison. He thought I might be able to help."

"Why would he think you could help?"

Max eased the ID case out of his pocket and placed it on the table beside John's drink. He now had a different card behind the window and the gold badge was authentic.

"You don't look like FBI."

"Yeah, well, so what does the FBI look like?"

Glasman didn't answer.

"When did Mitch start doing cocaine?"

The kid finally broke. Angered, he snapped, "Mitch didn't use drugs. They killed him! He was going to tell everything and they killed him." The kid put his face in his hands and kept mumbling, "They killed him."

Max had no doubt Cole had been murdered, but could only guess at the reason. Glasman knew very little about Cole's involvement with Gilbird or Tolinger, but did surmise that Linda Larkin knew he'd lied about his homosexual tendencies to get into the air force and by threatening to tell his commanding officer had blackmailed him into a breach of air force security. Blackmail was never a one-time deal. Over the last couple of years Larkin had won him over to her cause, probably made easier by Cole's brief association with a radical group of peace activists at Berkeley. These ties had somehow been over-looked or disregarded by the air force when making its investigation for the purpose of issuing a security clearance.

John had been present when the argument with Linda Larkin en-sued, after Larkin left, and according to him, Mitchell began downing drinks one after the other and started mumbling about people dying. When John asked what he was talking about, he just kept on mumbling about how thousands of people were about to die and how he had to stop it from happening, but he never mentioned how or when they would die. Glasman worked the graveyard shift at an all-night truck stop in Buellton and had left the Hitching Post at 11:15. He didn't know when or how Mitchell left the Hitching Post.

Max started to get up from the table, hesitated, and leaned close to Glasman, and conveyed a warning. "If these people think Mitch told you about their plans, and my guess is they will assume he told you everything, they'll come after you."

The kid threw down the drink Max had brought to the table and replied, "Who cares?"

"Nevertheless, I think you might be in danger and my advice to you is to get up right now and get as far away from this town as you possibly can."

Glasman sat quietly and just kept staring at the empty glass in front of him. As the band tuned up for their next set Max got up from the table and walked toward the kitchen.

Everyone in the bar had heard and seen the fight which ended when Larkin slapped Cole and stormed out. Tommy D. was of the opinion that she staged the fight, trying to make it look like a lovers' quarrel. He had answered questions for the police, but hadn't volunteered any information. The press either jumped to the wrong conclusion or Linda Larkin had insisted it was, indeed, an altercation between lovers. She was a regular customer, usually in the company of a couple of civilians who worked at the missile build-up and test facility. Often all three drank with Mitchell Cole.

"Was Cole alone when he left last night?"

"As far as I know, but he was really wasted. I think he was probably too drunk to even find his car, much less drive it away. My guess is that someone was waiting for him in the parking lot."

Max pulled two more fifty-dollar bills from his pocket and passed them to the bartender. He also let him see the FBI identification. "My guess is Cole was murdered to keep him from talking to the authorities. It might be healthier for you if you forgot you ever saw or talked to me."

"Got you covered, bro. And by the way, I had you pegged for a fed the minute you walked in."

"Yeah, well, I guess you can't fool an old pro, can you?" Tommy D. laughed and shook the hand Max extended.

The explosion blew a gaping hole in the wall, sending pots, pans, and broken dishes flying about the kitchen. The band stopped playing abruptly; people in the bar were either yelling and running toward the parking lot or screaming and pushing their way through the front door out onto the street.

Max didn't look in the parking lot. He knew what the explosion meant. It meant John Glasman, no longer at the corner table, had left to go to his job at the all-night truck stop in Buellton, got in his car, turned the ignition key, and died.

Max parked his Pontiac near the entrance to the Airport Hilton in Santa Maria. Greg Carlton hadn't been all that excited about getting out of bed in the middle of the night and flying to Sacramento. But when Max agreed to the price he quoted, Carlton became a bit more enthusiastic. At any rate, Greg was waiting and when he saw the TransAM pull into the parking lot, cranked up his van and drove over to where Max parked near the hotel entrance. Two hours later Greg set his twin Cessna down on a cropduster strip near Davis, about twenty miles southwest of Sacramento. Max had insisted they not land at either Natomas or Sacramento Executive.

The time spent waiting for a taxi was longer than the drive into old Sacramento—practically every city in the country had restored an older area as a tourist trap, always designated "Old Town." All the boutiques and gift shops were closed, but a few bars and a couple of trendy restaurants along the river were still open. The taxi dropped Max in front of the Gold Rush Saloon. He paid the driver and waited until the taxi was out of sight before heading toward the capitol buildings a half dozen blocks to the north.

The directory in front of the capitol directed him to the Immigration and Naturalization Services building. He doubted there was an alarm system, since legitimate visitors to the State Department buildings as well as janitors and service people came and went at all hours. Also, security was present on the capitol grounds twenty-four hours a day. The front door was easy enough. The door to Records was a snap. Hand vaulting the counter separating the waiting area from the work spaces, he found what he was looking for in one of the first cubicles—a computer terminal. He fired up the terminal and thirty minutes later had what he wanted. Linda Larkin was born Natasha Von Hegel, her birthplace was Semipalatinsic, USSR. Whoever had compiled information for her security clearance had left out, either accidentally or purposely, this bit of information. A large number of Soviet citizens fled their homeland each year. A great many of these refugees were granted U.S. citizenship and America was better off for having them, but a handful of spies slipped through as well. It would be interesting to get a look at the signature approving her clearance. He would lay odds the same person approved Cole.

During his walk back down Capitol Avenue toward Old Town he marveled at the vast amounts of data stored in computers and the ease with which information could be retrieved and with the right password altered or even deleted, allowing people to disappear and assume new identities. He thought about how easily he had pilfered the memory banks of DOD, CIA, FBI, DEA, and other computers from the privacy of his own home. George Orwell's warning flashed across his consciousness.

Dawn was breaking when Carlton stopped his van in the parking lot by the TransAM. Greg had wanted his money up front. Max had agreed, and paid willingly. Now he pulled a couple of hundred dollars more from his pocket and passed the money over to Carlton.

"Thanks. Anytime you need a pilot, I'm your man. Just let me get a little sleep in between flights next time. Okay?"

"I hear you." They shook hands and Greg drove away. Max had been awake for more than thirty-six hours. He was tired and needed a long rest, a rest he knew he couldn't afford to take; a couple of hours would have to do.

The trunk of the TransAM contained several neatly arranged bags and suitcases of various sizes. He chose a small shoulder bag, slammed the trunk lid shut, and walked across the parking lot toward the Hilton.

IN OVER HIS HEAD

He had a choice between the quietest room in the hotel, according to the desk clerk, and a nonsmoking room on the lower level next to the parking lot. Max wondered why nonsmoking rooms were always in the least desirable wing and on the lowest levels. He chose quiet. The room was, just as the desk clerk guaranteed, quiet and comfortable. He pulled the bedspread to the end of the bed and let it fall on the floor, removed his shoes, flopped on the bed, and was asleep almost immediately.

It was only three hours later that his wrist alarm summoned him from a deep sleep. After his wake-up ritual to assure no one was in the room, he stretched, wiped the sleep from his eyes, stripped off his clothes, stumbled to the bathroom, scraped off his two-day-old beard with the throwaway razor provided by the hotel, and using a plastic bag from one of the trash cans to keep the bandages on his left hand dry, took a long and refreshing shower. Now alert and rested, he donned a fresh set of clothes, stuffed the dirty ones into his shoulder bag, picked up the room key, and headed for the door.

The desk clerk gave Max a puzzled look and inquired, "You're checking out, sir?"

"That's right."

"But you checked in less than four hours ago."

"That's right."

"Is there a problem, sir?" Max figured the young man had the urge to run up and see if the furniture was still in the room.

"Not if you'll give me a receipt and point me towards a restaurant serving breakfast." The young man handed Max a copy of the room charges, along with a complimentary newspaper, and directed him to a restaurant just off the lobby. Thirty seconds after being seated by the hostess a waitress poured him a cup of coffee and took his order. He unfolded the newspaper and sipped the hot, steaming coffee. On the front page, along with pictures, were two columns on the car bomb that had killed John Glasman. No one had been arrested; however, authorities were looking for a man seen talking with Glasman just prior to his death. Investigators had little to go on as descriptions of the man were vague. Well, it looked like Tommy D. still wasn't volunteering information.

Police were also baffled, according to another front-page article, by the death of an unidentified man found in Pine Canyon. At first it was believed the man had lost control of his car and was killed when the car plunged into the canyon, caught fire, and burned. The coroner later concluded the man died from a gunshot wound. Similarities did exist in the two car bombings, but there was nothing to indicate the third death was tied to the car bombings or to Mitchell Cole. The article continued with speculation as to the man's identity and how he might have ended up in Pine Canyon.

The only other item of interest was an article confirming that the first test launch of the MX was scheduled for eight o'clock Saturday evening, less than thirty-six hours away.

The waitress arrived with his breakfast, which brought a smile to his lips as he thought about Sherry, knowing that if present, she would have frowned and lectured him on the adverse effects of eating food containing high fat and cholesterol. The smile faded as he wondered why she had taken time off from her job. He'd call later. Maybe she'd be home.

Putting Sherry out of his mind, he concentrated on the new pieces of the puzzle. There was something about the name Natasha Von Hegel that pricked his memory. Something familiar, yet he couldn't recall having ever heard the name. Natasha was Russian, Von Hegel was German. An East German had apparently married a Russian woman and the mother had given her daughter a Russian name. This seemed quite normal, except that in the Eastern bloc one did not move about at will. Semipalatinsk, a port city on the Irtysh River, with just over a quarter of a million people, was far removed from Germany and only three hundred miles from the Chinese border. A railhead at Semipalatinsk connected the rest of the Soviet Union as well as China, by way of the Irtysh River and the Kara Sea, to both the Atlantic and Pacific Oceans. There was little doubt Von Hegel had been forced by the State to move to Semipalatinsk, probably because of his expertise in transportation, either rail or shipping. His daughter had grown up under Communist control and influence, starting most likely with youth groups for the very young such as the October Cubs and the Young Pioneers, leading eventually to the Komsomol, and culminating in Party membership. She was now a KGB spy planning, according to Cole, to kill thousands of people. Max knew the killing in itself wasn't the goal of the KGB. The attitude of the public resulting from all the death and carnage was their goal. How did it all tie together? He had better start coming up with some answers.

He finished breakfast and found a telephone. The police snooping around Spic and Span might make several people very nervous, possibly nervous enough to make a mistake. A woman answered on the sixth ring. "Lompoc police department."

"I want to talk to the person investigating the circumstances surrounding the death of the man found in Pine Canyon."

"What's your name, sir?"

"I'm going to save you the trouble of asking the routine questions, so listen carefully. I have no intention of giving you my name, address, or telephone number. I could give you a phony name and address and cause you to waste time and effort trying to find someone who doesn't exist. So we can dispense with the customary dialogue and don't even think about putting me on hold so you will have enough time to put a trace on this call. If I'm not talking to somebody interested in what I have to say in exactly ten seconds I'm hanging up and you won't hear from me again. Do you understand?"

"Yes sir. Just a moment, sir."

Another voice identified himself as Detective Hooper and asked the same question the woman had asked and got the same answer. Hooper didn't waste any more time. "Okay, I'm the investigator assigned to the case, what do you have to tell me?"

Max heard the telltale click of another receiver being lifted from its cradle. "I'm only going through this one time and then I'm hanging up the phone, so you'd better start your tape recorder or prepare to take notes. The guy in the canyon is Jake Hatcher. Hatcher and a guy named Oscar Bell supply pushers throughout the area with cocaine. Bell works for John Gilbird, owner of Spic and Span Janitorial. You might also inquire into the whereabouts of Gilbird. Seems no one has seen him in over a month. Okay, that's it; color me gone."

The voice at the other end was cut short as Max hung up the phone. He walked back into the restaurant and asked the hostess for a paper cup. The hostess disappeared for a few seconds, then returned with a Styrofoam coffee cup and asked, "Will this be okay?"

"That will do just fine, thanks."

Max took the cup and headed toward his car. He considered the possibility that one of Larkin's cohorts had seen him talking with Glasman and followed when he left the Hitching Post and watched him get into his car. In which case the description of the TransAM and his license number might already be in the hands of the car bomber. With this in mind Max gave the Pontiac a cursory once-over before replacing his bags in the trunk and driving off toward the center of town.

Needing to make one more call that would require a handful of change, he pulled into a shopping mall in Santa Maria, and parked the TransAM near a video arcade. Even at this time of day several kids and a few adults were playing the video games. Pinball had come a long way. He fed one of the change machines two five-dollar bills, scooped up the quarters and dropped them into the Styrofoam cup. In a nearby restaurant he found a public telephone.

The operator asked for $3.85. He dropped sixteen quarters into the slot and waited. On the second ring Henri answered.

"What does the name Von Hegel mean to you?" Max asked, not wasting time on idle chitchat.

"You aren't referring to Erich Von Hegel?"

"Maybe. Tell me about him."

"At the close of World War II after FDR and Churchill gave Stalin half of Europe, a group of German rocket scientists and technicians at Peenemunde was moved to Kapustin Yar, a site similar to White Sands, where the Soviets had been engaged in rocket development prior to World War II. Erich Von Hegel was head of another German team of rocket scientists at Mitteiwerk in the Harz Mountains. Von Hegel and his team were transported to Semipalatinsk and began work on weapons that could be carried into space by the rockets being perfected at Kapustin Yar." Henri paused, then asked, "Why are you interested in Von Hegel?"

"The name turned up under very peculiar circumstances. I'll check out a couple more things and get back to you. In the meantime, if you want to listen to a little gossip on a party line I can give you some numbers."

"Well, you know me—I'm always interested in gossip." Max knew the term *party line* would assure a positive response. He gave Henri the numbers of the message phones in Florida, Nebraska, and D.C. "You're going to need a key and something to clear up the static." There was no reason for talking in riddles, but somehow, terms like *code* and *scrambler* seemed out of place in the conversation.

The operator cut in, "Please deposit two dollars and fifty cents for an additional three minutes." Max fed ten more quarters into the slot and got the recorded thank you. He talked with Henri for another minute or so, before hanging up.

Hesitating, wrestling with his emotions, he dialed Sherry's number.

"Deposit three dollars and twenty cents, please."

Three twenty? Hadn't he just called all the way across the country for three eighty-five? So, how could an instate call be three dollars and twenty cents? It didn't make sense. Nevertheless, he dropped thirteen of the fourteen remaining quarters into the slot. On the fourth ring her answering machine delivered the same message he had heard the last time he called, a message he was beginning to hear in his dreams—dreams that were now on the verge of becoming nightmares. Even so, he didn't hang up until the message ended. Her voice was music. He refused to consider that Sherry might be a KGB agent and he refused also to acknowledge his emotions were beginning to cloud his thinking—if mistaken, it could cost him his life. Halfway to the TransAM he swore under his breath. Suddenly aware of the quarter left over from the phone calls, carried clinched in his fist, he sailed the coin across the parking lot, and swore again, this time out loud.

The fresh-brewed coffee tasted like the proverbial cup of mud. The patio he found so restful at night and in the early morning sizzled under the blazing midday sun and the scorching Santa Anna winds. The normally booming surf had only enough energy from the unusually flat ocean to barely whisper. At present it was neither a pleasant nor a comforting place. Still, he continued to sit and stare at the Gilbird house. Sooner or later he had to get inside. Later was no longer an option. Something had changed—he didn't know what, but there was a difference in what he remembered and what he had been staring at for the last fifteen minutes. He walked to the wall at the back of the patio and watched the calm ocean for several minutes. With a disappointing glance at his coffee cup he dumped its contents over the wall and walked back into the house.

"That's it," he whispered.

"That's it!" he repeated the remark louder this time. There was no need to take a second look. He poured himself another cup of coffee. It tasted great. He had no idea what it meant, but at least he had a lead. One of the dish antennas had been dismantled and removed.

Viewing the videotape recording of the activity in front of his house took over an hour, but when finished he was positive he knew how the antenna had left and he was pretty sure where it was going. He still wanted to look inside the Gilbird house, but according to the videotape, not only was Evone Gilbird home but an unknown number had arrived in the Maxivan an hour before he got home. The dark-tinted windows of the van made it impossible to determine the number of people inside. Well, maybe he could eavesdrop on their conversations.

The "big ear" arrived in the same box as the telephone scrambler, but was more sophisticated than the average big ear, which picked up and amplified sound waves, allowing you to listen in on conversations a hundred yards away. Through the use of laser technology, the device Max had ordered operated somewhat like Doppler radar used by highway patrolmen to clock a vehicle's speed. The patrolman used his radar gun to bounce an RF signal off a moving vehicle and record the shift in frequency of the returning signal to determine the vehicle's speed. By the same principle, a continuous laser beam, when bounced off a window, was altered by any movement of the glass. Sound waves inside the room caused the glass to vibrate like a giant speaker which, in turn, caused shifts in frequency of the returning laser beam. The frequency shift was then used to reproduce the original sounds that caused the window to vibrate in the first place, making it possible to eavesdrop on conversations inside the room.

Max put on a pair of shorts and sunglasses and carried all the junk of an avid sun worshipper to the patio. After the standard sunburn lotion ritual he arranged things on the table so as to conceal, as best he could, his true purpose for being out in the hot sun.

He sighted the laser beam in on the larger of the two windows on the side of the house facing him, fit the tiny headset to his ears, and adjusted the volume. "Damn!" He repositioned the laser, focusing on the other window. After a moment he turned off the gadget and sat back in his chair. Any lingering doubts he might have had about the group's security were now gone forever. Noise generators had been attached to the windows rendering his eavesdropping device useless. Well, he had one hold card that just might pay off, but it would have to wait until dark. For the moment he might as well satiate his growing hunger and get some more rest.

The sound of a vehicle alerted him to the Maxivan passing in front of his house, Evone Gilbird followed behind in her station wagon. Was it possible luck was switching sides? Rest would have to wait, opportunity was knocking.

He stuffed the last couple of bites of pizza in his mouth, headed for the bedroom, stripped off his shorts, slipped on a pair of jeans, pulled on a T-shirt, and laced up his running shoes. After dressing, he immediately turned his attention to selecting items from the various bags and suitcases in the closet, placing them inside a day pack. From a dresser drawer he removed a Walther TPH in a spring-loaded, quick-release holster. He attached the holster to his belt just behind and above the right hip in what was known as a modified FBI position. He pulled the little gun from its holster, checking the quick-release mechanism, then removed, checked, and replaced the clip, and working the action, he jacked a round into the chamber, lowered the hammer to half cock and with the safety off eased the palm-sized gun back into its holster. Whereas everyone seemed to prefer the heavy stuff, like the .357 or .44 Magnum, he favored weapons at the other end of the spectrum. Handguns were close-range weapons and the only thing that really counted was being able to get the gun out of its holster and hit your target. Max could draw and put a 3-shot pattern within a 2-inch circle at fifty feet in less than half a second any day of the week whether sober, dead drunk, or awakened from a deep sleep. There were many other advantages to small handguns. They were lightweight, easy to hide, didn't show under a jacket, and .22-caliber ammunition was available anywhere in the world. He swung the backpack onto his shoulders, adjusted the straps, and headed toward the kitchen, where he drank a 32-ounce bottle of Gatorade. He knew the hot dry weather would dehydrate him rapidly.

At the back of his patio he climbed over the wall at a spot he had already determined to be the best place to begin descending the cliff. Rappelling gear would have made the descent quick and easy. Without it Max was slowed considerably and his lacerated left hand slowed him even more. Loose rocks and poor handholds rather than the difficulty of the descent itself caused him considerable concern. Still he reached the bottom in about ten minutes with little hardship.

Fate was still his ally. The ocean normally ran hard here, with driving surf that pounded against the bottom of the cliff face, but a minus tide and a calm ocean had left a narrow strip of sand, blocked in places by boulders and rock slides from the eroding cliff. Although the ocean prevented him from walking around most of the slides and boulders, forcing him to climb up and over, it was easy going compared to working his way across the face of the cliff, which he would have been forced to do had the tide been running high.

When the chain-link fence along North Vandenberg's southern perimeter became visible at the top of the cliff Max began working his way up the steep rockface. The designation's North and South Vandenberg were due to a highway running from Lompoc all the way to the ocean, splitting the base. A scattering of private property lay along the highway to the south, but to the north several sections of land, including Gilbird's house and the one he was renting, were in private hands. However, most of the private land between the north and south bases belonged to the railroad. Ten minutes later he lay in the tall grass at the cliff's edge, behind Evone Gilbird's house. The sun at his back, some twenty degrees above the horizon, shone through the windows, permitting fair visibility into the rear of the house, about fifty feet away. Ten more minutes passed and he was unable to detect any movement inside, yet it was impossible to be sure no one was on the premises. Less than an hour had passed since Evone had left home, but he had no way of knowing whether or not she had returned while he was below the cliff. And there was always the possibility someone who arrived in the van stayed behind. Assuming everyone had left and nobody returned, there were still obstacles to overcome. With every passing event his respect for their security grew.

Two television cameras, one at each rear corner, panned 270 degrees. One covered the rear while the second rotated toward the front, looking along the side of the house. As the first camera checked its side yard and looked to the front, the second rotated to cover the rear. He studied the cameras for a few minutes before lowering himself back over the cliff's edge and working his way toward the fence. Repositioned now, he assessed his chances and surmised that if he moved fast enough when the camera on this side of the house started panning away from the street toward the back, and the one on the far corner began panning away from the back and toward the opposite side yard, he would be able to reach the near corner undetected. And while standing underneath the one camera and around the corner from the second he would remain undetected. He would still have to get inside and no doubt overcome another silent alarm. However, he had an advantage here.

After leaving Jake, the Doberman, and the cocaine at building 5002 he'd returned to building 5001 and located the sensors and the transmitter used to send the alarm signal to other locations. An antenna of the same type, used for the alarm system at the buildings on North Vandenberg that housed the telephone/recorder and the cocaine, stood on a mast in the backyard. A coax, similar to television cable, fed through the wall and along the ground and up the mast to the antenna. Well, he'd planned long enough—it was time for action.

Standing against the wall at the corner he felt his timing and quickness had been good enough to avoid the searching eyes of the cameras thus far, but he would have to play hide and seek with the cameras several times before gaining access to the house. He removed the backpack and withdrew his Swiss army knife from one of the compartments. From another compartment he removed a roll of electrician's tape, cut off a 4-inch length, stuck it to the front of his T-shirt, and swung the pack back onto his shoulders. As the camera overhead started swinging away from the street and toward the rear, he slipped around the corner, grabbed the coax, and pulled another foot of cable out of the wall. He sliced through the cable about 6-inches from the wall and stripped away some of the insulation at each of the severed ends. He then twisted the center conductor and the mesh grounding shield together on the coax leading to the antenna and quickly taped the two ends together before pushing the coax back into the wall far enough to keep the taped ends from showing.

The camera was already sweeping across the backyard by the time he scurried back around the corner to safety. By merely looking one could not detect his tampering. The coax appeared exactly as before. This could be important should the cameras be monitored at other locations. He could enter the house now—the sensors would do their job and activate the alarm system, but the transmitter would be unable to convey his intrusion to any interested parties

He was getting more efficient at picking locks and very little time was required to get inside. He found the interior design of the house similar to his own, but the furnishings were quite different. It resembled Gilbird's office, with wall maps, telephones, and computer terminals with modems. One big difference, however, was that the telephones and modems used a radio transmitter to transmit and receive messages. Only one phone, with the number matching the one he had a tap on, used a regular telephone line. The absence of a computer mainframe suggested the one in Gilbird's office was the central processing unit for these as well as other terminals conceivably in different locations. In one bedroom he found a fire-control type of radar—radar designed to automatically lock onto and track a moving target. The output from a crystal controlled RF receiver as well as information from the radar was fed into a microcomputer and out through one modem to a central computer, no doubt in Gilbird's office, and back through a second modem to a transmitter. Max guessed the transmitter was capable of putting out somewhere around 500,000 watts. By comparison, the maximum power permitted by FCC to commercial television and radio stations is 50,000 watts. The transmitter had a feature incorporated into it that allowed the operator to transmit on either high or low power. This feature meant the operator could transmit at around 5,000 watts and would go virtually unnoticed by the FCC When an enormous burst of RF energy was desired, the operator could flip the switch to high power and transmit at 500,000 watts. It wasn't a question of whether or not this was a legally registered transmitter, no doubt, it was not. However, because of the transmitter's location it was likely the FCC would attribute any signals it might detect to the Air Force and would not investigate further. Still, it didn't add up, no matter how you looked at it, this transmitter was not powerful enough to override one of the Air Force missile control transmitters. So what could be its purpose if not to override the control transmitter? He didn't know and dared not venture a guess.

Evidence in another bedroom indicated that not only had one of the dish antennas been removed, but a transmitter, receiver, and microcomputer complete with modems, a setup identical to the one remaining, had been removed as well.

Utilizing a battery powered screwdriver from his backpack, Max removed the transmitter's rear access panel and set it aside. Reaching into his backpack again he removed a package of C-four, divided it into two equal parts, and then worked the gel into inconspicuous areas inside the transmitter. Next he pushed electronic detonators into the plastic explosive and hooked them to the high output side of the power selector switch and then replaced the rear access panel.

This would permit the transmitter to be tested for proper operation and function normally on low power, but the next time the selector switch was turned to high power the C-four would destroy the transmitter and perhaps level the entire building.

Max had no doubt whatsoever that the two transmitters, the one still here in Gilbird's house and the one that had left inside the Roach Coach, played a part in the recent missile failures at Vandenberg and would be used to perpetrate the final disaster—a disaster that would leave thousands dead and thrust the Soviet Union into the position of the world's only superpower. The question was still the same; what were they planning?

He resisted the temptation to boot up one of the terminals, fearing it might be detected. He contemplated leaving a few bugs around, but thought better of it. After they had found his bugs in Spic and Span, sweeping for listening devices might now be routine. If the bugs were found it could result in a more intensive search, which might lead them to the plastic explosive. Apparently they were still of the opinion the bugs found at Spic and Span were planted by the Drug Enforcement Agency; Max did not want to give them reason to think otherwise.

The garage door had been enlarged to accommodate oversized vehicles such as the Running Chef (mobile canteen) captured on tape by his video recorder as it left earlier this morning. A mechanics workshop, complete with power tools, provided technicians with everything they needed to remove the electronic components from the bedroom and re-install them in the roach coach. This gave the group not only a back-up system for their endeavor, but, a mobile one as well. All he had to do was figure out its intended use, and all evidence suggested he must do so before the MX launch.

His snooping was cut short by the sound of the garage door opening. Positive that no alarm signaling an intruder had gone out he assumed Evone Gilbird was returning home and was unaware of his presence. Hurrying to the back door he watched the cameras, waiting for the right moment. He heard a car pull into the garage and the engine shut off as he slipped out through the back door. Stopping at the spot where he had disabled the alarm system by severing the coax, he eased it out of the wall, removed the tape, reconnected the center conductors, and using the piece of tape wrapped the splice to prevent it from shorting to the grounding shield. After twisting the grounding shields together to complete the circuit he pushed the cable back inside the wall. His handiwork would not be discovered as long as no one pulled the coax out of the wall and exposed the splice. Evone had no doubt activated some remote control device disabling the alarm system, allowing her to enter the house. The system might automatically check itself for proper operation when next activated, this possibility necessitated reconnecting the coax. He barely made it to the corner before the camera swept into range. While he waited at the corner for the right moment to sprint to the cliff's edge and disappear over the side he heard the garage door close.

The sun was well below the horizon before he reached the top of the cliff behind his house and climbed back over wall and onto his patio.

Another frozen pizza, a quick shower, a change into his standard black sweats, and he was ready to play an ace he had been holding back.

Max drove past the pull-out overlooking Spic and Span for a couple of miles before making a U-turn, turning off his lights and heading back toward Lompoc. The moon, full now, and rising earlier each night was already well above the horizon making it easy to drive without headlights. He eased the TransAM into the pullout overlooking Spic and Span and cut the ignition. Standing beside the Pontiac he couldn't hear or see any cars in either direction. Crossing the road he climbed over the fence and started making his way up the hillside toward the tree with the radio/recorder. Whoever made the security sweep had discovered and deactivated the three bugs left in Gilbird's office. The tiny transmitters are fairly easily found if you are skilled and have the right equipment, it's almost as simple as walking into a room and finding a boom box with the volume turned to maximum, however, even with skill and equipment, finding a bug left in a passive mode would be similar to finding the smallest of portable radios well hidden and left in the "off" position. It is unlikely, after finding the three active bugs the search was extended to bugs in a passive mode. This being the case, the bug he left with a delayed startup time of forty-eight hours stood a good chance of surviving the sweep and was now sending any conversations in Gilbird's office to his little tape recorder hidden in a tree on the hillside.

The full moon lit up the countryside making it easy for Max to pick his way up the hill. A half-dozen cows that had been resting underneath the clump of trees ahead, apparently wary of the approaching man, got to their feet and began moving farther up the hillside. As one walked underneath the tree concealing the recorder, a loud explosion shattered the night. The unsuspecting cow was lifted ten feet off the ground and thrown twenty feet down the hill. She made a few feeble attempts to regain her footing, but soon gave up, her life quietly slipping away. Well, it looked like his ace in the hole wasn't going to pay any dividends, and he was running low on cards. There was no need to check the radio recorder; the only thing he would find was perhaps another booby trap.

Starting back down the hill, his attention was drawn to the warehouse below. Two cars were tearing out of the parking lot heading toward the highway. They would be at the pullout in another couple of minutes. Max hurried down the hill, crossed the road and was approaching the TransAM when a calm, cold voice warned, "Stop right where you are and don't move or I'll drop you in your tracks."

Max recognized the voice from the telephone conversations as Bell's. Max didn't speak but waited for the man to show himself. Bell had been hiding below the pullout, probably taking turns with others, waiting for someone to return and check the tape recorder, and when Max was out of earshot, used a battery powered radio telephone to alert someone at the warehouse—this would account for the two cars racing up the hill.

Someone had figured out the most logical spot for a person to position himself in order to listen to the bugs. Once the recording device was located all they had to do was wait; they knew it was only a matter of time before someone showed up to retrieve the tape. It was too bad for Bell that Max returned on his watch.

A super heterodyne receiver utilizes a variable oscillator to mix with the incoming RF signal to maintain a single frequency which made single button tuning possible—TRF (tuned radio frequency) radios, back when radio was in its infancy, required manually tuning each stage of amplification with a separate button. The function of an oscillator is to create a minute amount of RF energy, an undesirable downside is the fact that it also functions as a transmitter. So, after determining the general area where Max concealed his radio recorder, it was simple enough, using a very sensitive open-ended receiver to locate the eavesdropping device—during World War II many a German spy was caught because they were listening for instructions from Berlin on a heterodyne receiver.

The booby trap would in all likelihood, kill whoever returned for the tape, but, just to make sure, Bell was waiting.

Max did exactly as instructed, standing quite still, feet apart, the left slightly ahead of the right, similar to a karate "cat" position, not speaking or moving.

"Put your hands over your head." Bell walked out from behind the TransAM, about thirty feet away, as he spoke. The bright moonlight reflected off the gun in Bell's hand, the gun was pointing directly at Max, who still hadn't moved.

"I said get your hands up, Mister, and do it now!" Bell demanded and gestured with the gun.

To further reinforce whatever overconfidence the man may have already possessed, Max responded, in a frantic and startled voice. "Okay! Okay!

His strategy seemed to be working. Bell moved further away from the car and appeared unconcerned for his own safety; he was in charge and with obvious satisfaction in his voice, snapped, "Do it now!"

"I'm doing it, don't shoot, don't shoot!" The feigned panic in Max's voice was all that was needed to make Bell believe he had everything under control—he wasn't going to have any problems dealing with this frightened little man from the DEA. Bell continued walking toward the man dressed in black and was only ten feet away when Max pleaded again, "Don't shoot, don't shoot!" and at the same time moved with blinding speed. Bell was too slow to react. Max's hand flashed to his right hip then snaked out in front of him, all in one smooth, easy motion as the little Walther whispered 3 times. At about the same time the words "Don't shoot" reached Bell's ears, three Teflon-coated, .22-caliber bullets entered his brain. Bell stood for a few seconds as if nothing had happened, then his knees buckled, and he slumped forward, dead even before he hit the ground.

The sound of screaming tires, straining to maintain traction on the curves below, warned Max of the rapidly approaching vehicles. He caught sight of the headlights just three switchbacks below. He jumped in the Pontiac, turned the ignition key and slammed the TransAM into gear as the engine roared to life. The unpaved pullout provided poor traction and caused the Pontiac to fishtail as Max accelerated. The two cars topped the hill, a hundred yards away, just as Max reached the highway. When the wheels of the TransAM touched the solid pavement Max slammed the accelerator to the floor. With tires smoking, the Pontiac leapt ahead, leaving behind a smell of burning rubber. The lead car turned into the pullout while the second car zoomed past in pursuit of the TransAM. Max turned on his headlights, but left the rear lights off. By the time he selected the correct switches and engaged the hydraulic pump, the other car, having a running start, was almost on top of him. The Pontiac's engine was screaming, the tachometer read ten grand as Max shifted to second gear and left more rubber on the highway. As the engine RPM neared ten thousand turns for the second time, a red Nissan 300 ZX pulled along-side Max and a man with a gun leaned out of the passenger's window. Max shifted to third and the TransAm, now in its ground effects configuration, shot ahead. He saw a tongue of flame leap from the gun and heard both rear windows shatter as the projectile passed through the car behind his head. Another bullet shattered the rear windshield. The next switchback was coming up fast. Max went as deep into the turn as he dared before downshifting and braking hard. Since there were no brake lights showing, the driver of the Nissan was unaware of the TransAm's rapid deceleration. He realized his mistake too late and slammed on the brakes. Max hit the accelerator again and powered through and out of the turn. Unable to slow enough to negotiate the switchback, the driver lost control of the Nissan as the rear tires broke loose. The ZX spun out, skidded off the road, and rolled over several times before it crashed into a tree a couple of hundred feet down the hill.

On weekends most businesses keep extended hours, so it wasn't surprising to find an auto self-storage garage attendant still in his office at 8 p.m. in Santa Barbara on a Friday night. Max put-up a security deposit and paid for six month's storage, pulled his Pontiac inside the unit he had just rented, locked the door and took a taxi to the local Chevrolet dealer. The dealer had a large selection of used vehicles, including several different models of used trucks. Max chose a late model, dark brown, half-ton, short-bed with a 454 cubic inch engine, and a two speed transfer case that afforded the advantage of shifting to four wheel drive on the fly. The salesman watched suspiciously as Max counted out crisp new fifty dollar bills, but wasn't about to ask questions of a man paying more than the truck was worth without dickering over the price. At the storage garage he transferred the contents of the Pontiac's trunk to the space behind the Chevy's seat.

If anyone in Lompoc was watching for a Firebird TransAM with broken rear windows they probably wouldn't pay much attention to his new pick-em-up truck. At any rate, he needed some equipment still at his house; hopefully no one had yet associated his car with the Pontiac that traveled surf Road.

He finished the last of two sandwiches, hastily thrown together, poured himself a cup of coffee and opened the newspaper purchased from a vending machine while waiting for the salesman to complete the paperwork for his truck. Glancing at headlines, he passed over most articles quickly, showing only modest interest in others, but stopped abruptly when turning to the section pertaining to local news. He pushed everything aside and spread the newspaper out on the breakfast bar.

A full page layout of the MX, drawn to scale, showed how the fifteen bomb payload was deployed and explained how, with individual guidance computers, each bomb could be programmed for several different targets. A choice of pre-programmed targets could be selected either before launch or during flight. After the central guidance computer brings the Peacekeeper within range, the bombs would be dispensed in sets of five each, over three different target areas, the individual bombs would then begin homing in on their previously selected target.

Max sat in disbelief, unable to move, as the horror of it all left him numb. The plan was indeed ingenious; the Kremlin would reap benefits far beyond its immediate goals. The KGB had hit upon the one thing secretly feared by many people and forecast by others, a nuclear disaster within the United States. Although the warheads were high explosives and not nuclear—at least the shipping crates he saw, with the dummy warheads, were marked high explosive—the incident would be held up to the public as a preview of the disaster that would surely happen sometime in the future involving high-tech nuclear weapons.

The Kremlin would get everything it wanted at the disarmament talks. The public would rise up, not only in America, but around the world, in support of Gorbachev and against President Reagan. The anti-nuclear proponents have long predicted such a disaster, they would now have a field day with the help of the media—the media is always eager to publicize human suffering and propagate dissent. The USSR would emerge as the number one world power, at least in the short run, and possibly for decades to come. President Reagan would be forced to give away so much at the bargaining table that, in a worse case scenario, the United States would be weakened to a point beyond recovery. He saw it all now, except for one very important part.

The fifteen dummy bombs he'd found on his foray onto Vandenberg, along with the guidance systems, were the ones the Air Force intended to use for the test launch. The Air Force would never suspect, even in their wildest nightmares, that it was possible for anyone to remove the dummy bombs and replace them with live warheads, and with computers programmed to deliver those warheads to metropolitan areas in Southern California, rather than practice targets along the Pacific Missile Range.

The maps on the walls of Gilbird's home and office told the gruesome story. He remembered the cities circled and populations written in underneath the name of each city. Names he remembered included Long Beach, Anaheim, and Inglewood; he was unable to recall with certainty several others in and around Los Angeles. Further to the south were San Clemente, Oceanside, and San Diego. To further complicate the disaster and creating an international incident, Tijuana, Mexico was included. These cities were all planned targets. The computers were programmed to guide, with pinpoint accuracy, the warheads to highly populated areas within those cities. On a Saturday evening shopping centers and sporting events would be likely targets. This part of the plan was crystal clear—still, he wasn't convinced they could pull it off. The Air Force would, up until the exact moment of launch, monitor every aspect of the Peacekeeper and its payload. The computer programs would be checked and double checked continually throughout the countdown. After the launch all information would be sent back to the control center by telemetry, should any change in trajectory, contrary to the program in the guidance computer, be observed the destruct command would be transmitted resulting in the MX completely destroying itself. In the event the ICBM did not self-destruct after the command was sent, an airborne B-52 would be standing by to destroy the MX with an air-to-air missile.

In the fifties, the air force had developed a nuclear-tipped air-to-air missile that utilized a B-52 for a launch platform. The two-stage Thunderbolt used the same target-seeking radar as the land-based Bomarc—the target seeking-system had never failed during the testing phase. Fortunately it never became necessary to put either missile to the ultimate test. The two missiles were designed to knock out an entire squadron of enemy bombers approaching the United States—prior to the ICBM, a nuclear attack by long-range bombers had been the number one threat. The Thunderbolt was designed by the air force as part of the *Big Stick* policy and was the first line of defense—the ground-to-air Bomarc would pick off any bombers that managed to avoid the Thunderbolt.

The ground-based Bomarc fell victim to an early arms reduction treaty and all were destroyed. However, the Bomarc's little brother, the air-to-air Thunderbolt, was overlooked by the arms reduction committee and mothballed as the Big Stick was phased out.

In the early days at Cape Canaveral when we were playing catch-up with the Soviets in the space race, NASA became concerned that a complete systems failure might result in one of the huge rockets crashing into a highly populated area, and asked the air force to dust off the Thunderbolt and use it to back up the self-destruct system.

After successfully putting a man in orbit, NASA decided they no longer needed the Thunderbolt for a backup. However, the air force was developing an intercontinental ballistic missile and thought it made good sense to have a backup in case the onboard destruct system failed. Use of the B-52 with two air-to-air Thunderbolts began at Vandenberg when the first Titan was launched from an underground silo in May 1961.

It seemed obvious that KGB operatives were planning, somehow, to take control of the MX once it launched. This part of their plan he couldn't figure out.

To take control of the Peacekeeper would require a transmitter not only more powerful, but with a different wavelength from the one he had seen in Evone Gilbird's house. It seemed impossible. Even if they could take control, a Thunderbolt could still easily destroy the MX before it reached Los Angeles. There had to be something very simple he was overlooking. The KGB would not plan a project this complicated and daring without having every minute detail carefully worked out. Well, he wasn't going to take any chances of going it alone, there was too much at stake. He was in over his head and he knew it; he needed help.

The telephone rang only once before the automatic transfer tones were heard in the receiver and the phone rang a second time.

"Langley."

Henri was no doubt in a high-level meeting and all calls on his private line were being routed to the Watch Commander's office.

"I'd like to speak with Henri Tosi, please."

The man at the other end asked for an authenticator. When Max could not supply the proper codes, the man suggested he call back on the Red (regular) Line.

"It's urgent I speak with him immediately."

"I'm sorry, Sir, Mr. Tosi cannot be disturbed, may I take a message?"

"I'll call back in one hour. Please convey to Mr. Tosi it is imperative I speak with him."

"Yes sir, may I say who is calling?"

"Tell him his old friend J.J. just landed."

Max found it ironic, but perhaps proper, that without thinking he would leave a message similar to the one left for the President when it was learned Enrico Ferrmi had been successful in splitting the atom—the message had read, "The Italian navigator has landed."

Max lifted one end of a long skinny crate onto the tailgate of his truck then pushed it into the bed as far as it would go, about four feet stuck out past the tailgate. Returning to his bedroom he selected several items, carefully enclosing them in plastic bags, and placed them in his backpack, when finished, he carried the backpack and a canvas bag to the garage, and placed them on the passenger seat. Returning to the bedroom again, he selected a pair of black cotton sweat pants, a black cotton turtleneck sweater, heavy black cotton socks, and black running shoes, laying them all out neatly on his bed.

Finished with his equipment, he checked his watch, walked to the kitchen, turned on the television, poured himself another cup of coffee, and tossed another frozen pizza in the oven. Lately he'd seemed cursed with an insatiable appetite, his nerves were on edge, and a feeling of helplessness randomly invaded his consciousness. It was a new experience and he didn't like its implications. He wondered if these feelings were starting to cloud his thinking, as he was now beginning to fear the Commies just might succeed.

The eleven o'clock news began with on sight video of a man on a stretcher being loaded into a coroner's wagon, as a woman explained how a local resident had spotted the body beside the highway. Authorities were presently withholding the name of the dead man, however, the reporter had learned from the sheriff handling the investigation, the man had died from gunshot wounds to the head. The cameraman panned the area while the reporter explained, according to the sheriff, there were no witnesses, although evidence indicated a car had left the scene at high speed. The sheriff declined to speculate as to whether or not this apparent homicide was in anyway connected to the other four mysterious deaths of the last few days. Switching back to the studio, the anchorman reported, after running a pre-recorded interview with an Air Force spokesman, the countdown to the first launch of an MX Peacekeeper missile was going perfectly, with launch still scheduled for eight o'clock Saturday night, less than twenty-four hours away. When the oven timer sounded he shut off the TV and carried his pizza to the patio.

Max sat breathing in the fresh salt air, wondering if these were to be his last moments in this serene spot, bathed in moonlight above the Pacific Ocean. Thoughts and images drifted through his consciousness mingling with the sound of surf below. He closed his eyes and found himself on his big Bonzai board paddling hard to catch a giant wave roaring down on him like a freight train. His take-off was clean, he trimmed his board and shot the curl riding just ahead of the breaking white water. As the ride took him closer to Trestle Beach he saw a red-haired, green-eyed, bikini-clad girl sitting in the sand watching him. Startled, he wiped out. She had never been in his *quiet place* before. He opened his eyes and for one brief moment he wanted to find Sherry and flee to some remote island and leave the rest of the world to deal with the KGB. He'd already sacrificed almost half his life trying to prevent the Communists from taking over the world and nobody cared. Americans are told every day,

"The Communists mean us no harm." If they would only take a look at events of the last fifty years, and think about the way communism has changed the world, they would easily see the untruths in such illogical statements. But, thinking seems to be too much trouble for most people, they prefer to have radicals, liberal politicians, and the media do it for them. Well, to hell with them, to hell with them all, it was time they woke-up and started thinking for themselves, the Albanians, Ukrainians, Estonians, Latvians, Lithuanians, Poles, Czechs, Hungarians, Laotians, Kurds, and Vietnamese to name a few, could tell how the Communists meant them no harm. How many times has it been said, those who fail to learn from history are doomed to the same mistakes? Well, to hell with them, to hell with them all, it was time they woke up and learned how to think for themselves. Leaning back in his chair and clearing his mind, all frustrations vented, he took control of his emotions. If the KGB wasn't stopped, the death and destruction they were about to wreak would be passed off on the public as an accident, just as the Kremlin planned. All the other missile failures had only been a rehearsal; this time it was the real thing and the curtain was about to go up. Someone had to stop them and he was elected, honor and conscience gave him no choice; the free world was at stake.

Still unable to reach Henri, he called Sherry. Her answering machine played the same message he'd heard a dozen times in the last couple of days. The phone at his own apartment went unanswered. He had to trust someone, so with mixed emotions he dialed Sherry's number again. When the beep sounded he left Henri's telephone number with instructions to call and give him a simple message; the message would have no meaning to anyone other than Henri Tosi. When he added, "I love you," the words came easier this time.

WILDFLOWERS

Max eased the crate off the back of his truck and let it fall to the ground, pulled the Chevy forward a few feet and killed the ignition. The crate was fairly well hidden in the undergrowth, lush along this section of the Santa Ynez River, nevertheless, after placing his backpack and the canvas bag beside the crate, he cut some branches, and tossed them on its top until everything was completely hidden. There was very little chance the crate would be discovered, especially in the dark, but, why take the chance when it took only a few extra minutes to cut a few branches and camouflage the crate.

This accomplished, he returned to the truck, and leaving the headlights off, drove back along the railroad tracks until he reached Surf Road where it entered the eucalyptus grove. Off road driving appeared to be no problem for the four-wheel drive, his truck handled the terrain easily. With no other vehicles in sight, he switched on the lights and drove back to his house.

He parked the truck inside the garage and closed the door. He tried unsuccessfully to reach Henry one last time before resetting his security devices, and leaving by the front door.

The bright moonlight made running easy, still, he slowed and ran more cautiously after seeing a red diamond back rattle snake slither off the road into the chaparral. He intersected the railroad tracks, slowed to a walk and kept to the center between the rails until he reached the river then stepped off the railroad bed and followed his tire tracks back to the camouflaged crate.

Max removed the branches, then lifted the top off the crate and removed its contents. He assembled the metal tubes that supported the sail and attached the triangular-shaped rigging to the board. He smiled as he remembered the shop pro, a kid of about fifteen who asked if he'd ever been on a sailboard. When the answer was negative the kid suggested that perhaps he was a bit too old to take up the sport. When Max remarked that it probably wasn't much different than surfing the kid expressed doubts about his ability to ride a wave, after all the years Max had a few doubts of his own. When he discovered Max had ridden longboards before he was born, the kid became more affable and eagerly suggested the type of equipment best suited for what Max had in mind. They discussed board types and sizes, rigging, sails, harnesses, pads, masts, and lots of other stuff, most of which Max didn't know existed. After showing Max how to assemble everything the kid volunteered a few do's and don'ts as well as some how-to's and how-not-to's.

With everything assembled and ready to go Max pulled a neoprene dry suit from the canvas bag, removed his running shoes, put them in a plastic bag and arranged the shoes inside his backpack before slipping the dry suit on over his clothes. With the dry suit zipped up, and the Velcro fasteners secured at the neck he began perspiring, although the temperature had dropped considerably since sunset.

At the river's edge he checked the straps on his pack one last time before easing into the water with his sailboard. The offshore Santa Ana winds were light but steady. He climbed onto the board and found it a little difficult to balance with the fifty pound backpack. Pulling the mast up as the kid had instructed, he shifted positions, selecting the correct slalom pads, getting his feet well under the straps as the wind filled the sail. He leaned back to counterbalance the pressure against the sail and found himself moving smoothly across the small lagoon where the river widened before emptying into the ocean.

After making a couple of trips back and forth across the inlet he felt competent and headed out towards the open ocean. He wiped out on the first breaker. The sensation was that of walking out of the sunshine on a hundred degree afternoon into an air conditioned room as the perspiration inside the neoprene suit condensed.

He found it a little more difficult to right the board and pull up the mast in the rough water, but, once accomplished he made it past the breakwater and found the going much easier. An offshore breeze required him to keep his back to the shoreline and, even with the full moon, spotting landmarks required a great deal of concentration. The view from his sailboard was quite different from the one he'd had from Carlton's airplane. As the sound of crashing surf grew louder he knew he was nearing Purisima Point and sailed further out to sea, staying clear of the jagged rocks along this part of the coast. At last the sound of pounding surf was behind him and growing fainter with each passing second. Although surfing required good arm strength to paddle out and catch a wave and strong legs to keep your balance and maneuver the board as it slipped down the face of the wave, you always had the opportunity to lie on your board and rest while waiting for the next wave. If after a few rides you were extra tired you could always be more selective, passing over all but the really good waves. He found the sailboard a lot more demanding, pounding his legs continuously while the wind tried to wrench the sail from his grasp. He wasn't sure how many miles he had sailed or how much time had passed, but, his arms and legs were beginning to turn to jelly, and what had started as soft throbbing pains in his lacerated left hand, brought on by the heavy grip required to keep the sail upright were now shooting pains reaching all the way to his shoulder, he didn't know how much further he could go before resting.

He was relieved when a narrow strip of sand appeared along the shore line. As the strip of sand grew wider and several red lights, marking missile silos finally appeared faintly on the hillside he knew he was, at last, nearing his destination. This was the landmark he was seeking, Missileman Beach.

The wind had been falling off since he rounded Purisima Point and was barely keeping his board moving. His strength was waning as well. Turning into the wind he began tacking toward the beach, but was unable to maintain control of the board and was once again reminded not only of the necessity of the dry suit, but, of its comfort, as well, as the cold dark ocean closed over his head. The kid had certainly done him a favor by insisting on the dry suit. The water temperature along the California coast in winter varies a couple of degrees either side of sixty, without the suit he could have died of hypothermia between the Santa Ynez lagoon and Missileman Beach.

His arms were so weak he could barely hold on to the rigging in order to stay afloat. He finally managed to crawl onto the board letting the wave action carry him toward the shore. When the board nudged the sand he slipped back into the water and dragged the board a few feet onto the beach and sank to his knees. Maybe the kid was right, perhaps he was too old for this sport.

Slipping the backpack from his shoulders and using it for a pillow, he lay on his back listening to the waves roll ocean grinders back and forth amongst the pebbles along the waters edge, turning them slowly but surely into sand. His strength returning, he removed a bottle of Gatorade from his pack and drank leisurely. Several minutes passed before he sat up, returned the empty bottle to his backpack, and began stripping off the neoprene suit. He had been well protected in the cold water; still, by the time he reached the beach a chill had penetrated the suit. While lying on the beach recovering his strength the neoprene suit was cozy at first, but heat continued building until he had become uncomfortably warm. When he peeled-off the dry suit the moisture in his perspiration soaked clothing, exposed to the warm dry air, evaporated rapidly, functioning as an air conditioner and felt cool against his skin. Checking his watch he discovered to his surprise over two hours had passed since he climbed onto the sailboard at the mouth of the Santa Inez River. There was no more time for resting; he still had fourteen or fifteen miles to cover before dawn, and after that, a lot of unknowns.

He moved the sail board into the dunes, placed his neoprene suit underneath and camouflaged everything as best he could. Sitting on a driftwood log he brushed the sand from his feet and slipped on a fresh pair of socks from one of the plastic bags in his backpack before pulling on and lacing-up his running shoes. Max surveyed the area one last time before adjusting the shoulder straps on his backpack, and heading north towards a point about a half mile further up the beach where the sand ended and rugged cliffs once again dominated the coastline. When the sound of pounding surf reached his ears and he could see the foam and flying spray, glistening white in the moonlight as breakers crashed against the rocky cliffs, Max turned away from the ocean and walked into the dunes.

The photographs he had taken on the flight back from San Diego with Greg Carlton showed a parking lot just above the spot where the cliffs began climbing away from the dunes, a parking lot probably for use by air force personnel wanting to do a bit of beachcombing, swimming, sunbathing, or whatever one cares to do on a California beach.

Max found the parking lot without much difficulty. From there he cautiously made his way along an unpaved road, full of potholes, for a couple of hundred yards until it connected with a road that led inland to Vandenberg's center of operations. Fully recovered from his initiation to sailboarding he set an easy gait for himself and ran effortlessly on the smooth blacktop that paralleled the beach for a short distance before curving away and ascending onto a long broad mesa. The climb required an extra effort to maintain the pace he had set for himself, but, once on top he again ran with long, easy strides that ate up a mile about every eight minutes. The moon, although low on the western horizon, still lit up the country side providing excellent visibility.

An approaching vehicle forced him to break stride and temporarily abandon the roadway in order to conceal himself from its headlights— he would repeat this several times before reaching his destination.

Several miles later the road dropped off the mesa down into a narrow valley and followed a series of small ponds filled with reeds and lily pads, connected by a spring fed creek, before ascending the next mesa. In the valley Max felt a change in temperature, a reminder the

Santa Ana winds had died allowing the moisture laden marine air to move on shore. Already fingers of fog were moving along the low lying areas. Without the offshore breeze the cool ocean air would continue to flow inland over the warm land mass, creating a thick fog that would soon blanket the entire coastal area.

Max had studied the photographs and a detailed street map of the air base until every detail on his intended route was permanently fixed in his mind. When he reached the crest of the second mesa he knew his destination was only a couple of miles away. From the top of the second mesa he could see the runway approach lights about three miles away, the strobes created eerie patterns against the encroaching fog. Ten minutes later Atlas Road intersected on the right and angled off toward the airfield. Max slowed to a walk for the next couple of hundred yards so as not to miss a fire break cutting through the chaparral in the direction of, according to Pablo a Eucalyptus grove standing about a mile off to the left. The dirt road, even in the dark, was easier to find than he anticipated and was in good shape. He walked at a fast pace and reached the eucalyptus grove without any problems. When checking his watch he realized he had arrived none, too, soon, he had less then two hours of darkness left.

The trees were thick only along the perimeter, thinning after about fifty feet, to reveal three or four hundred houses on well lighted streets meandering about in all directions. This was military family housing. Max had purposely come through the back door, so to speak, to avoid the street lights and security—the military goes to a lot of trouble, even making a show of it, to secure the front door, but often leaves the back door unguarded—but, more importantly, it put him almost in the back yard of the house occupied by Colonel Howard Kent Tolinger. A near-by street sign, conveniently illuminated by an overhead light, provided a quick reference and was easily located on one of the maps he carried. Refolding the maps, he slipped them into his pack, and eased back into the woods. He was on the right street, but, had turned off the firebreak into the woods a little too early and was in the wrong block. A short time later he located the house and after double checking the street and the house number, waited in the woods in back for several minutes, observing the neighborhood and watching for movement inside the house. Satisfied, he moved toward the back door.

Less then a minute later he was standing motionless just inside the kitchen, waiting for his eyes to adjust to the interior, his other senses keen and alert. He could hear snoring from somewhere down the hall to his left. The only other sounds, a drip from a leaky faucet in a bathroom down the same hallway and the ticking of a near-by clock.

Slowly his sight adapted to the new surroundings and he moved silently to the dining room, eased his backpack off, and placed it gently on the large oak table. From the pack Max removed a mini-cassette recorder and two small leather cases.

Selecting a couple of ampoules of chloroform from one of the leather cases, he crossed the dining room into the living room and headed down the hallway towards the bedrooms. The snoring grew louder as he approached the open door to the master bedroom.

Except for his shoes, Tolinger lay on his back fully dressed with his head propped up against two pillows. A glass, only inches from his right hand, still smelled of bourbon. An empty bottle on the night stand beside an ashtray, filled with half-smoked cigarette butts, hinted that Howard Kent Tolinger was a very troubled man.

His snoring was uneven, broken by the mumbling sounds of unintelligible half formed sentences. His face contorted with each outburst. Max held one of the ampoules under Tolinger's nose, squeezing it until the thin glass broke allowing the chloroform to flow out onto the surrounding cotton. Even in his sleep the man seemed to sense that something was wrong as he breathed the vapors. His head jerked back and forth a couple of times before the anesthetic took affect. A check of the rest of the house found the other bedrooms unoccupied; things were working out better than he had hoped.

Before returning to the dining room Max crushed the second ampoule between his fingers and let Tolinger breath some more chloroform vapors, a precaution to make sure he didn't wake up and cause trouble before getting the injection of truth serum. From the second leather case he removed a syringe, attached a hypodermic needle, pushed the needle through the rubber cap of a vial containing a yellow tinged liquid, and slowly drew the liquid into the syringe.

Tolinger, under the affects of chloroform, never felt the needle slip into his arm. Tomorrow, he would question and might even guess the reason for his nausea, the soreness in his arm, the splitting headache, and the puncture wound on his skin. But, he would not remember anything that took place between the time he fell asleep and the time he awoke, if he remembered anything at all. The advantage of Sodium-Amytal with Benzedrine over Sodium-Pentothal, besides the subject's willingness to cooperate fully, answering any and all questions, is the subject's inability to recall the incident. The disadvantage was that sometimes the subject couldn't recall anything ever again. Max would not have cared whether Tolinger recovered from the drug or not except for the fact that when the time came he wanted the traitor to know why he was dying. And the time would come, that was a promise.

Waiting for the drug to take affect, Max looked through the refrigerator and found a half dozen unopened bottles of spring water. One he drank slowly, replacing the body fluids lost during the two hour run from Missileman beach. Two of the bottles went into his pack. The empty Gatorade bottle he had hauled all the way up from the beach went into the trash compactor. From the freezer he removed a box of Snickers ice cream bars. On the way past the dining room table he picked up the tape recorder, in the living room he stopped long enough to grab a cushion from the sofa, before walking on down the hallway to the master bedroom. After placing the ice cream bars on the nearest bedside table and using the cushion from the sofa to prop up the recorder on Tolinger's chest, he pulled up a chair and sat down. Leaning over from his chair, Max pushed the proper buttons on the recorder; a red light came on indicating the machine was in the record mode.

"How are you feeling, Colonel Tolinger?" Max asked in a calm and pleasant voice.

"Okay." Came the relaxed reply. The drug was working remarkably well.

Twenty minutes later Max finished the last ice cream bar and switched off the recorder. He had everything he needed. The one answer eluding him all this time was no longer a mystery. Gilbird's group had no intentions of trying to override the control transmitter. Their plan was much simpler and appeared perfect.

From the instant telemetry was switched from the ground monitoring umbilical system to the on board transmitter, the receiver in Gilbird's house on surf Road, as well as the receiver in their mobile rig, would track, monitor, and route the information through their computers where the identification authenticators would be retained, but the original data would be replaced with false information and then be sent via their five hundred kilowatt transmitters to receivers in the launch command center. The half million watt transmitters used by Gilbird's group would easily override the low output transmitter aboard the MX. Actually, they would not alter the data sent by the MX until the missile reached an altitude of 50,000 feet, at which time the first stage would separate. Precisely at that time they would alter the data, indicating to launch control, the second stage had failed. With little, if any, discussion with his crew the launch commander would order the missile destroyed. With the destruct signal sent, Gilbird's crew could then shut down their equipment and disappear, their job completed. The destruct signal would not cause the MX to destroy its self, it would instead instruct the missile to switch programs. This feature had been incorporated into the Peacekeeper's computer by

Linda Larkin. She and whoever assisted her were responsible for the new program that would guide the MX along the Southern California coast where it would drop fifteen bombs which would glide with deadly accuracy to highly congested targets in and around Los Angeles, San Diego, and Tijuana, Mexico. Larkin's tampering with the missile's computers had not been discovered mainly because of Mitchell Cole's cooperation. Cole was in charge of security at the missile check out facility where missiles are checked out in detail before being transported to the launch sites. After the MX had been inspected and deemed ready for launch Cole had secured the building, but delayed transportation long enough for Linda Larkin and her crew to switch the Peacekeeper's computers and to replace the dummy warheads with the real thing. Cole had later had a change of heart and was about to expose everything—his change of heart had cost him his life.

Backup destruction of an ICBM in case of power failure, or any other problem causing the destruct sequence to fail, was carried out by SAC. The Strategic Air Command was responsible for having a B-52 airborne and armed with Thunderbolt air-to-air missiles for every ICBM launch. Because of the unpredictable coastal fog, two B-52s were loaded with Thunderbolt missiles and flown to Nellis Air Force Base in Nevada, where they could be sure weather would not be a problem. Before the ICBM launched, one of B-52s would take off from Nellis, and remain in a holding pattern over the Santa Barbara Channel until released by launch control. The second B-52 remained on alert at Nellis in case a problem developed with the primary.

Only this time, should the crew of the B-52 find it necessary to let their Thunderbolts fly, they would find it impossible to arm the missiles—this bit of handiwork performed by another Communist agent who had somehow managed to infiltrate Air Force Security at Nellis.

A message on the telephone/recorder near SAC Headquarters in Omaha gave the saboteur at Nellis the aircraft numbers and the time they would arrive in Nevada.

Max was getting scared. He couldn't believe there were so many people in such sensitive DOD positions controlled by the KGB. Also, he was beginning to doubt everyone. Had General Wedemyer been correct when, answering the question of how long we had to turn back the tide of Communism, put to him by the House Committee on Un-American Activities, he answered: "Sir, my humble and honest judgment is that it is too late."

The thought troubled Max, but he would never consider it too late, as long as he was alive, but paranoia was definitely setting in.

He walked into the dining room, sat down at the table, removed a couple of maps from his backpack, chose one and spread it out on the table, and using his MINI-MAGlite studied the map intently before folding it up and replacing it, along with the rest of his equipment, back inside the backpack.

From one of the plastic bags in his pack he removed a brown five by eight-inch air bubble envelope with Henri Tosi's address already inscribed and the proper amount of postage affixed. He slipped the tape cassette inside, peeled the cellophane strip off the adhesive and carefully sealed the envelope. He slipped the pack onto his shoulders and adjusted the straps, wiped his fingerprints from everything he had touched, and departed by the backdoor.

The mailbox, located conveniently at the intersection where he first entered the housing area, had the same squeaky drop chute door associated with every mailbox in the world. In the still of this pre-dawn Saturday the squeak and the sound of metal slamming against metal as he closed the door seemed to reverberate throughout the neighborhood. The metallic thunder Max heard echoing about was only in his mind, brought on by his growing fear and paranoia. He imagined people jumping out of bed, grabbing the telephone, and calling security to report a prowler. His paranoia was growing, not from fear of being caught, but, from fear that somehow someone or something would prevent him from subverting the Communists and their grand plan to usurp American prestige and power through the deaths of hundreds of thousands, possibly several million people. He could see the headlines now, and the twenty-four hour around the clock television coverage of the carnage and of the anti-American demonstrations that would follow the first telecasts of the disaster. America would never recover and would be held hostage, as would the rest of the world, as the Kremlin's every demand would be met whenever and wherever they chose—without American power and prestige, the rest of the world would be held hostage as well. He dare not fail, but, if he should, at least his friend would know the truth and possibly, with the aid of the tape recording, bring to the world's attention what really happened and alert people to the realization that for Communists, the end really did justify the means.

Wispy fog drifted through the eucalyptus, growing denser with every passing second. By the time he broke out of the woods, lights from the airfield were no longer visible and it was impossible to spot any other landmark. Without the fire road he would have needed a compass just to keep from going in circles or wandering aimlessly about in the chaparral. The hard asphalt underfoot was his only in-dication that he had reached the road.

He crossed the pavement, so as not to miss Atlas Road, then turned right and walked along the shoulder, retracing his earlier steps until he once again felt asphalt underneath his feet. He found the street sign and using his MINI-MAG, made sure he had indeed reached Atlas Road.

The fog worked both for and against him. With dawn breaking, it would be more difficult to move about the air base unseen. The fog prolonged the advantage he had had during the hours of darkness, on the other hand, it heightened the possibly he would become lost in unfamiliar surroundings.

Considering the fog was now so thick he could no longer see the sides of the road he chose to walk rather than run and chance falling into the ditch. A broken leg would, in all likelihood, ensure success for the KGB. Also, the air force would immediately recognize sabotage, close the air base and conduct a thorough search. With a broken leg he would be unable, even with his skills, to avoid capture and eventually would be identified as Jack Johnson, deserter, traitor, and spy, not to mention being credited with the most villainous and dastardly deed in history. Henri could not come to his defense; to do so would indicate CIA involvement and possibly expose the Harte cover-up. He would be executed just as Henri had warned, by the same system he was trying to protect. He wasn't concerned for his own life—it only mattered if losing it meant the Communist plan would succeed.

An hour and a half later Max reached his first objective, a bridge over the railroad tracks—Santa Fe still maintained a right-of-way through Vandenberg. Just across the tracks a dirt road intersected on the right, a thousand yards beyond the intersection a fenced compound with armed guards and patrol dogs blocked the road to all traffic. A large sign proclaimed the area Restricted. The compound was of no interest to Max, except for the simple fact it was there and presented an obstacle. The road he wanted turned left only fifty feet from the guard shack. The guards were not a problem although the sun had already climbed above the eastern horizon and the fog was beginning to burn off making visibility considerably better. As a marine sniper in Southeast Asia, he had, on numerous missions, been required to lie, without moving, for hours in 100-degree heat with insects sucking his blood or forced to inch his way through muck and mire with little or no cover, sometimes at a rate of only a foot an hour just to get within range of his target. Getting past the guards presented no problem, the dogs with their keen sense of smell, however, were a different story.

The area he needed to reach, an abandoned maze of roads with old launch sites and rusted out gantries used in the early days at Vandenberg, lay approximately five miles beyond the compound, overlooking the coast. The only road into the area paralleled the compound along the front and down one side for about a hundred yards. Anywhere along the road paralleling the compound he stood a good chance of being detected by the dogs. He walked the short distance back to the bridge, stepped off the pavement and climbed down the embankment to the railroad tracks. Ten minutes later he scrambled out of the railroad bed and followed the slope of the land downhill toward the ocean.

He could smell the salt air long before he heard the surf, he was in the right area, but couldn't see any of the landmarks Tolinger mentioned while under the truth serum. Max strained his eyes searching for evidence of the abandoned launch sites and finally spotted a twisted, half fallen, steel tower looming ghostlike out of the fog. Five minutes later he was walking along the broken streets connecting the crumbling buildings and rusting gantries. The pavement was being reclaimed by sage grass, creosote bushes, and Monterey Cypress.

This was the place where the Roach Coach would set up operations, according to Tolinger's drug-induced statements. Tolinger had avoided the commonly used slang such as Roach Coach, Ptomaine Truck, and Gedunk Wagon, in referring to the Running Chef, the Air Force version of the mobile canteens roaming every military installation in the world selling sandwiches, soft drinks, pizza, et cetera, to people in isolated work places. If Tolinger was correct, and there was no reason to believe otherwise, Linda Larkin would not show up until the countdown had reached T minus thirty (launch time minus thirty minutes). The air force would have already finished their security sweeps of the area and with the countdown that far along she would stand little chance of being spotted. Max took in a long deep breath letting it out slowly, contemplating his options. It seemed simple enough, only two things left to do, actually three, considering the promise he made Tolinger, and come hell or high water, if still alive, he would keep his promise. But, first things first and for now all he had to do was wait around, undetected, until Larkin showed up—then do whatever was necessary to disable the transmitter hidden it the mobile canteen before the countdown reached zero. That would take care of numbers one and two, three would have to wait.

The old four story concrete launch control facility wasn't perfect, but, from the top he had a commanding view of the entire area and it would certainly be cooler and more comfortable than sharing the shade of a creosote bush with ants and sand fleas for the rest of the day. However, there were disadvantages, the chaparral was sparse near the building and provided very little cover should the need to abandon the facility arise. Also, the bottom ten feet of the rusted stairway that wrapped around three sides had been severed and removed, conceivably to discourage adventuresome curiosity seekers. Without inside stairs, exiting during daylight hours without being spotted by anyone searching the area would be next to impossible. Still, the advantages outweighed the disadvantages, but, with so much at stake he couldn't afford to overlook anything or make any mistakes.

An old cable bundle, still securely attached with stand-off bolts every couple of feet, ran up the side of the building providing a somewhat less than easy means of reaching one of the second floor windows. The other levels were easily accessible by the stairs. When the facility was operational the cables had probably attached to antennas on the roof connecting them with various receivers and transmitters on the lower levels. All equipment had long been removed and the building was nothing more than a shell. The third floor with windows on all sides proved to be the best level for surveillance. Max wasted little time selecting a spot on the concrete floor to get some badly needed sleep. Lying on his back using the pack for a pillow, he took in a deep breath, let it out slowly, and fell asleep.

His dreams were in psychedelic hue. Faces floated in and out, never quite in focus, some smiling, some laughing, and some crying. Sometimes his own face, distorted and frightened, would float out of the veil of ever changing colors. Unidentifiable aromas drifted about. He would feel the pain as someone, unrecognizable through the color mist, stabbed him from behind. The laughing, crying, smiling faces would gather around to watch him stagger and fall while trying to catch a glimpse of his assailant.

The faces would then close in around him, the sobbing and laughter growing louder each time he tried unsuccessfully to regain his feet. This scenario played over and over until the helicopter, swooping low over the building, jolted him from his fitful sleep.

For a moment after awakening Max sat on the crumbling temple floor unconcerned, comforted by the sound of the rotating blades; only friendly choppers plied the skies over the jungles of South Vietnam. The second helicopter, hovering just outside the old launch facility, brought him back to the present.

He watched the two aircraft work systematically sweeping back and forth across each designated sector before moving on to another. A glance at his watch told him the MX would lift-off in less than three hours, providing the countdown was still on schedule. Actually, the countdown was unimportant. His only concern for the moment was staying out of sight of the searching eyes inside the helicopters and remaining undetected until the Roach Coach arrived. Max was puzzled when the chopper that had earlier hovered beside the tower, where he lay hidden, touched down momentarily, near some old cypress trees, but dismissed it as unimportant.

Once the Helicopters moved off toward the ocean and began working the coast line Max stood up stretching slowly performing a series of tai chi exercises. He was sore all over, his muscles ached, his joints were stiff, and pains shot all the way to his shoulder each time he opened or closed his left hand. The kid was right. He was getting old.

It was seven forty, only twenty minutes before the Peacekeeper was scheduled to launch and Max was beginning to worry that maybe he was in the wrong place or that possibly there had been a last minute change of plans by Gilbird's Group when he spotted a dust cloud rising from the dirt road paralleling the fenced in compound. The dust cloud continued moving toward the abandoned launch sites. Twilight was fading into dusk, it was the time of day when light was tricky and even with binoculars Max wasn't able to identify the vehicle as the mobile canteen, but he had no doubt it was Linda Larkin. There were no lights of any kind on the vehicle not even headlights and the driver was forced to slow down upon reaching the abandoned launch sites to avoid the trees and bushes growing up through the crumbling streets connecting the rusted out gantries. Only then was Max able to make out the words, Running Chef. Max watched the Roach Coach as it passed within fifty feet and continued on for another half mile before stopping on a precipice overlooking the ocean.

Max turned up the last bottle of water and drank until it was empty, leaving the bottles in the corner—he didn't want clinking glass betraying his presence. Before donning his backpack he strapped on the little Walther just above his right hip near the small of his back. If the MX launched at eight o'clock he had less than ten minutes to reach the Roach Coach and disable the transmitter. He hoped Larkin was on schedule and the countdown had been held for those extra minutes.

The moon was just clearing the Sierra Madre and hung big and full in a cloudless sky, lighting up everything it touched. Following the same route the Roach Coach had taken Max exercised minimum caution on the hazardous road in an effort to reach the mobile canteen before eight o'clock. Even with the bright moonlight he was still unable to see all the holes in the road and tripped twice, falling hard each time. And each time pain shot up his arm as he reached instinctively with his left hand to break the fall. He was unaware the stitches had ripped through the flesh, reopening the already infected wounds. Just over six minutes had elapsed since he climbed down from his hiding place, and now, he stood within thirty feet of Linda Larkin, listening to her bark instructions at a Chinese guy. Apparently they were having a problem starting the motor generator that powered all their equipment. From the near sound of panic in her voice Max was fairly confident she had, for whatever reason, arrived late and the launch was going down as scheduled at eight o'clock. Another guy was busy connecting cables to various antennas set up in different locations around the vehicle. A large section on the ocean side of the Roach Coach had been opened up to expose the dish antenna which would track the MX and listen to the Peacekeeper's telemetry. The mobile canteen had been parked so the antenna would be looking down the Pacific Missile Range; the antenna was in the perfect position and would be ready to track the MX as soon as it was launched providing the Chinese guy could get the motor generator working.

An omni directional whip with a ground reflector, sat on a tripod twenty feet from the dish. This antenna was most likely hooked to a battery-powered radio tuned to the countdown that was being broadcast directly from Launch Control. This would account for the voices coming from a speaker inside the vehicle. Max surmised the unidirectional antenna aimed in the direction of Lompoc, transmitted data picked up by the dish after it had been re-coded by the computer in the Roach Coach to another antenna at the Spic and Span warehouse.

A similar antenna received the data back after it had been altered by the complex program in the mainframe computer in Gilbird's office. The data would once again be processed by the micro-computer and match-up with the original authenticator codes received from the MX with the false information. Max figured the other unidirectional antenna, looking in the direction of Tranquilian Peak where air force antennas would track the Peacekeeper and relay telemetry data to Launch Control, would be used to transmit these bogus signals. Their 500,000-watt transmitter would easily override the small transmitter aboard the MX—the data exchange between the Roach Coach and Spic and Span would use multiplexing and a frequency shift so as not to interfere with or be detected by Launch Control.

Their system obviously worked well, proven by the destruction of at least two Minuteman missiles, two Titans, and one Atlas missile. The system, although complicated in design, was simple in application. Signals were received and channeled through their equipment then transmitted to Launch Control exactly as they had been received until the moment of choice. At that time the computer in Gilbird's office at the Spic and Span warehouse would alter the data to indicate a systems failure. Launch Control would then transmit a coded self-destruct signal requiring the missile to destroy itself. This had accounted for the previous missile failures. Only this time the missile would not destroy itself, the destruct signal would instruct the MX to switch to its secondary program, the program designed to guide it along the Southern California coast. The previous failures had only been practice. This was for real.

It was easy to understand why they chose this spot for their mobile operation, to the north he could see the blinking lights outside the MX silo, to the southeast the lights of Lompoc were visible, and the missile range was entirely over the Pacific Ocean, west and southwest of this point. This was a perfect spot and because it was the perfect spot, Max guessed it to be their primary system while the setup at Evon Gilbird's house was their secondary. If this was true, it would certainly account for Linda Larkin's anxiety. The methods used by the Kremlin in dealing with failure weigh heavily on a KGB agent's mind at all times, and gruesome scenes from either episodes witnessed, stories told by others, or created out of fear by their own mindset, flash across their subconsciousness as previews of what lies ahead, should they fail. He figured Linda Larkin's imagination was in fast forward about now. Even if the backup system were to be needed and worked perfectly, failure to bring the primary system on line was not an option for her.

Well, at the moment everything seemed to his advantage, he certainly didn't foresee any problems taking out this operation with just two unsuspecting men and a woman about to go into panic mode. As he slipped the backpack from his shoulders and eased it to the ground Max became aware of blood dripping from the bandages on his left hand; reasoned unimportant, it was forgotten the same instant.

Somewhere behind him a twig snapped. He couldn't see anything and nothing moved. He accredited the sound to a deer, even thought he knew animals rarely step on a fallen branch, but there was no time to further analyze the cause of the disquieting sound. He put it out of his mind and moved quickly and quietly towards the mobile canteen.

The motor generator fit snugly into a compartment on the side of the Roach Coach making it difficult for the man to work on the unit. Larkin stood behind the guy, holding a flashlight, shining its beam into the area where the man worked. She continually reminded him of his incompetence and hinted at the consequences should he fail.

The guy double checking cable connections on the opposite side of the vehicle never saw the shadow moving silently but swiftly toward him. The non-reflective black clothing and grease paint made Max almost invisible, even in the bright moonlight, to all but the most observant. The man, satisfied the antennas were all hooked up and properly aligned, was unaware of Max standing only three feet away until he straightened up and turned toward the Roach Coach. It was too late, the last breath he would ever take rushed out through his lips with a soft hiss as a fist slammed into his solar plexus. A split second later a right hand shot upward with blinding speed and devastating force. The heel of an open palm caught his nose, driving bone and cartilage up into his brain. Max caught the dead man, as his knees began to sag, and without a sound eased him to the ground.

Fifteen feet from Linda Larkin and the Chinese guy Max froze in his tracks, chills ran up his spine as his blood turned to ice. The warning sound of a huge rattlesnake, coiled and ready to strike, only two feet from his left foot held his full attention. In these quiet surroundings the rattling sound was very loud and not only had his attention, but Linda Larkin's as well. Max recovered from the shock of almost stepping on the fangs of death, at about the same time a third man, alerted by the rattlesnake's warning, stepped from inside the vehicle holding a standard, military issue .45-caliber pistol pointed at the center of his chest. Max knew he had made a mistake in assuming no one was inside the vehicle. It really didn't matter. Max had no illusions of being a serious challenge to the quick draw artist, but on a good day he could get his weapon out and put a bullet on target in less than half a second, when his life depended on it he was probably a little faster.

The forty-five was a single action automatic requiring the man to either manually thumb back the hammer, assuming a round was already in the chamber, or work the action to cock the hammer and jack a round into the chamber. Either way, he would die with a bullet in his brain before he ever got off a shot. Max knew as soon as he moved, the rattlesnake would sink its fangs into his leg. He would have to deal with the snakebite later. Poised, ready for action, he filled his lungs with the fragrant night air and froze once again—the snapping twig was no longer a mystery, he also knew why the helicopter touched down behind the trees.

The aroma of soft desert flowers drifted on the breeze. This would not have been unusual in April or May, but in the winter, even in California, wildflowers rarely bloom, especially wildflowers with a hint of musk. The same flowers and musk he had detected on the fantail of the *Matanuska*, but, was unable to identify until this very moment, a fragrance that permeated not only his bedroom, but his dreams as well. A fragrance shipped directly from Paris to the red-haired, green-eyed beauty standing somewhere behind him with a twenty-five Beretta Spitfire automatic aimed at his back. All hope and caring dashed, he wondered why fate was so cruel to send him someone he could love and to give him a reason for living just to turn it all so treacherously against him.

He considered kicking the snake and letting nature take its course, but there was more at stake here than his life or his disappointments.

He would put Sherry out of his mind and deal with it later, for the moment she was just another obstacle to the success of his mission. She surely couldn't know he was aware of her presence. Just that much was an advantage. Maybe she could only hit paper targets on the police range and wasn't prepared to deal with real live targets that shot back. If he could dive into the clump of manzanita about six feet in front of him and to his right before Sherry put a bullet in his back he could still at least wreck Linda Larkin's plans and send the Soviet Union to the table without any new bargaining chips. A target moving left to right is more difficult to hit, for a right-hander, than one moving in the opposite direction—the same problem exists for a right-handed quarterback running left and throwing right. He would have to take out the guy with the forty-five at the same time he dove into the manzanita. Confident now, his thinking clear, ignoring the rattlesnake, he was set to dive head-first into the bushes when several things happened in rapid succession.

The night lit-up bright as day, the motor generator roared to life and the man thumbed back the hammer on his pistol at the very moment a dark hole appeared just above the bridge of his nose. Max still hadn't moved and the report from the Beretta had barely reached his ears when a second hole appeared just above the man's left eye; he was dead even before he fell. The little twenty-five automatic barked a third time and the snake's head disappeared.

There was no time to think about what had just taken place as Linda Larkin with her wits still intact and intent on carrying out her mission jumped inside the mobile canteen. Max sprang after her, reaching the door just in time to see her swinging a Mac-eleven machine pistol in his direction. The little Walther whispered twice and she slumped to the floor. Outside he heard the Beretta speaking again. That, he surmised, took care of the Chinese guy. Max grabbed the machine pistol and emptied it into the transmitter and computer. He wasn't about to take a chance some preset program would be set into motion by signals from the MX telemetry or by remote control from Spic and Span or some other location. First smoke and then flames erupted from the transmitter. Satisfied, Max turned and stepped outside just as the deafening sound of the rocket motor reached his ears.

There she was, his red-haired, green-eyed, guardian angel, in camouflage and grease paint. He had a lot of questions. He guessed she had some questions of her own.

HAVE A NICE DAY

"The best laid schemes 0' mice an' men, gang aft agley, an, lea'e us nought but grief an' pain, for promised joy!," so wrote Robert Burns, and so it had been for the KGB. Ambassador Harte had not made his speech in front of the United Nations General Assembly. The ultra liberal, socialist aligned candidate had been soundly defeated. The National Aeronautics and Space Administration recovered from the loss of Challenger as the world watched the new shuttle Discovery deliver a payload into space and return safely with its crew two months before the maiden voyage of the Russian shuttle "Snowstorm." Their complicated and carefully planed MX disaster had failed, and their data gathering apparatus in the United States had been badly damaged with many of their agents either dead or in custody and scores of others, exempt from prosecution through diplomatic immunity, had been deported persona non grata.

AT the latest arms limitation talks the Communists' demands and protests, of previous, meetings had turned into requests and cooperation. The Kremlin's problems were not all international, however, at home Soviet citizens were demanding an end to one party rule with free elections, separatists were speaking out in the Baltics, the Berlin wall was coming down, and the hard line Communists were scrambling just to maintain control.

Max believed he was partly responsible for the change in the way the Kremlin now operated both at home and abroad. Peter Deriabin, a former member of the KGB and the CPSU now living in the United States, once wrote, "Russia has a score to settle with Communism some day."

Max believed that day was close at hand, but he was afraid when the day arrived thousands of Soviet citizens would die, success would be measured by the cost to those willing to give their lives for the freedom of future generations.

Max felt good about himself as he left the Mezhdunarodnaya Hotel on Krasnopresnenskaya. He knew his part, if any, had been very small, but he liked to think he had, just as he promised himself as an eighteen year old kid standing in front of the Lincoln Memorial gazing into the reflecting pool at the Washington Monument, been a determining factor in those changes. If so, all the pain and disappointments in his life had been well worth the sacrifice. Walking toward the Smolenskaja Metpo Station he looked across the Moskva River at the city he knew better than any city in the world, a city that served as his prison for eight long years. No, he wasn't locked behind bars, he was as free as most Muscovites, but any attempt to leave the Soviet Union would have meant death or worse. He smiled, wondering on what page of the KGB most wanted list (death list) his name appeared or if perhaps they had bought the fake kidnapping of Ambassador Harte. His face crinkled with another broad grin as he thought about the number of Party members who would find it difficult to sleep tonight should they suddenly become aware Jack Johnson was back in Moscow. They wouldn't be afraid of any personal havoc he might wreak, they would fear instead, should he be apprehended, what he would tell the inquisition and in which direction his finger might point. If they slept at all they wouldn't dream of vacations at their dacha on the Black Sea, no indeed, their nightmares would be filled with the horrors of prison camps in Siberia.

He would have never, even in his wildest dreams, believed that having escaped the watchful eyes of the Communists, he would ever return to this city, at least not of his own free will. But he always kept his promises so here he was, once again, walking along the dimly lit streets of Moscow.

He remembered the promise well, even if Tolinger under the influence of truth serum did not, and he fully intended to be true to his word.

His life had changed considerably since the night of the first MX launch. He smiled again recalling the emotions that flooded through every fiber of his being as he stepped from the Roach Coach and gazed into the eyes of the woman he loved. They had stood looking at each other for what seemed like an eternity. He had taken only a single step toward her before she threw herself into his open arms. They embraced without talking, oblivious to the MX riding on a column of fire as it climbed into the California sky and headed southwest toward its target, 5,000 miles away, somewhere along the Kwajalein Atoll in the Marshall Islands.

With the Peacekeeper a faint speck in the nighttime sky the sound of the rocket motor had died away, the only thing Max could hear was the distant surf and the sound of his own heart. He opened his mouth to ask the obvious question when Sherry put her fingers gently to his lips. "Please, can it wait? I'll tell you everything."

He hesitated only slightly before kissing the soft fingers pressed so delicately against his lips and nodded, his head moving up and down, just once, ever so slightly. With a slow deep breath she closed her eyes for a moment. Tears formed at the corners, but, when her sea-green eyes reopened the twinkling lights that had always shown so brightly, but extinguished since that fateful night in San Diego when he chose to lie rather than trust her, were once again alive and dancing.

They stayed clear of the compound and the sensitive nose of any guard dog that might be patrolling the perimeter, upon reaching the railroad tracks Sherry, without an explanation, turned right toward the lights of Lompoc, Max followed without asking any questions. Three hours later they passed through the chain link fence marking the southern boundary of North Vandenberg. They continued along the tracks for another half hour before Sherry, still in the lead, turned right toward the ocean. When they intersected Surf Road, Sherry turned back toward North Vandenberg and the end of the road. It was obvious to Max, Sherry not only knew her way around Vandenberg she also knew where he lived.

It was well after mid-night when they spotted the emergency equipment around what was left of Gilbird's house, two California Highway Patrol cars, an ambulance, a fire engine, a coroner's wagon, and a Lompoc police car, as well as vehicles from local television stations were parked along the road. The plastic explosive had certainly done the trick.

With all the excitement and everyone's attention focused on the house at the end of the road, no one noticed the two shadows cross the patio and disappear inside the house two hundred yards away. Neither did they notice the previously dark windows were now glowing ever so faintly.

Max was, too, wound up to sleep, he sat alone on the patio in the predawn quiet drinking coffee, listening to the surf, contemplating the constellations, and reflecting on past events. He had slipped out of bed without waking Sherry, pulled on some sweats, and made himself breakfast. She, unlike him, had gone more than forty-eight hours without sleep; he had managed to sleep on the concrete floor of the abandoned launch facility while waiting for Linda Larkin. Even though exhausted, she had insisted on revealing to him every detail of her life, or so it seemed, from the day she was born to the present. So they talked and made love until, convinced there were no more questions to be answered, she fell asleep. Every word she had spoken, every act, every touch was imprinted permanently in his brain.

A Sound of Freedom

"You don't remember me at all, do you?" She spoke for the first time as they washed away the perspiration and grease paint, taking turns in front of the shower head as they shared soap and shampoo. Of course he remembered, he remembered everything about her, from that magic afternoon she escorted him to his new apartment in San Diego to the painful night he'd left her sleeping without any parting words or explanations. She continued before he could even gather his thoughts or formulate an answer.

"Of course you don't. Why should you? I was only sixteen years old and you had your groupies running after you all the time, not to mention that cheap little French tart Jeanne Jouve. That little hussy followed you everywhere and was always draping herself all over you like a cheap suit. I hated her."

Max had no idea what she was talking about or why she seemed to be upset with him. Obviously she was referring to a period in his life sometime prior to his disappearance behind the Iron Curtain. Before he could respond she kissed him and continued, her voice softer now, "I hated you, too, at first, when my father started dragging me away from my friends on weekends, chasing all over Europe just to watch you race that stupid little red car. But, after I started reading about you and seeing your picture in racing magazines, I found myself keeping all the race programs. Pretty soon I started a scrapbook which I shared with my girlfriends. They all thought you were cute, and wanted to come with me to the races. I persuaded my father to let me bring two friends each weekend. He would get us pit passes and we would hang around the garage watching the cars being readied for the race and fantasize about the drivers. I suppose by then I had a real crush on you even though you didn't know I existed. Do you remember when you lost a wheel in the chicane at Spa-Francorchamps, shunted and hit the wall? Do you remember the candy striper that brought you cookies and flowers and magazines and the like, while you were in the hospital recuperating?"

He did remember a skinny little freckle-faced girl with her hair in a ponytail who showed up everyday with all sorts of goodies, followed usually by two other little girls who kept whispering and giggling all the time. It seemed so long ago and in another world, a world mostly forgotten. How did she know about all these things? He was surprised he remembered so much about the little candy striper. Besides the cookies and magazines, she'd brought a get well card everyday and flowers twice a week. Also, there were more personal items, like stuffed animals, and he recalled some expensive slippers and a crocheted pillow. He recalled also the little girl in the red and white striped dress, who was almost a nuisance at times, had green eyes and the hair pulled back in a ponytail was flaming red. Could it possibly be the same girl? How else would she know all these things? He held her at arms length watching the water cascade over her breasts, her wet body glistened and her eyes sparkled even in the low intensity light. Well she certainly wasn't skinny now; she had grown in all the right places and in perfect proportion.

"Did you really crochet that pillow?" In less than a heartbeat her arms were around his neck and her body pressed against his, as her arms pulled his lips to hers, she whispered, "You do remember, you do, you really do."

A half hour passed, perhaps longer, before either spoke again. Max lay in bed with his head propped up with a couple of pillows, Sherry lay in his arms.

"I cried for weeks after I learned you had defected to the Soviet Union. I tore up my scrapbook, even the programs and pictures you signed for me. I threw out everything and told myself I hated you, but I didn't. I could never bring myself to believe you were a traitor. I kept telling myself it was all a mistake. Eight months ago my father called me in Berlin, insisting it was urgent that I come to Washington. I arrived late in the evening and my father picked me up at the airport and took me straight to his apartment. After dinner he became pensive, apprehensive, and a bit mysterious, and yet there was an air of excitement surrounding him as he handed me a very large manila envelope across the table. 'You have every right to hate me. I hope you won't. I hope you'll understand I couldn't tell you the truth. You were right all along.'

It was so unlike my father, I knew he loved me as I loved him and I couldn't imagine anything he could do that would make me feel otherwise. Although he had been a bit over protective at times he was generous to a fault, and had never denied me anything within reason. Without responding I opened the envelope and then I understood. For a moment I did hate him, but within a second or two we were hugging each other and crying. Inside the envelope, everything carefully pasted back together, was the scrapbook I had torn up and thrown away. Every single thing I had collected was there. All the race programs, the pictures you autographed for me, even the posters I had ripped from my bedroom wall. Before I could ask any questions he pushed me away holding me by the shoulders and looking directly into my eyes, a broad smile on his face, stated, 'He's going to need a Candy striper for a while. Are you interested?'

Somewhere nearby a coyote yipped, breaking his concentration. Finding his coffee cup empty, Max returned to the kitchen, refilled his cup, and walked back outside. Standing by the wall at the rear of the patio he breathed in the cool salt air and listened to the restless ocean below. The moon had already slipped below the horizon and the stars were beginning to fade, dawn would soon be breaking. He lay back on the comfortable lounge chair, took a sip of coffee, and returned his thoughts to Sherry's life story as she had revealed it to him over the last few hours. It read, in part, like a Harlequin Romance, with a "love-lost-love-found" theme, but the one thing tying it all together was the biggest surprise yet—her father.

Fate can be cruel or kind and for Sherry it had been both on more than one occasion. Her father, twenty-year-old Corporal Andrew Lee Dale, had died when the car he was driving blew-up two weeks before she was born. Her mother, nineteen-year-old Sherry Lynn, died in the delivery room, leaving her without parents and without a name. Her biological father was the military driver for the man who adopted her, the only father she had ever known, Lieutenant Colonel Thomas Paul Boaden. The car bomb, planted by terrorists, had been intended for Colonel Boaden.

The kinder side of fate provided two loving and dedicated parents in Colonel and Mrs. Boaden, who adopted and christened her Sherry Lee. But, at age twelve tragedy struck again when Mrs. Boaden died of cancer. Her father, now a Brigadier General, devoted every minute of his spare time to her, and they became very close. By trying to spend as much time as possible with his daughter he unintentionally piqued her interest in Jack Johnson.

According to Sherry, the General had always wanted a son, but he and Mrs. Boaden could not have children. When her father met with Henri Tosi and Jack Johnson he saw in the young marine the son he had always wanted, but could never have, and so gave into a fantasy, Jack Johnson became his make-believe son. This of course, Sherry made crystal clear, was only speculation on her part, but she attributed her father's sudden fascination with auto racing, which led to her being dragged all over Europe on weekends and to the eventual meeting of Candy Striper and patient, to this presumed interest.

After Jack Johnson's well-contrived defection to the Soviet Union, Sherry had been sent to a private school in Geneva, Switzerland. She had attended college at the Sorbonne, and later studied at the Spanish University in Madrid. One advantage of growing up in several different countries is the exposure you have to their languages. Sherry was fascinated by the languages she encountered, she studied them at every opportunity, majoring in foreign languages. Her fluency in seven different languages helped land her a job with the U.S. Ambassador's office at the United Nations. Two years later, after completing the FBI training course at Quantico, she applied for a position with the secret service and was accepted immediately.

Her first assignment kept her in D.C. as part of a team responsible for the security of visiting Heads of State. Her job brought her in contact with Clarence Elmore Kennthly, a Washington dignitary living in Georgetown; over time they became romantically involved and were married.

The highlight of entertainment at the wedding reception turned out to be an uninvited guest, a process server who surprised everyone by delivering a writ to the groom, naming him in a palimony suit. He had been living with a prominent Georgetown socialite who was not about to fade away graciously after being dumped for another woman. The incident somehow made the morning paper and was picked up by the wire service and found its way into newspapers across the country. The following evening, as they were about to depart on their honeymoon, two federal agents showed up with bigamy warrants for her husband's arrest. He had conveniently forgotten to tell her about the wives in Dallas, Seattle, and Los Angeles.

After the annulment she asked to be transferred to any available position abroad, a week later she arrived at the U.S. Embassy in Paris, once again serving as an interpreter. As coincidence would have it, Henri Tosi was on assignment in Paris using the Embassy as a line of communication to Langley. During this time Henri, a long time friend of her father's, persuaded her to join the company. When, almost a year later, problems with security in the U.S. Embassy in East Germany became apparent she was asked to transfer to the embassy in East Berlin. At the embassy, just off Unter den Linden, almost within the shadow of Brandenburg Gate and a couple of blocks from the Russian Embassy, she uncovered another sex-for-secrets exchange. A marine sergeant serving as an embassy guard had been caught in the KGB net by a young woman working for the East German secret police, STASI. It was a case with shades of Jack Johnson and Jeanne Jouve, and she could not help thinking perhaps the stories she had heard were true and he was a traitor after all. Still, she could not fully accept the notion that Jack had betrayed his country, or perhaps, she couldn't bring herself to believe it because it would then become a personal betrayal and like her father, she had fantasies. Another six months passed before she received the telephone call from her father urging her to return to Washington.

Sherry had arrived in D.C. a day after Maxwell Alexander Kayne checked into Siempre Primavera. Henri had arranged everything for Sherry in San Diego just as he had made all the arrangements for Max. Henri was ninety-nine percent certain his old friend had told him the truth about everything, in which case he would probably need someone to help him adjust to his new life, and who better than

Sherry. There was also a one percent possibly the KGB had, with mind altering drugs and numerous other methods of brainwashing, turned Jack around and possibly through hypnosis and drugs sent him unknowingly on a suicide mission—another Manchurian Candidate—in which case she would also be nearby. Her mission was to get close to Max and observe and report, but while carrying out her mission she'd fallen in love.

Jack had been unaware of the two microchips placed in his upper torso by Doctor Chekhov and his staff as they simulated injuries received by David Harte. The good doctor had taken care in placing the microchips underneath his left clavicle, while simulating injuries to the left side of his head, neck and shoulders with several jagged cuts, supposedly the result of flying glass. The hair cut very short all over his head and shaved around the injuries, most of which required stitches, would be the area given most attention, or so Doctor Chekhov surmised. He thought it highly unlikely anyone would make a detailed examination of other areas. Jack might possible have some discomfort in his left shoulder, but was unlikely to suspect anything amiss. Even if he did associate the pain and the slight budge protruding from the area underneath his collar bone with the implications, where could he go, what could he do, who could he ask for an explanation or assistance? He certainly could not take the chance he might be discovered as a fraud and traitor to his country. His only hope would be to continue with the plan outlined for him by the KGB.

Doctor Chekhov, unaware of the sophisticated medical equipment available in the west, had not counted on the medical staff at the Naval Hospital in Bethesda ordering a CAT scan. The examination, even with a CAT scan, had Henri Tosi not intervened, might not have been thorough enough to detect Doctor Chekhov's handiwork. The tiny devices, no thicker than a dime and half the size, with highly sophisticated amel chromel junctions for power had been removed by Surgery's Chief of Staff under the watchful eye of Bethesda's Commanding Officer. After an alternate power source had been attached to keep the microchips operational, they were turned over to Henri, with no questions asked, no records kept; there would be no discussion of the surgery by anyone outside the operating room.

The AC Junction is a device originally designed to detect temperature changes in remote and hazardous areas. When the ends of two wires, one made of amel the other chromel, are connected and heat is applied, electrons flow from one metal to the other and the flow increases or decreases as the temperature changes. By connecting the other ends of the wires to a device capable of detecting the amount of change in electron flow, the related change in temperature at the junction could be observed and recorded from a safe location. Experimental laboratories hidden deep within the confines of the KGB apparatus had made use of the AC junction and adopted it to their own devious needs. By using loops of amel chromel wire thinner than an eyelash they designed a power supply that used heat generated by the human body that was capable of powering a microchip. Once, successfully implanted, barring physical damage, the microchip would continue to operate as long as their host was alive.

One of the microchips implanted in the soft tissue under Jack Johnson's clavicle, was an electronic beacon in the super-high-frequency wavelength. The device was limited to a range of no more than a hundred yards and required a supersensitive receiver to detect, but, still powerful enough to permit KGB Agents in the U.S. to remain alert to his whereabouts. The KGB agents knew where the Ambassador lived and if they should lose track of him all they had to do was wait near his apartment; fortunately for the KGB Harte lived alone.

The other device, capable of being detonated by remote control, contained a lethal poison similar to curare, but more deadly. At the first hint of a double-cross, or perhaps shortly after his speech in front of the U.N. General Assembly the device would have been exploded, releasing the poison into his system. The case could than be made that the ambassador had been silenced by the CIA or some other governmental organization. Perhaps a scheme had been devised with false documents already in place to implicate the president. At any, rate Jack Johnson had been expendable. This came as no surprise to Max, the KGB considers everyone expendable, as the Communist Party slogan, coined by Emma Goldman, an American anarchist deported to Russia in 1921 for her active involvement in Communism, suggested, as she wrote of Lenin's strategies: "The end justified all means."

Max smiled, thinking how a song, made popular in his teenage years by Bob Dylan, more accurately echoed present-day times in the Soviet Union: "The times they are a-changing."

In the hands of the true masters of deceit eight years was a long time, so Max wasn't bothered that his friend had not trusted him a hundred percent, had the tables been turned he would have done exactly the same. How could he be upset, even for a moment, with a friend who answered his call for help, provided a new identity, and as it turned out, actually saved his life? Jack Johnson had had no intention of following the prescribed KGB plan. Had Henri not been there watching out for him the KGB agents assigned to observe and report on Jack's movements and actions would have informed their bosses back in the Kremlin of any sign of a double-cross. Should there be even a question of Jack's loyalty to the Communist Party the KGB elite would have made sure there would be no naming of names. Orders would have come down to the agents monitoring Jack and they would have exploded the microchip sending the poison into his bloodstream. This became evident when the alleged kidnappers leaked to the press in Beirut that Ambassador Harte, obviously confused and disoriented, was claiming to be a victim of mistaken identity.

The entire charade, simple as it may have been, worked flawlessly. Jack Johnson had been kept in the hospital until a CIA surveillance team identified known KGB agents from the Russian embassy keeping an around the clock vigil near the hospital. Everything had been made as easy as possible for them to pick up the signal generated by the microchip they believed to be implanted in Jack's body. Actually the tiny devices, embedded in shockproof material inside a small box made from plastic used for the construction of radomes, sat on a table by an open window in an empty room, empty except for the men watching the nearby streets via video cameras and television monitors. Once positive identification of the KGB agents had been made, Ambassador Harte, after a short speech and an equally short question and answer session with the press, left the hospital in a government-chauffeured limousine.

The papers had been full of the Ambassador's intended trip, including departure time, so there were no surprises when the limo headed for Andrews Air Force Base. The unsuspecting Soviet agents followed, but lacking the proper clearance to enter the air base watched as the limousine turned off the road and passed through the main gate. The two spies were obviously convinced that David Harte departed as advertised. However, only the microchips in the pocket of a CIA operative boarded the airplane; Jack Johnson went home with Henri Tosi.

A couple of weeks after the fake kidnapping, the location where Harte was supposedly being held reached the KGB via a double agent in the GRU—a branch of the KGB concerning itself with military intelligence gathering. This GRU agent was under the control of the Central Intelligence Agency. When it had been established the Soviets had setup surveillance near the kidnapper's alleged hideout and were once again monitoring the signal from the microchip transmitter, the news of Harte's reference to mistaken identity was released. The media speculated the ambassador had probably been tortured and was delirious which accounted for his confusion. The media had a way of making a lot out of nothing.

Fewer than forty-eight hours passed after the first broadcast before the device containing the poison exploded. Starting twenty minutes later the power supply for the microchips was slowly cranked down and then turned off. The signal from the transmitter faded slowly at first, than ceased entirely, shortly afterwards the KGB agents packed up and left, hopefully, to report their mission accomplished. Neither David Aaron Harte nor Jackson Jefferson Johnson would ever be heard from again, and Maxwell Alexander Kayne was born a free man at age 37.

Sherry, awaking from a long and restful sleep lay unmoving, her well tanned body golden in the rays of the late-afternoon sun filtering through lace curtains covering the sliding glass door that opened onto the patio. Like a cat she stretched leisurely and slowly kicked free of the covers. The last few hours before sleep came were still fresh in her mind; she rolled to the center of the bed and reached across to the other side only to discover she was alone. She opened her eyes and was surprised to find she had slept almost twelve hours. Walking slowly through the house she found Max asleep in another bedroom. She hesitated for a moment or two, resisting the urge to crawl into bed and snuggle up against him, before continuing into the kitchen where she picked up the telephone and dialed a local number. The phone rang only twice before it was picked up at the other end. The conversation was brief, a mere thirty seconds. A few minutes after she replaced the receiver back in its cradle a helicopter lifted off from North Vandenberg and headed south.

Returning to the master bedroom she showered, first hot and than cold. Stepping from the shower, it occurred to her the only clothes she had with her were the cammies she wore the night before which lay soiled and wrinkled in the bottom of the clothes hamper. Searching through the bureau drawers she found and pulled on a T-shirt that came down to mid-thigh. Looking at herself in the mirror she shrugged. It wasn't all that flattering, but it was a lot less revealing than the minidresses she had worn in the past. She stopped at the door to the bedroom where Max slept and stood watching him for a few seconds before walking back into the kitchen and opened the refrigerator door.

"I should have known." She said to herself, "Junk food, I'm going to have a hard time retraining that man."

Max, oblivious of time, had sat on the patio recalling episodes in his life and contemplating the future. The sun had climbed well into the sky, its warming rays probed the patio, knocking down the early morning coastal chill, and drowsiness began to overtake him. So as not to disturb Sherry he chose another bedroom, pulled the covers back, and eased into bed. His sleep was deep, his dreams were pleasant, and he awoke relaxed and rested. Neither the traffic to and from what remained of Gilbird's house nor the helicopter touching down and still parked in the turn-a-round at the end of the road had disturbed him. The first sounds to reach his ears were men's voices, muffled and indistinct, floating through the open door of the bedroom. He walked quietly to the master bedroom. Sherry was gone, her dirty clothes were still in the hamper and the Beretta lay on the table where she placed it when they arrived sometime after midnight. He picked up the Walther and an extra clip from the top of the bureau, eased back out into the hallway and moved silently towards the voices. As he neared the living room he recognized Henri Tosi's voice. Anxious to see his old friend he relaxed and walked out of the dark hall, crossed the living, and entered the dining room, where Sherry was pouring coffee for two men setting at the table. Max approached Henri from behind and was about to speak when the man sitting opposite him looked up from the forms and papers he was carefully arranging in a single stack. Max froze in his tracks, more than thirteen years had passed, but he still recognized the man, and for a moment he was a marine sergeant just introduced into the company of a General; his heels clicked as he snapped off a smart salute. The General stood up, returned the salute, and extended his hand. "I should be saluting you son, welcome home."

Max stepped forward and shook the General's hand.

"Or maybe I should say welcome to the family. My daughter tells me she intends to marry you."

All three men turned and looked at Sherry. Her face turned red, almost matching the color of her hair. She opened her month to speak, but before she could utter a sound the general put his arms around her and she hid her face against his shoulder. "And my daughter always gets what she wants, at least that's been my experience; I've certainly never been able to refuse her anything."

"I doubt that I shall either, Sir." Sherry pulled away from her father and almost knocked Max off balance as she rushed into his arms. Looking into her shining eyes, only inches from his, he asked, "Does this mean you accept?"

She didn't speak; she only smiled and tightened her arms around his neck as she buried her face against his chest. "Do you approve, Sir?"

General Boaden laughed and extended his hand again, "Congratulations, son."

Sherry pulled away from Max and kissed her father on the cheek. Thanks dad, you're the best."

Henri Tosi leaned back in his chair and looking at each of the trio one after the other, shook his head and stated: "I've witnessed some strange things in my life, but this has to be one of the strangest. I'm not exactly sure of what just happened."

Henri pointed to everyone in turn as he sorted it out. "The best I can figure is he proposed, she accepted, and you gave your blessing. If that's the case," Henri stood up and extended his hand, "I'd be honored to be your best man."

Max grabbed Henri's hand. "I wouldn't have it any other way." Laughter and more hugging followed Henri's comments. Only a few seconds passed before he asked, "Okay, if that's all settled can we move on to some serious matters?"

"You always were the sentimental one, Henri."

Sherry's teasing brought one last round of laughter that quickly dissolved into solemnity.

Henri continued, almost as he had over thirteen years ago with the first words Max ever heard him speak, as he asked, "Shall we get started?"

The debriefing was recorded on tape, to be transcribed later and took the rest of the day and the better part of the night. General Boaden climbed back in the awaiting helicopter and departed after about two hours, but not before presenting Max with a gift he never expected.

A service or an organization often claimed that it took care of its own—yet it was difficult to find evidence to support such claims. In one case at least, an exception had been made. Jack Johnson was gone forever, but had he remained in the marines he would now be able to retire with full benefits. The pension and benefits would have been lost, except for the efforts of General Boaden. Great care had been taken to create a file on one Maxwell Alexander Kayne, complete with duty stations, promotions, and citations. Anyone desiring to check the personnel files in the army's central computer would find Colonel Kayne was honorably retired at the end of twenty years of service, and was now living in San Diego, California; Max would be forever grateful.

He was grateful also, for the marriage proposal the general so quickly and easily solicited for his daughter, otherwise he might still be contemplating the question, waiting for the right time or place or still fumbling for the appropriate words.

The honeymoon, emulating a dream, had been long and beautiful carrying them from desert island beaches to remote mountain tops. They traveled in motor homes, cruise ships, and high flying jets, hiked wilderness trails, canoed wild rivers, and climbed glaciers; neither Max nor Sherry had ever been happier. But now an uninformed observer might wonder what chilly wind had extinguished the flame that only days ago had burned so intensely it spilled over and warmed others. The aura previously surrounding the lovers had vanished. They sat in the observation lounge of a river cruiser without speaking or touching or even looking at each other.

The moment Sherry feared most was rapidly approaching. The fear was not for her except perhaps in a selfish way. She had known, even before they were married, this day would eventually arrive, Max had made it absolutely clear, but she had locked it out of her mind. Now, that day had arrived and if anything went wrong she would never see her husband again.

Her fear began when they boarded the cruise ship in Leningrad and continued to grow with every passing day until it was almost unbearable. From Leningrad the ship crossed Lake Ladoga and followed the river Svir into Lake Onega, then turned south via the Volga Baltic Channel, passed Goritzky, continued on across Lake Ribinsk, entered the Volga again at Uglich, and now it was turning into the Moscow Channel.

The Intourist bus, complete with guide, was waiting dockside to take the tour group to their hotel. Next morning a welcome breakfast, compliments of Intourist, started a three-day tour packed adventure for the tour group; everyone was excited except Sherry. She feared the worst.

Max was excited in a different sort of way, but the first three days were filled with boredom and time dragged by ever so slowly for him. He had seen Red Square too many times already, as well as the Faberge egg collection in the State Armory. The circus and the folklore shows were interesting, but he had seen them many times over. Little had changed. Finally the time arrived he had been waiting for. He skipped the ballet for obvious reasons—many a night he had sat in the Bolshoi Theater and watched Lara dance. Only party members, their guests, and tourists normally can get seats to the ballet and opera. High-ranking state officials with their own private boxes were regulars. On occasions when these state officials were unable to attend, escorts would be arranged for their wives and girlfriends. In years past Captain Jack Johnson, officer in the KGB, defector from the imperialist west, was continuously in demand. These women liked being seen on the arm of the young American and enjoyed his conversation over dinner; some of these women demanded more of Captain Johnson than dinner. Actually, this worked out very well for Jack, tickets were hard to come by for junior officers, so in return for an evening talking about movie stars and Hollywood lifestyles, he was able to watch the beautiful and talented Lara dance, enjoy gourmet dinners at private tables behind closed doors through which only generals and members of the politburo passed and occasionally pick up a bit of information to send back to the CIA. He would have liked to see Lara dance one last time, but he was too familiar a face at the Bolshoi, even after plastic surgery he dared not take the chance one of his previous escorts might spot him; they had a habit of watching the tourists through their opera glasses.

Now the waiting was over, he began to tingle with excitement; adrenaline was flowing at an ever increasing rate. Tomorrow morning at six o'clock his tour group would board an Aeroflot flight to Helsinki and it would all be over, his promise fulfilled. Several times in the past few days he had considered aborting his plan and forgetting about it entirely because of the anguish he was causing Sherry. They had discussed all of this before they were married and she had agreed; now he was thinking it too selfish of him to cause her so much grief, but he had come too far and the window of opportunity was closing. Even so, two hours earlier he told her he was calling it off. Sherry desperately wanted him to call it off, but fearing, if she agreed, it might come between them sometime later, insisted he continue as planned. However, she did agree to board the plane without him if he failed to return. Whether or not she would, Max didn't know. After tonight it would be finished and they could return to the life they had shared for the past year, in a world where nothing mattered but the two of them and their own happiness. He knew even as the thought entered his mind it could never happen; they were both dedicated to the same cause, and that cause would always put them in harm's way.

Henri Tosi knew it also; his parting words had been, "By-the-way Max, how's your Arabic?"

Muscovites weren't any different from the inhabitants of any other city on a Saturday night. Young people were out, mostly in groups, looking for discotheques, moving from one to another or standing in line to get into one of the more popular clubs. Older couples and sometimes entire families stroll through parks and along streets, going from nowhere to nowhere. The streets aren't crowded, but a lot of people are out moving about, and with the exception of street venders hustling tourists, no one paid much attention to anyone outside their own group. Max did not fear being stopped or questioned; only a senior officer would ever question the purpose or intent of anyone wearing a Lieutenant Colonel's uniform with the dark blue trim of the KGB. Full Colonels and higher ranking officers, having their own state-issued cars and drivers, would not stop to check on an officer whose uniform was perfect in every detail. Even if they should, his identification would pass anyone's scrutiny, and he knew State Security well enough to satisfactorily answer any questions they might ask. Any junior officer stopping him on the street would receive a dressing down he might very well remember for the rest of his life. The uniform

Max wore had been purchased, for a souvenir of course, on the black market in Leningrad. The ID had been supplied by Henri Tosi.

The brightly lit Smolensicaja Metpo, clean and modern with marble halls, chandeliers, and gleaming mosaics was more like a museum than a subway station. The underground was one of the Communist showpieces. Max joined the crowd on the platform and moved, as was expected of a KGB officer, to the front as people moved aside. The station on Marx Prospekt, across from the Moskva Hotel, had a great deal more activity than other stations; this was part of his plan. It would be even more crowded in a couple of hours at which time he would change into dinner clothes, exit the station, cross the street, and walk along Gorky Uiltza to the Bolsohi where the Intourist bus would be waiting to return his group, now attending the ballet, to their hotel. Max would mix with his tour group as they left the theater. Sherry would slip the ticket with the section, row, and seat number reserved for Max by Intourist into his pocket; the ticket would bear the proper validation marks proving Max attended the performance. If the need should arise, enough of the group would remember he was on the bus, and the state tour guide would certainly recall his generous parting gift. Yes, it would indeed end well.

Max checked his bag with the lady tending the "water closet," asked her name, inquired about her job and commended her attentiveness. He knew, by asking her name, the lady would make sure nothing happened to the bag that belonged to a KGB Colonel; she would worry until he returned. Max took the numbered identification tag the lady handed him and dropped it into his pocket. Later he would retrieve the bag, pay her for a shower, refresh himself, change clothes and meet-up with his tour group.

Outside he crossed the street without concern for traffic, at night traffic is sparse at most, few people fortunate enough to own a car use them for pleasure; gasoline isn't expensive in the Soviet Union, but neither is it plentiful. All but a few of the vehicles on the streets at night were state owned. The two guards at the nearby Rossiya Hotel saluted smartly and held the door open as Max approached. The lift operator looked up from a copy of Tass and stiffened as Max walked toward him. Max entered the lift, the operator closed the doors and started the cage on its upward journey, awaiting, although anticipating the KGB Colonel's instructions. Max didn't need to ask directions, he had been a guest at the Rossiya for several months and knew the hotel well. He knew the floor he wanted and could almost guess the suite. The operator stopped the lift as directed and opened the doors. Max stepped out into the corridor and recalled his emotions of ten years past when he saw if for the first time. There was no question as to the room he wanted, two guards stood outside the door. The young privates snapped to attention, a hint of fear in their faces. To the private a KGB colonel was nothing less than equal to God, and they hoped they wouldn't or hadn't made any mistakes. Sensing the young men's anxiety, Max sought to put them at ease; he would be better served by having the young soldiers as allies, rather than having them apprehensive and uncertain of the proper action to take. Max returned the salute, pulled a package of cigarettes from his pocket and asked in Russian, "Do you have a match?"

He removed a cigarette from the pack and stuck it in his mouth then invited the young soldiers to join him. The privates apologized, almost in unison, for not having a match, explaining they couldn't afford cigarettes and had no reason to carry matches, however they looked longingly at the pack of cigarettes Max held in his hand. Max took the cigarette from his mouth, stuck it back in the package and replied, "It's just as well, I'm trying to quit anyway. What's your name son?" he asked of the soldier closest to him.

"Private Kulakova, Comrade Colonel, sir." he quickly replied.

"What's your first name?"

"Yurik, sir," came the reply just as quickly as before, but without the previous formality and with less tension in his voice.

"Well Yurik, since neither of us have a match, how about doing me a favor and getting rid of these cigarettes for me.

"Yes sir!" Max knew the cigarettes would not be destroyed. Even if the kid didn't smoke they would bring a good price on the black market.

"How's our guest tonight, Yurik, resting comfortably, I hope?"

"I don't know, sir. He ate dinner about two hours ago. I would imagine he's sleeping, sir."

Max wasn't surprised that the man might be sleeping. He remembered how in his early days as a guest of the KGB, after twelve or fourteen hours of interrogation interspersed with propaganda films and lectures, sleep and nightmares were your only friends. Yes indeed, he remembered—he would never forget.

"Well, I'd better look in on him; we certainly wouldn't want our distinguished guest to want for comforts, would we?"

"No, sir."

"I'll only be a few minutes."

"Yes sir."

Max closed the door, placed his hat on the entry table and took a slow look around the suite. It was just as he remembered, elegantly furnished in antiques, but with the air now, just as it was then, stale and musty. Tolinger lay on his back in a bed that possibly had belonged to royalty and dated back to the time of the Czars. From the looks of the bed it wasn't a restful sleep. The covers were mostly on the floor and he had both hands around a pillow squeezing it as though he was trying to choke someone. Between the snoring and wheezing, he muttered unintelligible words and phrases.

When Tolinger opened his eyes the only thing he could see was Max Kayne's face, only a foot away from his own. Speaking English for the first time since entering the hotel, Max asked, in a soft, calm voice.

"Good evening, Comrade Colonel, have you found your accommodations comfortable?" Tolinger clutched at his neck underneath the pillow that Max held firmly in place, his eyes were popping almost out of his head, and his face was a ghostly white. His mouth opened and closed, but no words came forth, only a soft gurgling sound could be heard.

"Your friends in the United States Air Force and the Central Intelligence Agency asked me to look in on you to see if you needed anything. Feel free to refer any requests to me personally, my name is Maxwell Alexander Kayne, or perhaps you know me by my former name, Jack Johnson, or possibly the code name Spider means something to you. But forget the name; I'm just here to personally make sure you get everything you deserve."

Tolinger couldn't speak or move, he could only stare into the face that smiled sinisterly at him from only inches away. He blinked to keep the face in focus.

There were many things Max wanted to say to this despicable man, but he didn't have the time, every second he spent in the room was an unnecessary risk. Hell, he wasn't there to try and rehabilitate the SOB, anyway.

Max walked to the door, picked up his hat, turned and walked back to bed where Tolinger lay; his eyes blinked several times as he tried to focus, otherwise he did not move.

Once again Max leaned close to the man as he asked dispassionately. "By-the-way, Comrade Colonel, do you know what woke you?"

Then, answering his own question, said, "You just had your throat cut. Have a nice day."

The End

www.ingramcontent.com/pod-product-compliance
Lightning Source LLC
Chambersburg PA
CBHW070518260626
47161CB00004B/1584